MONUMENT 14

MONUMENT 14

EMMY LAYBOURNE

FEIWEL AND FRIENDS

NEW YORK

S

A FEIWEL AND FRIENDS BOOK
An Imprint of Macmillan

MONUMENT 14. Copyright © 2012 by Emmy Laybourne.
All rights reserved. Printed in the United States of America by
R. R. Donnelley & Sons Company, Harrisonburg, Virginia. For information,
address Feiwel and Friends, 175 Fifth Avenue, New York, N.Y. 10010.

Library of Congress Cataloging-in-Publication Data Available

ISBN: 978-0-312-56903-7

Feiwel and Friends logo designed by Filomena Tuosto

First Edition: 2012

2 4 6 8 10 9 7 5 3 1

macteenbooks.com

FOR MY BROTHER

CHAPTER ONE

TINKS

YOUR MOTHER HOLLERS THAT YOU'RE GOING TO MISS THE BUS.
She can see it coming down the street. You don't stop and hug
her and tell her you love her. You don't thank her for being
a good, kind, patient mother. Of course not—you launch yourself down the stairs and make a run for the corner.

Only, if it's the last time you'll ever see your mother, you
sort of start to wish you'd stopped and did those things. Maybe
even missed the bus.

But the bus was barreling down our street so I ran.

As I raced down the driveway I heard my mom yell for my
brother, Alex. His bus was coming down Park Trail Drive,
right behind mine. His bus came at 7:09 on the dot. Mine was
supposed to come at 6:57 but was almost always late, as if the
driver agreed it wasn't fair to pick me up before 7:00.

Alex ran out behind me and our feet pounded the sidewalk
in a dual sneaker-slap rhythm.

DAY 1

"Don't forget," he called. "We're going to the Salvation Army after school."

"Yeah, sure," I said.

My bus driver laid on the horn.

Sometimes we went over to rummage for old electronics after school. I used to drive him before the gas shortage. But now we took our bikes.

I used to drive him to school, too. But since the shortage everyone in our school, everyone, even the seniors, took the bus. It was the law, actually.

I vaulted up the bus steps.

Behind me I heard Mrs. Wooly, who has been driving the elementary–middle school bus since forever, thank Alex sarcastically for gracing them with his presence.

Mrs. Wooly, she was an institution in our town. A grizzled, wiry-haired, ashtray-scented, tough-talking institution. Notorious and totally devoted to bus driving, which you can't say about everyone.

On the other hand, the driver of my bus, the high school bus, was morbidly obese and entirely forgettable. Mr. Reed. The only thing he was known for was that he drank his morning coffee out of an old jelly jar.

Even though it was early in the route, Jake Simonsen, football hero and all-around champion of the popular, was already holding court in the back. Jake had moved to our school from Texas a year ago. He was a real big shot back in Texas, where football is king, and upon transfer to our school had retained and perhaps even increased his stature.

"I'm telling y'all—concessions!" Jake said. "At my old high school a bunch of girls sold pop and cookies and these baked potatoes they used to cook on a grill. Every game. They made, like, a million dollars."

"A million dollars?" Astrid said.

Astrid Heyman, champion diver on the swim team, scornful goddess, girl of my dreams.

"Even if I could make a million dollars, I wouldn't give up playing my own sport to be a booster for the football team," she said.

Jake flashed her one of his golden smiles.

"Not a booster, baby, an entrepreneur!"

Astrid punched Jake on the arm.

"Ow!" he complained, grinning. "God, you're strong. You should box."

"I have four younger brothers," she answered. "I do."

I hunkered down in my seat and tried to get my breath back. The backs of the forest green pleather seats were tall enough that if you slouched, you could sort of disappear for a moment.

I ducked down. I was hoping no one would comment on my sprint to catch the bus. Astrid hadn't noticed me get on the bus at all, which was both good and bad.

Behind me, Josie Miller and Trish Greenstein were going over plans for some kind of animal rights demonstration. They were kind of hippie-activists. I wouldn't really know them at all, except once in sixth grade I'd volunteered to go door to door with them campaigning for Cory Booker. We'd had a pretty fun time, actually, but now we didn't even say hi to each other.

I don't know why. High school seemed to do that to people.

The only person who acknowledged my arrival at all was Niko Mills. He leaned over and pointed to my shoe—like, "I'm too cool to talk"—he just points. And I looked down, and of course, it was untied. I tied it. Said thanks. But then I immediately put in my earbuds and focused on my minitab. I didn't

DAY 1

have anything to say to Niko, and judging from his pointing at my shoe, he didn't have anything to say to me either.

From what I'd heard, Niko lived in a cabin with his grandfather, up in the foothills near Mount Herman, and they hunted for their own food and had no electricity and used wild mushrooms for toilet paper. That kind of thing. People called Niko "Brave Hunter Man," a nickname that fit him just right with his perfect posture, his thin, wiry frame, and his whole brown-skin-brown-eyes-brown-hair combo. He carried himself with that kind of stiff pride you get when no one will talk to you.

So I ignored Brave Hunter Man and tried to power up my minitab. It was dead and that was really weird because I'd just grabbed it off the charging plate before I left the house.

Then came this little *tink, tink, tink* sound. I took out my buds to hear better. The *tinks* were like rain, only metallic.

And the *tinks* turned to TINKS and the TINKS turned to Mr. Reed's screaming "Holy Christ!" And suddenly the roof of the bus started denting—BAM, BAM, BAM—and a cobweb crack spread over the windshield. With each BAM the windshield changed like a slide show, growing more and more white as the cracks shot through the surface.

I looked out the side window next to me.

Hail in all different sizes from little to that-can't-be-hail was pelting the street.

Cars swerved all over the road. Mr. Reed, always a lead foot, slammed on the gas instead of the brake, which is what the other cars seemed to be doing.

Our bus hurdled through an intersection, over the median, and into the parking lot of our local Greenway superstore. It was fairly deserted because it was maybe 7:15 by this point.

I turned around to look back in the bus toward Astrid, and everything went in slow motion and fast motion at the same time as our bus slid on the ice, swerving into a spin. We went faster and faster, and my stomach was in my mouth. My back was pressed to the window, like in some carnival ride, for maybe three seconds and then we hit a lamppost and there was a sick metallic shriek.

I grabbed on to the back of the seat in front of me but then I was jumbling through the air. Other kids went flying, too. There was no screaming, just grunts and impact sounds.

I flew sideways but hit, somehow, the roof of the bus. Then I understood that our bus had turned onto its side. It was screaming along the asphalt on its side. It shuddered to a stop.

The hail, which had merely been denting the hell out of our roof, started denting the hell out of us.

Now that the bus was on its side, hail was hammering down through the row of windows above us. Some of my classmates were getting clobbered by the hail and the window glass that was raining down.

I was lucky. A seat near me had come loose, and I pulled it over me. I had a little roof.

The rocks of ice were all different sizes. Some little round marbles and some big knotty lumps with gray parts and gravel stuck inside them.

There were screams and shouts as everyone scrambled to get under any loose seats or to stand up, pressed to the roof, which was now the wall.

It sounded as if we were caught in a riptide of stones and rocks, crashing over and over. It felt like someone was beating the seat I was under with a baseball bat.

I tilted my head down and looked out what was left of the windshield. Through the white spray outside I saw that the grammar school bus, Alex's bus, was somehow still going. Mrs. Wooly hadn't skidded or lost control like Mr. Reed.

DAY 1

Her bus was cutting through the parking lot, headed right for the main entrance to the Greenway.

Mrs. Wooly's going to drive right into the building, I thought. And I knew that she would get those kids out of the hail. And she did. She smashed the bus right through the glass doors of the Greenway.

Alex was safe, I thought. Good.

Then I heard this sad, whimpering sound. I edged forward and peered around the driver's seat. The front of the bus was caved in, from where it had hit the lamppost.

It was Mr. Reed making that sound. He was pinned behind the wheel and blood was spilling out of his head like milk out of a carton. Soon he stopped making that sound. But I couldn't think about that.

Instead, I was looking at the door to the bus, which was now facing the pavement. How will we get out? I was thinking. We can't get out. The windshield was all crunched up against the hood of the engine.

It was all a crumpled jam. We were trapped in the demolished sideways bus.

Josie Miller *screamed*. The rest of the kids had instinctively scrambled to get out of the hail but Josie was just sitting, wailing, getting pelted by the ice balls.

She was covered in blood, but not her own, I realized, because she was trying to pull on someone's arm from between two mangled seats and I remembered Trish had been sitting next to her. The arm was limp, like a noodle, and kept slipping down out of Josie's grip. Trish was definitely dead but Josie didn't seem to be getting it.

From a safe spot under an overturned seat, this jerk Brayden, who is always going on about his dad working at NORAD, took out his minitab and started trying to shoot a video of Josie screaming and grabbing at the slippery arm.

A monster hailstone hit Josie on the forehead and a big pink gash opened on her dark forehead. Blood started streaming down over her face.

I knew that the hail was going to kill Josie if she kept sitting there out in the open.

"Christ." Brayden cursed at his minitab. "Come *on*!"

I knew I should move. Help her. Move. Help.

But my body was not responding to my conscience.

Then Niko reached out and grabbed Josie by the legs and pulled her under a twisted seat. Just like that. He reached out and pulled her two legs toward him and brought her in to his body. He held her and she sobbed. They looked like a couple out of a horror film.

Somehow Niko's action had broken the spell. Kids were trying to get out and Astrid crawled to the front. She tried to kick through the windshield. She saw me on the ground, under my seat, and she shouted, "Help me!"

I just looked at her mouth. And her nose ring. And her lips moving and making words. I wanted to say, "No. We can't go out there. We have to stay where there is shelter." But I couldn't quite piece the words together.

She stood up and screamed to Jake and his people, "We've got to get into the store!"

Finally I croaked out, "We can't go out! The hail will kill us." But Astrid was at the back of the bus by then.

"Try the emergency exit!" someone shouted. At the back of the bus Jake was already pulling and pulling at the door, but he couldn't get it open. There was mayhem for a few minutes; I don't know how long. I started to feel very strange. Like

DAY 1

my head was on a long balloon string, floating above everything.

And then I heard such a funny sound. It was the *beep-beep-beep* sound of a school bus backing up. It was crazy to hear it through the hammering hail and the screaming.

Beep-beep-beep, like we were at the parking lot on a field trip to Mesa Verde and the bus was backing up.

Beep-beep-beep, like everything was normal.

I squinted out, and sure enough, Mrs. Wooly was backing up the elementary–middle school bus toward us. It was listing to the right pretty bad and I could see where it was dented in the front from smashing into the store. But it was coming.

Black smoke started pouring in through the hole I was looking through. I coughed. The air was thick. Oily. My lungs felt like they were on fire.

I should go to sleep now was the thought that came into my head. It was a powerful thought and seemed perfectly logical: Now I should go to sleep.

The cries of the other kids got louder: "The bus is on fire!" "It's going to explode!" and "We're going to die!"

And I thought, They're right. Yes, we'll die. But it's okay. It's fine. It is as it should be. We are going to die.

I heard this clanking. The sound of metal on metal.

And "She's trying to open the door!"

And "Help us!"

I closed my eyes. I felt like I was floating down now, going underwater. Getting so sleepy warm. So comfortable.

And then this bright light opened up on me. And I saw how Mrs. Wooly had gotten the emergency door open. In her hands she held an ax.

And I heard her shout:

"Get in the godforsaken bus!"

CHAPTER TWO

SPACE BLANKETS

I WAS SLEEPY WAS THE THING. I SAW THE KIDS SCRAMBLE BACK toward Mrs. Wooly. She helped them get down on all fours and scoot out the emergency door, which was sideways.

There was a lot of shouting and people helping one another over the battered seats and slipping on the hail on the floor, slipping because everything was sticky, now with the blood of the kids who had been crushed and Mr. Reed and maybe also motor oil or gasoline, maybe . . . but, see, I was so warm and sleepy.

I was all the way up at the front of the bus, at the ground level, and the black smoke was encircling my head in these rich, ashy tendrils. Like arms from an octopus.

Niko came scrambling up the aisle, checking to see if anyone was left. As I was mostly under a seat, he didn't see me until he was just about to turn back.

I wanted to tell him I'd be fine. I was happy and comfortable and it was time for me to go to sleep. But it was so far to go, to get to those words and then pull them up to my throat and my lips and then form them. I was too far under.

Niko grabbed my two arms and started pulling.

"Help me!" he shouted. "Kick your legs!"

I tried to move my legs. They were so thick and heavy. It was like I had the legs of an elephant. Like someone had replaced my lower half with a big sack of lead.

Niko was gasping now, the smoke getting thicker and thicker. He grabbed my hair with one hand and smacked me across the face with his other hand.

"Push with your legs or you're gonna die," he shouted.

He smacked me across the face! I couldn't believe it. You see it on the tab but to have someone do it to you was just shocking.

So it worked, that smack. I came up from the sleepiness. I was up from down under. I was awake.

I pushed out from under the seat and stumbled up to my feet. Niko half dragged me through the hail, down the "aisle" that was not an aisle but was actually the space above the seats (because, remember, the bus was on its side).

The hail was still crashing and pounding through the windows. It seemed to have a gait now. Small hail, small hail, then a couple whoppers. Little, little, brutal.

I saw Niko take a big one to the shoulder, but he didn't even react.

Mrs. Wooly had the front door of her bus pulled right up to the back of ours. Niko pushed me through the emergency door. Mrs. Wooly hauled me up and pushed me up the steps of her bus.

Jake Simonsen then grabbed my arm and pulled me down the aisle and put me into a seat. Then I got dizzy and my vision got all sparky, and before I knew it, I threw up on Jake

Simonsen. Football star. King of the beautiful. And the vomit was, I am not kidding you, black like tar. Oatmeal and tar.

"Sorry," I said, wiping my mouth.

"Doesn't matter," he said. "Sit down."

Mrs. Wooly's bus was in much better shape than ours. There were giant dents in the ceiling. Her windshield looked nearly opaque, it was so crosshatched with cracks, and most of the back windows were broken from the hail flying in; but it was Air Force One compared to our bus.

Josie was slumped next to a window. Astrid was trying to stop the flow of blood from Josie's head. Brayden had his tablet out of his backpack and was trying to power up.

Niko started coughing up gunk up in the first seat.

And that was us.

There had been at least fifteen kids on the bus. Now it was Jake, Brayden, Niko, Astrid, Josie, and me.

Mrs. Wooly put the bus in gear and it lurched toward the Greenway.

The hail was changing now. Changing into a heavy, frozen rain. The quiet of the rain was so strong I felt it in my bones. A steady, heavy *whoosh*.

They say that your ears ring after you listen to something loud, like a rock concert. This was a continuous GONGONGON-GONGONG. The quiet hurt as much as the hail.

I started coughing hard. Sort of a cross between coughing and vomiting. Black gunk, gray gunk, brown gunk. My nose was running. My eyes were pouring tears. I could tell my body was trying to get the smoke out of me.

Suddenly everything got orange and bright. The windows and the thin window frames stood out, illuminated against a silhouette of fire and . . . BOOM, our old bus exploded.

Within seconds the entire behemoth was engulfed in flames.

DAY 1

"Well," Jake said. "That was close."

I laughed. That was funny, to me.

Niko just looked at me like I was crazy.

Brayden stood up and pointed out the window at the flaming wreckage that had once been our bus.

"Class A friggin' lawsuit, my friends," he said. "Right there."

"Sit down, Brayden," Jake said.

Brayden ignored him, and stood, counting us.

"The six of us," he continued. "We're suing the Board of Education! Where my dad works, they have plans for this kind of stuff. Emergency plans. There should have been a plan. A drill!"

I looked away from him. Clearly, Brayden was a little crazy at this moment in time but I couldn't blame him. He had every right to be unhinged.

The bus reached the store. I thought she'd stop it outside and we'd walk in, but no, just as she had before, Mrs. Wooly drove it right through the hole where the glass doors had been and then we were inside the Greenway, in a bus.

Surreal upon surreal upon surreal.

There were no Greenway employees around so I figured they must not have come to work yet.

The elementary and middle school kids were grouped together in the little Pizza Shack restaurant-within-the-store area.

I saw Alex through the bus window and he stepped forward, squinting to try to see me. The bus sputtered to a stop on the shiny linoleum. Mrs. Wooly got off, then Niko, then me. I stumbled over to Alex, my legs still weren't working completely right, and then I hugged him hard. I got char and vomit all over him but I didn't care.

He had actually been pretty clean before I hugged him. They

all were. The little kids were scared, of course, but Mrs. Wooly had gotten them out of harm's way in a hurry.

One thing that bears explaining is that the middle school and grammar school in Monument were right next to each other, so for some of the little pocket neighborhoods, like ours, they had one bus collect the kids for the two schools. That's why there were eighth graders and kindergarteners mixed together on Mrs. Wooly's bus.

From the five-year-olds to the eighth graders, the kids from her bus looked fine.

Not us. We looked like we'd been in a war.

Mrs. Wooly started barking out instructions.

She sent an eighth grader named Sahalia and a couple little kids to the Pharmacy section of the store to get bandages, first aid cream, that kind of thing. She sent two kindergarteners to get a cart full of water, Gatorade, and cookies.

Niko said he'd go get some thermal blankets to help prevent shock. He was looking at Josie when he said it and I could see why.

Josie was definitely looking worse for the wear. She was sitting slumped on the steps of the bus, keening and rocking back and forth. The bleeding on her forehead had slowed, but the blood was thick and clumpy in her hair and dried on her face in patches. She looked totally terrifying.

The remaining little kids were just standing and staring at Josie, so Mrs. Wooly sent them off to help Sahalia. Then she looked at Astrid.

"Help me get her into the Pizza Shack," she said.

Together they lifted Josie to her feet and led her to a booth.

Alex and I sat together at one booth. Brayden and Jake and the rest just kind of slumped at their own tables.

DAY 1

We all started talking. It was all along the lines of I can't believe what just happened. I can't believe what just happened. I can't believe what just happened.

My brother kept asking me, "Dean, are you sure you're okay?" I kept saying I was fine.

But my ears were funny. I heard this rhythmic clattering sound and the *boom-boom-boom* of the hail was still in my bones.

Sahalia and the little kids came back with a cart loaded with medicines and first aid stuff.

Mrs. Wooly came and looked at us one by one and gave us whatever she thought might help.

Josie took the most of her attention. Mrs. Wooly tut-tutted over the gaping cut on Josie's forehead.

The chocolate hue of Josie's skin made the gash look worse. The red of the blood was brighter, somehow.

"It's gonna need stitches, hun," she told Josie.

Josie just sat there staring ahead, rocking back and forth.

Mrs. Wooly poured hydrogen peroxide over the cut. It bubbled up pink and frothed down over Josie's temple, down her neck.

Mrs. Wooly blotted the cut with gauze and then coated it with ointment. She put a big square of gauze over it and then wrapped Josie's head with gauze. Maybe Mrs. Wooly had been a nurse in her youth. I don't know but it was a professional-looking job.

Niko returned with some of those silver space blankets hikers use. He wrapped one around Josie and offered me one.

"I'm not in shock," I told him.

He just looked at me calmly, his hand outstretched with the blanket.

I did seem to be shaking somewhat. Then it occurred to me

that the strange sound I was hearing might be the chattering of my own teeth.

I took the blanket.

Mrs. Wooly came over to me. She had some baby wipes and she wiped off my face and neck and then felt all over my head.

Can you imagine letting your grammar school bus driver wipe your face with a baby wipe and look through your hair? It was absurd. But everything had changed and nobody was teasing anybody.

People had died—we had almost died.

Nobody was teasing anybody.

Mrs. Wooly gave me three Advil and some cough syrup. She also gave me a gallon bottle of water and told me to start drinking and not stop until I hit the bottom.

"How are your legs?" she asked. "Seemed like you were walking funny before."

I stood up. My ankle was sore, but I was basically fine.

"I'm okay."

"I'll get us some clothes," Niko volunteered. "We can change and get cleaned up."

"You sit down," Mrs. Wooly ordered him.

He sank slowly into one of the booths, coughing black gunk onto his sleeve.

She looked Niko over and wiped down his face and neck, just like she'd done for the rest of us.

"I'm gonna tell the school about what you did back there," Mrs. Wooly said to him quietly. "Real heroic, son."

Niko turned red. He started to get up.

Mrs. Wooly pressed a bottle of Gatorade into his hands with some Advil and another bottle of cough syrup.

DAY 1

"You're sitting," she told him.

He nodded his head, coughing up more gunk.

Jake was pressing the screen of his minitab repeatedly.

"Hey, Mrs. Wooly, I'm not getting a signal," Jake told her. "It's like it's out of juice, but I know it's charged."

One by one, pretty much everybody took out a minitab and tried to turn it on.

"Network's probably down," Mrs. Wooly said. "But keep trying. It'll come back."

Alex took out his minitab. It was dead—blank. He started to cry. It seems funny now. He didn't cry during the storm, he didn't cry seeing me all beat up, he didn't cry about the kids who'd been killed on my bus—he started crying when we realized the Network was down.

The Network had never, ever gone down.

We had all seen hundreds of commercials aimed at reassuring people that the National Connectivity was infallible. We had to believe that because all of our files—photos, movies, e-mails, everything—were all kept in big servers "up in the sky."

Without the Network, you had no computer. You just had a blank tablet. Maybe fifteen dollars worth of plastic and scrap metal. You had nothing.

And there were supposed to be a thousand backups in place to make the Network impervious to natural disasters—to nuclear war—to anything.

"Oh, for Christ's sake!" Brayden started railing. "If the Network's down, who's going to come and get us? They won't even know where we are!"

Jake started talking in his deep, chill-out voice, telling Brayden to calm down. That everything would be okay.

But Alex slid out of the booth and started kind of screaming,

"The Network can't be down! It can't be. You don't know what this means!"

Alex was locally famous for being good with computers and machines. People we hardly knew dropped by with malfunctioning tablets to see if he could debug them. On the first day of high school, my English teacher pulled me aside to ask if I was Alex Grieder's brother and did I think he would look at her car's GPS.

So if anyone among us was going to get the implications of the Network being down, it was Alex.

Mrs. Wooly grabbed Alex by the shoulders.

"Grieder Jr.," she said. "Go get some clothes for Grieder Sr."

By Grieder Sr. she meant me, of course.

"But you don't understand," Alex wailed.

"Go get clothes for your brother. And for these other guys. Take a cart. Go right now," she directed. "Sahalia, you go with him and get stuff for the girls."

"I don't know their sizes," Sahalia protested.

"I'll go with you," Astrid said.

Mrs. Wooly opened her mouth to tell Astrid to sit down and then closed it again. Mrs. Wooly knew her kids, you see. She knew that Astrid wouldn't be told what to do.

So Astrid and Alex and Sahalia went.

I drank my water.

I worked real hard on not throwing up any more.

A couple of the little kids pawed at their minitabs. They kept pressing the screens on their dead minitabs and cocking their little heads to the side. Waiting, waiting.

They couldn't figure out what the heck was going on.

It was weird, changing with Brayden and Jake in the bathroom. These were not guys I was friends with. Jake was a senior. Brayden

DAY 1

was a junior, like me. But they were both on the football team and were built. I was neither.

Jake had always ignored me in a genial kind of way but Brayden had been downright mean to me.

For a moment I considered going into a stall to change. Brayden saw me hesitate.

"Don't worry, Geraldine," he said. "We won't look if you're shy."

Dean . . . Geral*dine* . . . Get it?

He'd started the Geraldine thing back in grammar school.

Then, when we were in eighth grade, he'd had this bit about my hair. That it needed "styling." He'd spit in his hands and work it into my hair, like the spit was gel. By the end of the year, he would just spit right on my head and mash it around with his hand.

Real stylish.

I understood Brayden was considered handsome by the girls. He had that olive color of skin that always seems tan, and brown, wavy hair and very thick eyebrows. Kind of Cro-Magnon-man eyebrows to me, but I gathered that the girls thought he looked rugged and dangerous. I gathered this because every time he was around they'd twitter and preen in a way that sort of made me hate everyone.

What I'm saying is—me and Brayden—we were not friends.

I didn't go into a stall, I just shucked off my dirty shirt and jeans and started washing up at the sink.

"Can you believe that hail?!" Jake said.

"It was unbelievable," Brayden answered.

"Totally unbelievable," I agreed.

"I know!"

Jake asked me about a particularly foul welt on my arm from a hailstone.

"It really hurts," I said.

"You're okay, Dean," Jake said, and he clapped me on the shoulder. Which also hurt.

Maybe he just got swept up in the good feeling. Or maybe he was trying to take care of me and be a leader. I didn't care if it was a put-on. It was good to feel normal for a moment.

"Hey, Jake," I said. "Sorry about the puke."

"Man, don't think another thing about it," he said.

I tossed him the sweatshirt Alex had gotten for me from the racks out in the Greenway.

"Here," I said. "I picked it out just for you. It'll go nice with your eyes."

Jake laughed with a start. I had surprised him.

Brayden laughed, too.

Then our laughter chuckled along until it got completely out of hand, until we were all gulping air, tears in eyes.

It hurt my throat, which was still raw from the smoke, but Jake and Brayden and me, we laughed for a long time.

After we had changed, Mrs. Wooly held a kind of a makeshift assembly.

"It's maybe eight or nine," she told us. "The Network is still down and I'm a little worried about our friend Josie here. I think she's in shock, so she'll probably come around in a day or two. But it might be something more serious."

We all looked at Josie, who stared back at us with a weird, detached interest, as if we were people whose faces and names she couldn't quite place.

"Here's what we're going to do," Mrs. Wooly continued. "I'm going to walk on over to the ER and get some help."

A chunky little girl named Chloe started to cry.

DAY 1

"I want to go home," she said. "Take us home! I want my nana!"

"Nonsense," Mrs. Wooly told her. "The bus has two flat tires. I can't take you anywhere. I'll be back with help lickety-split."

Chloe didn't look at all satisfied with this answer, but Mrs. Wooly went on.

"And look here, kids, your parents are going to have to pay the store back for whatever you guys use, so go easy. This ain't Christmas.

"I've decided to put Jake Simonsen in charge. He's the boss until I get back. For now, Sahalia and Alex, I want you to go and help the little kids pick out some good games and puzzles from the Toy Department."

The little kids cheered, especially Chloe, who made a big show of jumping up and down and clapping her chubby little hands. She seemed a little fickle, emotion-wise. And a little annoying.

Sahalia sighed with irritation and got to her feet.

"Why do I have to do everything?" she complained.

"Because these guys nearly died and you didn't," Mrs. Wooly snapped.

The grammar school kids went off to the Toy section.

"Look," Mrs. Wooly told us big kids after they had gone. "The ER's not too far. I can probably walk it in a half hour to an hour. I might get a ride, which would mean I'll be back much quicker. Keep Josie hydrated and every so often ask her what year it is. What's her name? What kind of, I don't know, pop does she like? Cookies. That kind of thing."

She ran her hand through her wiry gray hair. Her gaze drifted past us, to the entrance to the store and the broken sliding-glass doors.

"And if people come, don't leave here with anyone but your parents. Promise me that. Right now, you guys are my responsibility.

"And—not that I think there is going to be—but if there's any rioting or looting or anything, you guys get all the kids together here in this pizza area, and you just stay together. Big kids on the outside and just stay together. You got me?"

Now I understood why she had sent the younger kids away. She didn't want them to hear about a riot.

"Now, Mrs. Wooly?" Jake said. "What do we do if the people from the store come?" He gestured toward the damaged bus sitting in the midst of the empty shopping carts in the entrance foyer. "They're gonna be pissed."

"You'll tell them that it was an emergency and the school board will take care of the damages."

"I can make us lunch if need be," Astrid said. "I actually know how to run the ovens in the Pizza Shack because I had a job here last summer."

I knew she'd had a job at Greenway. It had been a summer that involved a lot of superstore browsing for me.

"A hot lunch!" said Mrs. Wooly. "Now you're talking."

The little kids came back with board games.

Mrs. Wooly got ready to go.

I went to the Office Supply section and picked out an eight-dollar pen and the nicest, most expensive, executive-brand notebook on the shelf. I sat down right there and started writing. I had to get the hailstorm down while it was fresh in my memory.

I've always been a writer. Somehow, just writing something down makes anything that happens seem okay. I sit down to write, all jammed up and stressed out, and by the time I stand up, everything is in the right place again.

DAY 1

I like to write actual longhand, in a spiral notebook. I can't explain it, but I can think on the page in a way I can't do on a tablet. But I know that writing by hand for anything beyond a quick note is weird, seeing as we're all taught to touch-type in kindergarten.

Brayden stopped and watched me for a moment.

"Writing by hand, Geraldine?" he said with scorn. "Real quaint."

We all lined up to say good-bye to Mrs. Wooly at the entrance to the store. The sky had returned to its normal resting shade of crisp blue clear. Like my mom used to say, "Colorado skies just can't be beat."

The hail was a foot deep most everywhere. At places where there was an incline, the hail had run off somewhat, depositing itself into huge drifts.

You would think it would have been fun to play in—like the outdoors was a giant ball pit. But the big chunks of hail, they had bumps and lumps and stuff stuck inside them like rocks and twigs. They were sharp and dirty, and no one wanted to go out and play. We stayed in the store.

There were a couple of cars in the parking lot. They looked absurd, all crunched in, like a giant had taken a hammer to them. Mrs. Wooly's bus had sustained a lot less damage.

"If all the cars in town look like that," Alex said to me, "we're going to be walking home."

I thought about walking home right then. I could have just waited until Mrs. Wooly left and then went home. But she'd told us to stay and I followed directions, and also, Astrid Heyman was at the Greenway, not at our dull, cookie-cutter house on Wagon Trail Lane.

The names of the streets in our development were all like

that. Wagon Gap Trail, Coyote Valley Court, Blizzard Valley Lane . . .

I have to say that never once did I walk down our street and mistake it for a country lane cutting through some frontier prairie. Who, exactly, did the developers think they were fooling?

I could hear distant sirens. There were some pillars of smoke rising up in other places. A column of smoke was still rising from our burnt-out bus so I had a pretty good idea what the others were from.

I remember thinking that our town had really taken a beating. I wondered if we'd get some National Crisis assistance. We'd seen images of the San Diegans receiving boxes of clothes and toys and food after the earthquake in '21. Maybe now that would be us and our town would be besieged by the media.

Mrs. Wooly was taking nothing more than a pack of cheap cigarettes and a pair of knee-high rain boots.

Brayden stepped forward.

"Mrs. Wooly, my dad works at NORAD. If you can get a message to him, I'm sure he can send a van or something to get us."

I was probably the only one who rolled my eyes. Probably.

"That's good thinking, Brayden," Mrs. Wooly said in her gravelly voice. "I'll take it under advisement."

She looked us over.

"Now, you kids listen to Jake. He's in charge. Astrid's gonna make you all a nice pizza lunch."

She stepped through the door frame and out into the parking lot. She took a few steps forward, then turned to her right, looking at something on the ground we could not see. She seemed to recoil, gagging a bit.

Then she turned and said, with force, "Now go on inside.

DAY 1

Go on! Don't come out here. It's not safe. Get inside. *Go.* Go have lunch."

She shooed us back in with her hands.

Mrs. Wooly had such authority, we all did what she said.

But out of the corner of my eye, I saw Jake step out to see what it was that she'd seen.

"You too, Simonsen," Mrs. Wooly said. "This ain't a peep show. Get back in there."

Jake walked toward us, scratching his head. He looked sort of pale.

"What?" Brayden asked. "What's out there?"

"There's some bodies out there. Looks like a couple of Greenway employees," Jake told us quietly. "I don't know why they went out there in the hailstorm, but they sure are dead now. They're all mashed up. Bones sticking out all over the place. I've never seen anything like it. Except maybe for that mess back on the bus."

He took a deep breath and shivered.

"Tell you one thing," Jake said, looking at me and Brayden. "We're staying inside till she comes back."

CHAPTER THREE

METAL GATE

"WHO LIKES PIZZA?" ASTRID YELLED.

The little kids answered with a chorus of emphatic me's, their arms shooting up like it was a hand-raising competition.

"Pizza party! Pizza party!" they chanted.

Their excitement was catchy and Astrid looked beautiful talking to them, hearing about their favorite kinds of pizza, with the wind picking up the tendrils of her hair and bringing a flush to her cheeks.

Listen, the tragedy of the day and the destruction of our town wasn't lost on me—and I was worried about my parents and my friends and how the hail might have affected them— but I will admit that I savored being near Astrid.

My mom believed that you make your own luck. Over the stove she had hung these old, maroon-painted letters that spell out MANIFEST. The idea was if you thought and dreamed about the way you wanted your life to be—if you just envisioned it long enough—it would come into being.

DAY 1

But as hard as I had manifested Astrid Heyman with her hand in mine, her blue eyes gazing into mine, her lips whispering something wild and funny and outrageous in my ear, she had remained totally unaware of my existence. Truly, to even dream of dreaming about Astrid, for a guy like me, in my relatively low position on the social ladder of Lewis Palmer High, was idiotic. And with her a senior and me a junior? Forget it.

Astrid was just lit up with beauty: shining blond ringlets, June sky–blue eyes, slightly furrowed brow, always biting back a smile, champion diver on the swim team. Olympic level.

Hell, Astrid was Olympic level in every possible way.

And I wasn't. I was one of those guys who had stayed short too long. Everyone else sprang up in seventh and eighth grade but I just stayed kid-size through those years—the Brayden-hair-gel years. Then, last summer, I'd grown, like, six inches or something. My mom delighted in my absurd growth spell, buying me new clothes basically every other week. My bones ached at night and my joints creaked sometimes, like a senior citizen's.

I'd entered the school year with some hope, actually, that now I was of average—even above-average—height, I might rejoin society at an, um, higher level. I know it's crass to talk about popularity outright, but remember, I'd had a thing for Astrid for a long, long time. I wanted to be near her and working my way into her circle of friends seemed the only way.

I thought my height might do the trick. Sure I was skinny as a rail, but still, my inventory of looks had improved: green eyes—good asset. Ash-colored hair—okay. Height—no longer a problem. Build—needed major improvement. Glasses—a drag, but contacts gave me chronic conjunctivitis, which looked a lot worse than glasses, and I couldn't get Lasik until I stopped growing, so that was out for a while. Teeth and skin—fair. Clothes—sort of a wreck but getting better.

I thought I had a chance but the sum total of our communication to date were the two words she'd said to me on the bus: *Help me*.

And I hadn't.

We all went back inside and Astrid got the Pizza Shack oven going and turned on the slushie maker.

Josie was still sitting in a booth, wrapped in her space blanket. I headed toward the soda dispensers to get her a drink, but I saw that she already had two Gatorades and a water on the tabletop in front of her.

The slushie maker was too high up for the little kids to reach, so after watching them jumping up to try to reach the handles in a cute but utterly futile way, I went over and offered to make each kid whatever kind of slushie they wanted.

They cheered.

They had never known you could combine the flavors, so they were impressed with the layered slushies I made for them.

"This is the best slushie I ever had!" gushed a towheaded first grader named Max. He had a preposterous cowlick in the back of his head that made his hair stand up like a little blond fan.

"I had a lot of slushies in my life 'cause my dad's a long-distance trucker and he's always takin' me on the road," Max continued. "I probly had slushies in every state of America. One time my dad took me out of school for a week and he almost took me into Mexico but then my mom called him and said he'd better haul me back on up to Monument before she called the cops on him!"

I liked Max. I like a kid who holds nothing back.

DAY 1

One kid was Latino. I put him at about first grade, maybe kindergarten. He was chubby and jolly looking.

"What's your name?" I asked him.

He just smiled at me. He had two big holes where his top front teeth should have been.

"*Cómo se llama?* Your name?"

He said something that sounded all the world to me like, "You listen."

"I'm listening," I said.

"You listen," he said, nodding.

"Okay, I listen."

"No, no," he said.

"His name is You-list-ease," said Max, trying to help. "He's in first grade with me."

"You-list-ease?" I repeated.

The Mexican kid said his name again.

And suddenly I got it. "Ulysses! His name is Ulysses!"

The Spanish pronunciation, let me tell you, sounds a lot different than the English.

Ulysses was now grinning like he'd won the lottery.

"Ulysses! Ulysses!"

A tiny, hardscrabble victory for him and me: Now I knew his name.

Chloe was the third grader who had been whining when Mrs. Wooly said she was going for help. Chloe was chubby and tan and very energetic. I made her a blue-and-red-striped slushie, like she wanted. However, it was not good enough for her.

"The stripes are too thick!" she complained. "I want it like a raccoon tail."

But it turns out it's really hard to make a slushie with thin stripes, as I discovered after five or six tries.

I handed Chloe my very best effort.

"Not like a raccoon's tail," she remarked. She shook her head sadly, as if she were a teacher and I hopeless student.

"This is as 'raccoon tail' as I can do," I said.

"All right." She sighed. "If it's your best work."

Chloe, I had already decided, was a piece of work.

The McKinley twins were our neighbors, actually. Alex and I sometimes shoveled their driveway for their mom, who I guess was a single mother.

She paid twenty dollars, which was okay money.

The twins were a boy and a girl both with red hair and freckles. They had the kind of back-to-back freckles that overlap so they hardly had any other kind of skin, just a bit of white peeping through the thick be-freckling.

At five years old, they were the youngest kids, and they were the smallest by far. Their mom was small herself, and the kids were just tiny. Perfectly formed but, like, knee high. Neither of them spoke much, but I guess Caroline talked a little more than Henry. They were just completely adorable, to use a word that is most often used by girls and maiden aunts.

I did not really save the best for last because Batiste, the lone second grader, was a real handful. He looked vaguely Asian and had glossy black hair that was cut very close to his head, like a brush.

For one thing, Batiste was from a very religious family, so he considered himself the authority on sinning. I had already overheard him reprimand Brayden for cursing ("Taking the Lord's name in vain is a sin!"), tattle on Chloe for pushing Ulysses ("Shoving is a sin!"), and inform the other little kids that not saying grace before eating was a sin ("Before we eat, God wants us sinners to give thanks!").

He was always watching everyone, waiting for them to screw up, so he could point it out. A real charming quality, I

DAY 1

tell you. I guess being a little self-important know-it-all was not considered a sin by his people.

The other two kids from the grammar school bus were my brother, Alex, and Sahalia.

Sahalia was advanced, for an eighth grader. She had a very cutting-edge idea of fashion. Even I, someone who had worn sweatsuits and only sweatsuits to school until seventh grade, can identify someone with style when I see one. On the day this all went down, she was wearing tight jeans held together up one side with safety pins and a leather vest of some kind over a tank top. She also had a leather jacket—a big one, much too big for her, lined with red-checkered material. She was three years younger but far, far cooler than me.

Many people were cooler than me. I didn't hold it against her.

It looked like she'd gotten into the makeup section. I swear when we first arrived at the store, she didn't have any on. But now her eyes were lined with black and she had on very red lip gloss.

She was kneeling up on the booth seat next to where Brayden and Jake were eating. She was sort of watching them eat and trying to be a part of their group at the same time. It was a sort of a sideways approach to being included in a clique. You get near them, and hope they'll invite you in.

No such doing for Sahalia.

Brayden looked up at her and said, "We're trying to talk. Do you mind?"

Sahalia slipped away and went to hang out near Astrid. She walked like she didn't care. Like it was her plan to go to the counter all along. I had to admire her slouch.

Niko was eating alone.

I should have invited him to sit with Alex and me, but by the time I'd gotten the slushies made, and remade in Chloe's case, the pizza was done. I was hungry enough to forget my manners.

Alex and I wolfed down our first pieces of pizza. The square, heavy Pizza Shack pizza had never tasted so good. I licked the red sauce from my fingers and Alex got up to get us seconds.

By the time he came back, though, I was watching Josie.

She was sitting sideways in her booth, with her back to the wall. Mrs. Wooly had wiped her face and hands clean, but Josie still had dried blood on her arms and her body and the space blanket was sticking to it in places. She was still wearing her old clothes. I felt bad for her; here we were all having a nice pizza lunch, and she was clearly still back on the bus.

I took my pizza over to her and sat opposite her in her booth.

"Josie," I said quietly. "I got some pizza for you. Come on, Josie. Food will make you feel better."

She just looked at me and shook her head. One of her giraffe hair bumps had come unrolled and the hair was sort of listing and drooping over, like a broken branch.

"Have one bite," I bargained. "One bite and I'll leave you alone."

She turned her face toward the wall.

"Well, it's here if you want it," I said.

Astrid slid a large tray with some Sicilian pepperoni out of the oven. I was still somewhat hungry, so I went to the counter.

"Like pepperoni?" she asked me.

My heart was pounding.

"Yeah," I said. Suave.

"Here you go," she said, putting one on a paper plate.

"Thanks," I said. Real suave.

Then I turned and walked away.

DAY 1

And that was my second conversation with Astrid. At least this time I responded.

I was walking back to my booth when we all heard the rumble of a machine. A heavy, rolling, clanking sound.

"What's that?" Max stammered.

Three heavy metal gates were rolling down over the gaping hole at the front of the store. One, two, three, side by side they descended. The two on the sides covered the windows. The center one was a bit bigger and covered the entire space of what had been the sliding doors.

The gate was perforated so we could still get air and see out, but it was kind of scary.

We were being locked in.

The little kids lost it. "What's happening?" "We're trapped!" "I want to go home!" That kind of thing.

Niko just stood, watching the gate come down.

"We should like get something under it. To like wedge it open," Jake shouted.

He grabbed a shopping cart and rolled it forward, under the central gate.

But the gate dropping just pushed the cart out of the way.

The three gates settled with a heavy CLANK that rang with finality.

"We're locked in," I said.

"And everyone else is locked out," Niko said quietly.

"All right," Jake said, clapping his hands. "Which one of you little punks is gonna teach me how to play Chutes and Ladders?"

Alex came up beside me and tugged at my shirt.

"Dean," he said, "wanna go to the Media Department with me?"

* * *

All the bigtabs in the Media Department were dead, of course. They ran off the Network, just like our minitabs. But Alex found the one old-fashioned flat-screen TV. It was hung down low, near to the floor, off to the side.

I'd never really understood why anyone would want to buy a plain television, when bigtabs were only just a little more expensive and you could watch TV on a bigtab and use it to browse and text and Skype and 'book and game and a million other useful things. But every big store kept a couple televisions on display and now I knew why. They worked without National Connectivity. They were picking up some kind of television-only signals. And though the screen was kind of grainy and stripy at times, we watched eagerly.

Alex turned it to CNN.

The rest of our group filed over, drawn, I guess, by the sound of live media.

I expected the story of our hailstorm to be all over the news. It wasn't.

Our little hailstorm was nothing.

There were two anchors working together and they explained it very calmly, but the woman was shaken. You could see she had been crying. Her eye makeup was all smeared around her eyes and I wondered why nobody fixed her makeup. It was CNN, for God's sake.

The man in the blue suit said he would repeat the chain of events for anyone just joining the broadcast. That was us. He said a volcano had erupted on an island called La Palma, in the Canary Islands.

Shaky, handheld images of ash and a fiery mountain appeared on the screen behind the anchors.

DAY 1

The woman with the bad makeup said that the western face of the entire island had exploded with the eruption of the volcano. Five hundred billion tons of rock and lava had avalanched into the ocean.

They didn't have footage of that.

Blue Suit said the explosion had created a "megatsunami."

A wave a half a mile tall.

Moving at six hundred miles per hour.

Bad Makeup said that the megatsunami had grown wider as it approached the coast of the U.S. Then she stopped talking. Her voice caught in her throat, and Blue Suit took over.

The megatsunami had hit the Eastern Coast of the United States at 4:43 a.m. mountain time.

Boston, New York, Charleston, Miami.

All had been hit.

They couldn't estimate the number of fatalities.

I just sat there. I felt completely numb.

It was the worst natural disaster in recorded history.

The most violent volcano eruption in recorded history.

The biggest tsunami in recorded history.

They played some footage.

It played so fast they had to slow it down so you could see what was going on.

From the street, a shot of the Empire State Building and a tall cloud drawing closer and closer, frame by frame, but it wasn't a cloud—it was a wall of water—and then the image went blank.

A beach and you're looking out at the water, only there is no water, just a boat stranded about a mile out into the ocean bed and you hear a voice praying to Jesus and then the image is shaking, shaking, and a wave so high the minitab can't see the top thunders up. Then darkness.

Chloe said she wanted to watch kid TV. We ignored her.

Bad Makeup said the National Connectivity was down because three of the five satellite centers had been located on the East Coast.

Blue Suit said the president had declared a state of emergency and was safe at an undisclosed location.

We watched, mostly in silence.

"Turn it to *Tabi-Teens*," Chloe whined. "This is bo-ring!"

I looked at her. She was totally clueless. She was listlessly picking at a label stuck on the minitab counter.

None of the little kids seemed to understand what we were learning. They were just kind of slowpoking around, hanging out.

I had to keep watching the TV. Couldn't think about the kids.

I felt gray. Washed out. Like a stone.

Bad Makeup said the megatsunami had triggered severe weather conditions across the rest of the country. Her voice caught on "rest of the country." She mentioned storms called supercells, sweeping across the Rockies (that was us).

I looked over at Josie. She was watching the screen. Caroline had crawled onto Josie's lap, and Josie was stroking Caroline's hair absentmindedly.

CNN showed more footage from the East Coast.

They showed a house carried up the side of a mountain. They showed a lake full of cars. They showed people wandering around half naked on streets in places that should have looked familiar, but now looked like locations from war movies.

People in boats, people crying, people washed down rivers like logs on a log float, people washed up along with their cars and garages and trees and trash cans and bicycles and god-knows-what else. People as debris.

DAY 1

I closed my eyes.

Near me, someone started to cry.

"Put it to *Tabi-Teens*!" Chloe demanded. "Or *Traindawgs* or something!"

I took my brother's hand. It was ice cold.

We watched for hours.

At some point, somebody turned off the television.

At some point, somebody got out sleeping bags for everyone.

There was a lot of whining from the little kids and not a lot of comforting coming from us.

They were really bothering us. Especially Chloe and Batiste.

Batiste kept talking about the "end of days."

He said it was just like Reverend Grand said would happen. The judgment day was upon us. I wanted to punch him in his little greasy face.

I just wanted to think. I couldn't think and they all kept crying and asking for stupid things and clinging to us and I just wanted them to shut up.

Finally Astrid bent over and grabbed Batiste by the shoulders.

She said, real clear and kind of mean, "You kids go and get candy. As much as you want. Go do that."

And they did.

They came back with bags from the candy aisle.

That was the best we could do for them that night: candy. We took the bags and ripped them open and made a big pile in the middle of the floor, and everyone gorged on fun sizes of all brands and types.

We ate it like it was medicine. Like it was magic candy that could somehow restore us to a normal life again. We ate ourselves numb and got in our bags and went to sleep.

There was a lot of crying from the little kids and occasionally one of us would yell, "Shut up!"

That's how we got by, that first night.

DAY 1

CHAPTER FOUR

EIGHT POINT TWO

WE WERE SHAKEN AWAKE AROUND EIGHT.

It wasn't that thing that happens where you're dreaming that you're running through a forest chasing a fox or something and suddenly a tree grabs you and starts shaking you and you begin to wake up and realize it's actually your mom shaking you and your alarm is going off and you're late for school.

Not at all.

This was: You're in a sleeping bag on the floor of a giant superstore and suddenly the floor starts pitching and heaving and you're getting bounced around like a piece of popcorn in a hot pan and things start falling off the shelves and everyone is screaming and scared out of their minds and you're one of everyone.

It was more like that.

And here's the hilarious part—it was a FORESHOCK. Apparently, that's what happens when you're about to experience an 8.2. It's an earthquake so big it sends messengers ahead.

"Get to the Pizza Shack!" Niko shouted. "Under the tables!"

I grabbed Alex with one hand and picked up Ulysses the first grader with the other and ran for it. Stuff was falling off the shelves or had fallen. From the Food section and elsewhere you could hear glass bottles crashing off the shelves and onto the floor.

The rest of the kids were right behind me. I saw that all the big kids had grabbed one or two little ones. Astrid was escorting Josie. Tripping and falling and hurrying as best we could, we made it to the Pizza Shack and got under the tables. They were bolted down, which was why Niko wanted us there.

"We'll be safer here," I told Alex and Ulysses, whose nose was streaming wet snot.

"Hold tight to the table legs," Niko shouted.

"This is dumb," Brayden growled. "The earthquake is over. Why are we hiding here—"

And his voice began to shake.

Because the ground had begun to shake.

And he sure did grab himself a table leg.

The quake was less scary than the foreshock, in my opinion. We were ready for the quake. We were awake already.

We started shaking and shaking and you could hear things falling and crashing all around us.

It's a miracle the store didn't cave in, but, as we would discover, the store was built like a safe. It held. Rock solid. Pretty much everything was tossed to the floor and lots of the shelves toppled over, but the damage to the store was not as bad as it could have been.

"Is everyone okay?" Jake asked.

"Um, I would say, no," Astrid answered. "The world as we know it is gone. We're locked in a Greenway and an EARTHQUAKE just smashed the store to pieces!"

DAY 2

She was furious and she looked gorgeous.

"I know that, Astrid!" Jake snapped. "Obviously everything has gone to hell but I am supposed to be in charge so I just thought I'd ask!"

The kindergarten twins burst into new sobs. I saw that they, like Ulysses, had lots of grime and mucus on their weary little faces. All the little kids looked pretty bad off.

"Jake is doing the best he can so why don't you back off, Astrid?" Brayden said.

"Screw you, Brayden! You're the last person I want to be stuck here with!" she answered.

Josie had her hands over her ears. The little kids were crying and Chloe was starting to scream.

"All right, everyone just settle down," Jake said. "Astrid, you're out of control. Pull yourself together!"

"Excuse me," Henry said to Jake. "Me and Caroline have decided. We want to go home."

Henry and Caroline wanted to go home. Like it was some sleepover that had gone wrong and now he'd like Jake to call their parents so they could get picked up.

"Yeah! I want my nana!" Chloe yelled.

"Guys, we gotta wait for Mrs. Wooly," Jake said calmly.

But the little kids were in a full-blown meltdown now. Crying, noses running, snorting with sobs, the works.

Ulysses was near me and he nodded his head, agreeing with the shouts and demands and wails of the other kids. These tears, fat like jelly beans, plopping out of his eyes and running down his face, were so profuse they were actually washing his face because he kept wiping at them with the sleeve of his sweatshirt.

"It's going to be okay," I told him.

He just shook his head and cried all the harder.

I got up. Determined to go find a godforsaken Spanish-English dictionary.

"Don't go yet," Niko told me. "More aftershocks."

He was right. The floor started to pitch and I dropped down and ducked under the nearest table. It just so happened to be the table Astrid had ducked under, too.

This was certainly the closest I'd ever been to her. I held the center pole under the table. Her hands were just below mine.

Her head was bowed and it was all a blur of blond hair and purple sweater until the tremors stopped.

She looked up at me and there was this moment of plainness between us. Like she saw me and I saw her. She looked scared and young, like a little girl, and there were tears in her eyes.

I don't know what she read on my face. Probably that I was totally hers. That I loved her with everything worthy inside me.

I guess she didn't like what she saw, because she brushed away tears with the back of her hand and turned away from me. Her jaw was clenched and she looked like she wanted to punch me in the throat. That's the truth.

I got out from under her table.

"Screw this," Sahalia said. "I'm going home."

"No, you're not, Sahalia," Jake said. "Mrs. Wooly told us all to stay here and stay together and we're gonna do exactly that."

"Are you kidding?" Sahalia said. "Mrs. Wooly's not coming back. We're on our own. And frankly I'd rather take my chances out there than stay here with you losers."

Alex spoke up. "How are you going to get out? The gate is down."

Sahalia pointed to the wall, past the Pizza Shack, near the Grocery section.

DAY 2

Duh.

There was a door with a red, illuminated Exit sign above it. How had we missed it until now?

"They have to have emergency exits," she said.

Then she walked over and pushed it.

"Let me," Brayden said.

"Bray!" Jake yelled, but Brayden had already sprinted over. He bashed his weight against it.

"No good," he said. "It's locked."

"Like I said," Jake repeated, eyeing his friend. "We're staying here until Mrs. Wooly comes back."

"I'll find a way out," Sahalia said. She stomped off.

"Excuse me, but Sahalia is my neighbor," said Chloe. "If *she's* going home, I'm going with her."

"Me, too," said Max. "I can hitch a ride."

Jake was losing patience.

"You heard what Mrs. Wooly said! We stay here until she comes for us. It's simple."

"But why does Sahalia get to go?" whined Chloe.

"Sahalia's not going anywhere," Jake answered. "The doors are locked!"

"But I want my nana!"

Jake bent down and got up in her grill.

"Stop talking about going home. There is no going home until Mrs. Wooly gets back."

"But I want—"

He poked Chloe in the chest.

"Stop it."

"My nana—"

He poked her again. "Stop."

She stopped. Then she rubbed the spot on her chest where he'd poked her and glared at him.

So we were lucky that the Greenway was solidly built, but, man, the mess was incredible. Almost everything had been tossed from the shelves. The shelving units themselves hadn't fallen over, since they were bolted down. That was nice. But everything was a mess and most things made of glass were history.

We all picked our way through the merchandise, headed back to our sleeping-bag "home" in the Media Department.

"Gonna be a big cleanup," Alex said to me.

"It'll be good," I said. "Something to keep us busy until they come for us."

Alex shrugged.

The bigtabs that had been on the walls of the Media Department were now on the floor of the Media Department.

Pretty much everything in the Media Department was now on the floor of the Media Department.

The display wall itself was hanging partially off the concrete wall behind it.

The bigtabs were lying facedown on the floor, overlapping like roof shingles. Bits of black glass and plastic framing were scattered all over the place.

Everyone was standing around, forlorn and crestfallen, looking at the debris as Alex and I walked up.

"We just had the one crappy television," Brayden complained. "And now it's toast. We have no way of knowing what's going on outside!"

"I think we need to start thinking about an exit strategy," Astrid said.

"Shhh!" Alex interrupted her.

"No, I really do," she continued, surprised that Alex would cut her off.

"I hear the TV," Alex said.

DAY 2

We all shut up. If you listened very closely, there was a buzz, a hum. A tiny, tiny hum.

Brayden and Jake stepped forward and began digging through the bigtabs.

"Careful," Alex said. "You could get a shock!"

Jake found the TV.

He stepped back over the mound of dead bigtabs, holding the TV carefully at its sides.

The screen was smashed. Strange, glowing inkblots of color surged over the monitor helter-skelter.

Alex took the set and placed it on the floor.

He pushed along the lower edge of the frame. That was how you changed the channel—something I didn't remember since we'd switched out our TV for a bigtab when I was, like, seven.

Alex made some adjustments and the static got louder and louder.

Then a voice came on.

"Yes!" Jake said.

The little kids cheered.

"Quiet," Niko said.

"Shhh, you guys!" Astrid added.

It was a man's voice. Sounded like an interview.

"Entirely unexpected as this area is not on a fault line. It's unthinkable, really. And a quake of this magnitude is unprecedented. There is no doubt in my mind that it was triggered by yesterday's megatsunami."

Alex sat down in front of the TV. We all just took random places nearby, except for Chloe, who said she was going to get some food.

The voice on the TV changed.

"Excuse me, Professor. We have breaking news. There are reports coming in of a leak. A chemical leak. Chemical warfare compounds.

"There are reports that several chemical warfare agents may be leaking from NORAD's storage facilities."

"Quiet! Quiet everyone"—the voice was yelling to people in the studio, it seemed—"This is from NORAD: Attention, residents of Colorado and neighboring states. At 8:36 a.m. today, Wednesday, September 18, 2024, chemical weapon storage facilities at the North American Aerospace Defense Command Department have been breached. Residents in a five-hundred-mile radius of NORAD are urged to get indoors and seal all windows immediately."

Niko stood up. He looked wired, flushed. Panicked almost.

"Guys, we have to cover the front gates." Niko said. "Right now."

We zigged and zagged through the store, cutting our way through the fallen boxes and crashed-up merchandise. Niko started giving orders left and right.

"Jake, get plastic sheeting. Brayden and Dean, get duct tape."

"Plastic sheeting, like what?" Jake asked, panic in his voice.

"Shower curtains could work," Alex suggested. "Or plastic drop cloths, like painters use."

"Alex, help Jake. Figure it out. Astrid, keep the little kids out of the way."

"Don't stick me with the kids," she protested. "I'm just as strong as you guys are!"

"Just do what I say!" Niko hollered.

She did.

* * *

DAY 2

Brayden and I found the duct tape and cursed that we didn't have anything to carry it in, like a cart or a basket. The most either of us could carry in our hands was, like, ten rolls.

"I have an idea," I said. I stripped off my rugby shirt.

"What are you doing, Geraldine?" Brayden asked. His voice was flustered. "Screw you, I'm going."

He took off with his ten rolls.

I made knots in the sleeves and started loading the tape into it. Maybe it would have taken as long to find a bucket or a bag or something but I got at least thirty rolls in my shirt.

When I made it to the gate, Niko and Jake were trying to push the bus back from the gate, to make more space to work in. It didn't budge.

"Forget it," Niko said. "We'll work around it."

Brayden was ripping open the packets of plastic sheeting.

"I'll do that," Niko said. "Go back for more tape. We're going to need lots more—"

I arrived and dumped out the rolls of tape.

"Excellent," Niko said. "Open 'em up."

I started to tear the plastic wrappers off the rolls when Brayden elbowed me in the ribs.

"Nice abs, man," Brayden said. "You work out?"

He started to laugh. Jake stopped unfolding the sheeting and was on Brayden in about two strides. He shook him. Hard.

"We're gonna die from friggin' NORAD and you're busting on the booker about his friggin' physique? What's wrong with you? Come on, man!" Jake let go and Brayden stumbled backward.

I struggled to untie the stupid knots from my shirt.

Now I knew what Jake thought of me. The booker. Okay. Whatever that meant.

Meanwhile, we had sheeting to put up.

"This is going to be much faster," came my brother's voice. He came sliding over to us on the linoleum, holding two staple guns and a box of industrial-size staples.

Jake and Niko manned the staple guns. Me, Brayden, and Alex held the sheeting taut.

Two layers of shower curtains. One layer of wool blankets (Alex's idea). Then three layers of plastic drop cloths. The whole thing sealed along the edge with multiple layers of duct tape.

Astrid came striding over, trailing little kids. They swarmed past the bus and looked at our makeshift wall.

"Not bad," Astrid said.

"It'll do the trick," Jake said.

He grabbed Astrid and got her head under his arm.

"Hey, kids," he said. "Free tickles!"

The kids chirped and crowed, trying to tickle her.

"Let me go, you jerk!" she said, but with a laugh.

She pulled away from Jake, pushing the kids away.

"Get off me, you little monsters!" she shouted good-naturedly.

Her shirt rode up during the scuffle and I caught sight of her lower back. Tan, muscled, gorgeous.

She was in better shape than me. By far.

"Let's get more blankets," Niko said. "And do another layer. Then I want to see if there's some plywood and make it more sturdy."

I wiped the sweat off my head and the air felt nice and cool on my forehead. It made me realize something and the something hit me like a fist in my gut.

DAY 2

"The AC," I whispered. Then I shouted, "The AC!"

The AC was on. The huge industrial AC unit was sucking in the air from outside. It was why we all felt so nice and cool after working so hard.

"Son of a bitch," Niko said.

CHAPTER FIVE

INK

"WHERE'S THE MAIN CONTROLS?" NIKO ASKED ASTRID. "DO YOU know from when you worked here?"

"There's some kind of security office in the back," she stammered. "In the storeroom."

The little kids clung to Astrid so she stayed behind while the rest of us raced with Niko toward the back of the store.

We headed through two giant metal double doors into the storeroom.

It was dark back there. Most of the storeroom was filled with crashed-over boxes and toppled shelving units. Lots of smells mixed together: fruit juice, ammonia, electricity, dog food.

Set into the back wall were two giant loading bays, each with two huge metal doors.

I hadn't even considered that there would be loading bays but of course there would be. Safety gates had come down over the huge doors, just like up front.

To one side of the big, cavernous space was a booth with

the words Operations Center on the door. It had had glass walls before the earthquake, but now it just had glass debris scattered everywhere.

"Bingo," said Brayden, king of stating the obvious.

The door to the Operations Center was locked but since the glass in the door had been smashed to pieces, Niko just ducked through the jagged-edged door.

There was a row of security cameras, seeing into every corner of the store, though most looked focused on the Media Department.

"This is awesome," Brayden murmured. He pointed. "Look, you can see into the women's changing rooms!"

"Focus, Brayden," said Jake. "We need the controls for the AC."

Alex pointed. There were four panels, built into the wall. One controlled the solar harvest system on the roof. The function lights were steady green, which confirmed what we already knew: We had power.

One was about the gates. A flashing override message read, "Remote Trigger—Riot Gates." And one had to do with water pressure. That seemed fine.

And there was the one we needed: AC.

We all scanned the panel.

It was all numbers and zones. Percentages and lots of icons that were impossible to decipher. One looked like a lightning bolt. Another looked like an upside-down smiley face. One looked like someone mooning you, I'm not kidding. It was a totally indecipherable.

"Oh man," Alex said anxiously.

Brayden started pressing elements on the flat screen randomly.

"Don't—" Alex started, but Brayden cut him off.

"One of these buttons will turn it off!"

"But you can't just press them all like that," Niko objected. "You could just be—"

As if on cue, the AC picked up intensity, blasting us with cold air.

"Making it worse."

Brayden threw up his hands.

"We're going to have to find the unit and shut it off manually," Niko said. "That's the fastest way."

"It's probably on the roof," Alex said.

We all looked at him blankly for a moment.

"I'll go," Niko said.

"Me, too," Alex added.

I couldn't let my little brother go and not go myself.

"Me, too," I said.

"I'll be right back," Jake said. "Wait!" He ran off into the store for something.

"How do we get on the roof?" Alex asked.

"Up there," Niko said, pointing.

A perforated metal staircase ran up a wall and led to a hatch in the ceiling.

The hatch was open and yellowish sky shone through.

"What the—?" I stammered.

"Sahalia," Niko answered. "She must have found the hatch."

I was about halfway up the stairs when Jake came bounding toward me.

"Here," he said, handing me three industrial-strength air masks. He'd gotten them from the Home Improvement Department.

"Thanks," I said and looped their straps over my shoulder.

"I guess you better get some for you guys," I suggested. "Just in case."

DAY 2

Jake raised an eyebrow at me giving him a direction, no matter how gently put.

"Already on it, man," he said.

I stepped through the hatch, up onto the roof.

How can I describe what I saw?

First off, the roof was covered in hail and the surface had huge pits in places.

More importantly, there was Sahalia. She was sitting on the ledge of the roof, looking out at the sky. She had a box next to her. A home safety fire-escape ladder. It was still unopened.

Sahalia was staring straight ahead.

Niko and Alex were standing behind her, staring in the same direction.

I stopped in my tracks and the masks slipped from my fingers when I saw what they were seeing.

In the distance, near the mountains, a thick streak of pitch-black rose up, twisting like a ribbon through the air. It went up in a line, up until it reached cloud level, and then it gradually expanded out, shaped like a funnel.

It looked like a stream of ink being poured up, pooling in the sky.

Cold water from the hail was seeping into my sneakers and wetting the bottoms of my pant legs. I didn't care.

The black cloud was growing and growing, this ball of nighttime spreading out over the horizon.

"What is it?" Alex murmured.

"Ask Brayden," Niko answered.

Sahalia murmured, "They made something evil over at NORAD."

The ink cloud was now as big in the sky as the mountain

range behind it. It looked like an inverted mountain, tethered to the ground by its long black plume.

"AC units," Niko said. "Now."

Brave Hunter Man had spoken.

We scrambled to obey.

The units were easy to find. They stood right in the middle of the roof. Four giant, van-size boxes. They had slits in the sides to let in the clean air and then metal ducts branching out from each machine and connecting into one giant duct. The giant one went in through the roof of the Greenway.

"Shoot," Niko said. "The ducts."

The ducts were the problem. They had taken a major beating in the hail. They were battered and perforated. They had big holes in them and were sucking in the regular air along with the processed air from the units.

"Even if we shut off the unit, the bad air will come in through the broken duct," Alex said. There was panic rising in his voice. He was getting scared.

"We gotta seal off the vent," Niko said. He turned to Sahalia. "Go get a sledgehammer. If it's too heavy to carry, get Jake to bring it up."

"I can carry a stupid sledgehammer," she sassed.

"Well, go get it then!" Niko yelled.

She hurried to the hatch.

Niko stepped over to the giant duct, about four feet away from where it went into the roof. He shimmied up on top and jumped up and down. *BOOM*. The metal echoed. *BOOM*. And it gave, just a little.

"Help me," he said to me and Alex.

My brother and I got up there and we started jumping on

DAY 2

that duct together. It might have been fun, if we weren't watching a black cloud spread like an oil spill over the sky.

We jumped and together the three of us started to make a dent in it. (Pun unintentional, I promise.)

Sahalia came dragging the sledgehammer. We got off the duct.

Niko took it and *WHAM*. He started beating down the metal. The sledgehammer was much more effective than our jumping. The muscles in his back were straining and I really had to respect the guy. Niko was strong and tough.

The light went very, very green. Everything looked alien and underwater.

BAM. BAM. BAM, went the sledgehammer, denting down the air vent.

The chemical cloud was sweeping the air along in front of it like a summer rainstorm. Only this air was bitter and my eyes began to sting.

"You guys, go," Niko shouted. "I'll be right there."

"No!" I said. "You need our help—"

Suddenly I realized I'd left the masks by the hatch.

I ran to get them.

I guess Alex and Sahalia thought I was making a run for it. They followed me.

I grabbed the masks, and Alex and Sahalia slipped past me and into the hatch. They started down the stairs, coughing and cursing.

"I'll be right there," I shouted.

I turned to start back to Niko . . .

When I felt sick.

Sick in my throat and body and mind. I felt like my blood was on fire. I was so scratchy and irritated I wanted to kill someone. I really did. I wanted to kill somebody and the some-body I wanted to kill was Niko.

I saw him there, hitting the vent with that sledgehammer and I wanted to throttle him. End his whole noble, heroic no-sense-of-humor thing.

I lurched at him with the mask.

I roared at him.

Then I fell over, facedown in the hail. I'd been tripped.

Someone had me by the foot and I was furious. It was my brother. He had an air mask on and he was pulling me into the hatch.

I swung at him. I'd kill him. Tripping me like that. I'd rip his head off.

I grabbed handfuls of hail and I threw them at him.

He dragged me toward the hatch and pulled me in.

I started beating him with the mask I was still holding. He wouldn't let go of my leg and was dragging me down the stairs.

I swung at him, wanting him to lose his balance. I tried to get his mask off. I grabbed his hair and pulled. I bit my brother on the arm and drew blood.

I saw red, like people say they do. A sheet of blood red was over my eyes and I couldn't think. Just pummel. Pound, tear, destroy.

We reached the bottom of the staircase and Alex tried to squirm away from me. I launched myself at him.

Jake tackled me.

I hit the cold cement and I cursed him and raked at his face.

"Jesus Christ!" Jake cursed. "What happened up there?"

I roared at him. I had no words.

"What happened to your brother?" Jake demanded of Alex.

DAY 2

Alex was crying. I had made him cry.

"He's an animal!" Jake said, pinning me to the ground with his knee in my stomach. My arms were behind my back, somehow. In addition to football, Jake had also been on the wrestling team. And he had maybe fifty pounds on me—I was pinned.

We didn't hear Niko until he was standing right beside us.

"I sealed it," he said. "It's done. But we're gonna need to cover the hatch with plastic sheeting and the loading-bay doors back here, too. I'll get the staple guns if you guys get the—"

I must have growled or barked or something.

He gestured to me.

"What's wrong with Dean?"

I swear to God, I wanted to rip his throat out.

CHAPTER SIX

THE GATE RATTLER

JAKE STRAINED TO KEEP ME PINNED. RAGE HAMMERED IN MY heart. I wanted up!

I heard this weird whine. A panicky whine.

It was coming from Brayden.

"What is he?" Brayden said. His upper lip was curled back in an expression of disgust. "What is he? What is he made of?"

"What are you talking about?" Jake said, still struggling to keep me pinned.

Jake must have weighed two hundred pounds. I was flattened against the cold cement floor.

"Look at him!" Brayden cried. "There's smoke coming off him. He's straight from hell!"

"What are you talking about?" Alex said. He sounded scared. He sounded like he was crying but I couldn't see him from where I was pinned.

Brayden was pulling at his hair, looking all around.

"It's everywhere!" he cried. "Smoke from hell."

DAY 2

He backed away from us and huddled against a stack of giant boxes.

"Brayden, there's no smoke," Niko said. "Everything's okay."

"There is evil everywhere!" Brayden wailed.

"Dude, you're flipping out," Jake said.

Niko went over to Brayden.

"Don't touch me!" Brayden screamed.

"Look," Niko said to Jake. "His pupils are completely dilated."

"Get away from me," Brayden said.

"It must be the air." Niko came over to look at me. "The air went all green. We must have been breathing in the chemicals. Some kind of psychotic agent in the air."

Niko looked funny, too, though I wasn't quite up to saying so.

He had blisters around his eyes, like a raccoon mask. And his hands, when he touched me, were covered with tiny blood blisters, like he was wearing red lace gloves.

He started to cough. It sounded wet in there.

He coughed into his hand and came up with a blob of red phlegm. Then he caught sight of his hands and he looked at them with this expression of puzzlement so exaggerated I started to laugh.

Not a cool, ironic laugh but kind of a mad cackle.

I'm telling it like it happened, okay?

Brayden was seated on the floor, curled in a little ball, sobbing hard, jagged sobs.

Good.

I closed my eyes and listened to my heart beating. It was loud, like I had the heart of a gorilla.

All I could say was "Agghrr . . ."

I was trying to say Alex. But it didn't come out.

"We've got to get cleaned up," Niko said. He had his shirt

off and was examining his skin. A tapestry of blisters was developing over his skin. It followed the underlying veins. He was starting to look like a biology class illustration of the circulatory system.

I tried again. "Agghhrr . . ." I wanted to say I was sorry.

"We need soap and water," Niko said. "And I think I should take some Benadryl."

"I'll get it," Alex offered.

"Sahalia, you should change, too," Niko said. Sahalia looked freaked out. Her makeup was running down her cheeks. She headed toward the doors back into the store, giving Brayden a wide berth.

"Hey, would you mind getting us some clothes, too?" Niko asked.

She looked back at all of us.

"Sure," she said. "Whatever."

I tried to say, Let me up, I'm fine. But what came out was *grrrrag*. I strained against Jake's bulk.

"Chill out, Dean!" Jake shouted in my face.

Alex skirted by. He glanced at me, then looked away. He had welts across his face where I had clawed him and there was blood caked near his nose. His eyes were red.

"Hey, little man, do me a favor," Jake said to my brother. "Get me some rope so I can tie up the Hulk over here."

There is something very wrong with being tied up with rope your own brother brings from the Sporting Goods section.

After they tied me up, Jake took Brayden back into the store. He and Niko thought maybe the air in the storeroom was still polluted.

Niko stripped off his clothes and threw them in a trash

DAY 2

can. He told Alex to do the same. They took the antibacterial soap and spring water that Alex had brought, and stripped and washed down. They just stood there on the cement floor and scrubbed down together.

"Are you okay?" Niko asked Alex.

"I think so," Alex said.

"That was pretty scary."

"Yeah."

I hated hearing that. I hated hearing Niko comforting him. He was my brother. I should be the one comforting him. Only I had attacked him, you see.

"Here!" came Sahalia's voice, and some garments came flying through the door.

She had picked out pink tracksuits for us, complete with fluffy pink slippers.

I was starting to feel like myself again.

"Guys," I croaked, my voice horse and scratchy. "Guys . . ."

Niko stopped dressing to cough into the trash can.

"Are you okay?" Alex asked Niko.

Ask me, I wanted to say.

Niko nodded, wiping spit from his chin.

"The blistering is going down. Washing was a good idea. I think if I'd been up there any longer it could have been really bad."

Alex nodded sympathetically.

"Guys!" I said from the floor.

"Okay, Dean!" Alex snapped at me. "Just wait!"

Niko examined his chest. The blisters were fading away. Vanishing almost.

After they'd both dressed, they came over to look at me.

I saw Alex had my glasses sticking out of his shirt pocket. He must gave grabbed them during our scuffle. Pretty considerate, after I'd tried to tear his scalp off.

"You're feeling better?" Niko asked me.

"Yeah," I croaked. "Well, I feel like a buck fifty. But I feel like myself."

"Who is the president? What day is it? What's Mom's favorite flavor of ice cream?" Alex asked me.

"Cory Booker. Wednesday. She's lactose intolerant."

They let me up.

When we came out of the storeroom and walked back to where the others were waiting, we must have looked really funny in our pink sweatsuits.

Astrid started to ask us if everything was all right, then she burst into laughter.

"Hey, kids, look, it's the ladies' track team!" Astrid announced with a flourish, and they all cracked up.

Jake and Brayden joined in laughing. Alex, too.

But I still had some weird stuff happening in my body.

What I wanted was Astrid. She looked so good to me I wanted to take her, in a dark and terrible way.

Pardon my bloodlust. It's just a little something they whipped up over at NORAD.

I swallowed. Tried to get my breath back.

"We made you guys some pizza," Max said.

"Then we ate it all so Astrid's making you some more," Chloe added.

While Jake, Niko, and Brayden filled Astrid in on what had happened, I took a look at my brother, who I had really done a number on. The shopping cart of medical supplies was still in

DAY 2

the Pizza Shack area, so I poked around, but I didn't see what I wanted.

"Alex, please, come with me," I said. "So I can fix you up."

I knew what I needed to do the job right: Bactine. Our mom swore by it. She never used anything else to clean scrapes or cuts or what have you. She even carried it, in a small travel bottle, in her purse.

So I motioned for Alex to follow me and we headed back toward the Pharmacy section.

I felt horrible.

I had clawed him across the face. So brotherly of me. And he had a huge bruise developing along his jaw. Such familial tenderness. His eyes were red from crying. Because of me.

I rummaged through the fallen merchandise until I found the good stuff. I also grabbed a bag of cotton puffs.

"It wasn't me," I said, swabbing the first of his many scrapes. "Something in the air made me go crazy. You know I'd never attack you like that."

Alex nodded, looking at the floor.

"Please," I begged. "Say you forgive me. I feel so horrible. I couldn't feel any worse."

Tears welled up in my little brother's pale eyes.

"It's just . . . ," he said, his voice getting thin. "It's just that I wasn't scared before . . ."

And now he was.

Thanks to me.

"I don't understand what's happening," he said. "Why you acted like that. Why Niko got those blisters and Brayden started seeing things."

"We'll figure it out," I told him. "And I won't . . . I won't let myself get exposed to the chemicals in the air again. I promise."

"But, Dean, if you can't go outside, how are we going to find Mom and Dad? How will we go home?"

I could have lied. But Alex was smarter than me.

"I don't know," I said.

After I got him cleaned up we walked back together toward the others. He had forgiven me, but he was still kind of stiff with me. Wary, I guess. Or maybe he was just physically sore from the beating I had given him.

As we approached the Pizza Shack we heard: "I did too go to Emerald's!" from Max.

There was this big disconnect between what the big kids were dealing with and what the little kids were thinking about. For example, while I was patching up my brother after having tried to rip him apart due to a chemical compound–induced mania, Max, Batiste, Ulysses, and Chloe were discussing Emerald's, a strip club located near an off-ramp at the outskirts of town.

"He's lying. You never went to Emerald's. They don't let little kids in there," Chloe protested.

"They do if your uncle's the bouncer!" Max countered.

"What do they do in there, anyway?" Batiste wanted to know. "Our church is always trying to get those sinners to repent. But I don't even know what kind of sinning they're doing."

"Probably cursing," offered Chloe.

"Tons of that!" said Max.

"That's a sin." Batiste sighed.

"And drinking liquor?" Chloe asked.

"Totally," said Max. "They have these little glasses in all kinds of flavors like watermelon and peach passion and hot apple. But they taste horrible. Sweet and horrible. I had three of them

DAY 2

one time and then I puked them all up, right on the bar, and my mom said if my uncle ever takes me there again, she's gonna call the cops."

"Drinking is a sin," said Batiste.

"Wow," Chloe murmured.

"I don't want to go back, anyways," Max continued. "Boring. Just a bunch of moms dancing around in their string underwear. Big whoop."

I stifled a laugh.

"What?" Chloe said. "What's so funny?"

"Oh . . . Alex was just telling me a joke," I said.

"Tell us!" she demanded. "We love jokes."

Alex shrugged, lost. "I forget."

"Come on!" they pleaded.

"Okay, okay," I said. "How do you make a tissue dance?"

"How?" Max said.

"You put a little boogie in it!"

Nothing. Not even a groan.

"That's the worst joke I ever heard," said Chloe.

"I don't even get it," said Max.

Alex and I left the grade schoolers to discuss the finer points of adult entertainment and went over to where the big kids were gathering. We crossed past Josie, who was sort of slumped in a booth. Still not saying much. Well, anything.

"How are you, Josie?" I asked.

Alex nudged me toward the other big kids. He wanted to hear what they were thinking about the chemicals. I did, too . . .

"I don't understand," Astrid said. "It made Niko blister up, Dean turned into some kind of a monster, and Brayden started having hallucinations. But Sahalia and Alex and Jake were fine?"

"It doesn't make any sense but, yeah," Jake said, scratching his head.

"Maybe they attack based on age or something . . . ," Brayden said.

"I noticed that the effects seemed to wear off very quickly," Alex piped up. "It makes me think they attack the central nervous system."

"That anyone could make this kind of poison is just horrible," Astrid said. "The people at NORAD should be shot."

"Hey! That's my dad you're talking about," Brayden said.

"But why would they make such awful things?" Astrid asked us. "I mean, a chemical that makes people turn into savages? Or makes them blister up and die? It's evil."

"They made them to protect us."

"Protect us from what? From who?" Astrid demanded.

"From our enemies!" Brayden answered.

"It's inhumane," I spoke up. "Just making those compounds violates the Geneva Convention. It's illegal."

"Nothing's illegal if the government itself is doing it," Brayden asserted, like an idiot.

"That's just amazingly wrong," I said.

"Hey, Brayden," Astrid said. "What exactly does your dad do for NORAD, anyway?"

I'd been wondering that exact thing. I had sort of fantasized that Brayden's dad was like a janitor.

"That's classified, Ass-trid," Brayden replied.

Then we heard some rattling.

Chinka-chinka-chink.

"Hello?" came a distant voice.

We jumped up.

Someone was at the gate!

DAY 2

Beyond the plastic sheeting and the blankets, someone was rattling the gate.

"They came!" shouted one of the little kids. "They're here for us!"

"Anybody home?" came the voice from outside. "Hello!"

We rushed to the gate. Everyone started clamoring at once: "Hi! Hello! We're in here! Who are you? Hello! Hello!"

"Open the gate!" the voice shouted. "I hear you in there."

"Yes, yes! We're trapped inside, we want to get out! We want to go home!" shouted all the little kids in a big jumble.

Chloe turned to Niko and commanded him. "Take down the plastic. He's here for us!"

"Don't you touch it!" Niko growled. I'd never heard him so intense.

"Well? Open up! Come on! I'm hungry!" came the voice from outside.

The little kids were still bouncing with excitement, but I saw the others stiffen.

Listening real attentively. Something about his tone.

"We can't open the gate," Jake yelled. "It's stuck."

"You can! You can open it if you try! Come on!"

Chinka-chinka-chink.

"We're locked in," Jake tried to explain.

"Who's in there?" the voice shouted.

"We're kids from Lewis Palmer!" Jake continued. "We took shelter here from the hail and—"

"Open the gate, little kiddos!" the voice shouted.

"We can't open it, dude!" Jake yelled. "It's some kind of a security gate. But we want to get a message to our parents—"

"Get them a message?" The voice started to laugh. "Sure.

That's a great idea. I'll get them a message. Open the gate, so we can make a message!"

There was something very, very off in this voice. I exchanged a glance with Alex. He knew it, too.

"Like I told you, we can't!" Jake yelled again.

"Open it, you little twits! Come on, I'm hungry! Just open it. Open it."

"We can't—"

"OPEN THE F—— GATE! OPEN IT!!! OPEN, OPEN, OPEN!"

And the man outside started rattling the gate again. *Chinka-chinka-chink.*

I could see the fear wash over the little kids. Their faces, one moment ago bright with hope, went cold and pale.

Caroline and Henry, standing behind me, each clutched on to one of my legs at the exact same moment. I pried them off and crouched down, hugging them to me.

When the man outside shook the gate, our wall of plastic and blankets bobbed with the air pressure.

"Our wall," I said to Niko. "Is it going to let the air in?"

"I don't know. I don't think so," he answered.

"Go away," Jake shouted, his voice gruff.

"LET ME IN!" the man shouted. "BY THE HAIR OF MY F—— CHIN, LET ME IN OR I'LL HUFF AND I'LL BLOW YOUR EFFIN' GREEN-WAY DOWN!"

He was shaking the gate now.

Chinka-chinka-chink. CHINKA-CHINKA-CHINK. CHINKA-CHINKA-CHINK. *Wobble-wobble-wobble* went the sheeting.

Astrid stepped in front of the little kids.

"Come on, guys," she said. "Who likes puppet shows? I'm going to do a puppet show for you guys."

DAY 2

No one moved.

Obviously their failure to move had nothing to do with their feelings about puppet shows. They were rooted to the spot in utter horror and shock.

"OPEN THE DOOR, YOU LITTLE SONS A BITCHES!"

"Go away!" Jake yelled. "Go away and leave us alone!"

CHINKA-CHINKA-CHINKA-CHINKA-CHINK.

"Guys!" Astrid yelled. "Free candy! Come on. Whatever toys you want! Let's party! Come on."

She was working so hard.

"OPEN THE GATE OR I WILL KILL YOU. I WILL TEAR YOUR LIT-TLE KIDDO HEADS OFF AND I WILL MAKE A SOUP OUT OF YOUR LITTLE SMART-ASS KIDDO BRAINS AND——"

I started to sing.

Yes, sing.

"I'm a Yankee Doodle Dandy. Yankee Doodle Do or die."

I let go of Henry and Caroline and started marching, like I was the leader of a parade.

"An old old something something la la la, born on the Fourth of July." So maybe I didn't know the words, exactly.

Alex joined in. Astrid, too. All three of us marching like idiots.

"You're my Yankee Doodle sweetheart, Yankee Doodle do or die."

I led the three of us, making up the words somewhat and we walked in front of the gate, getting between the eyes of the little kids and the plywood, just trying to break the terror spell of the monster outside.

Who now started to yell, "YOU SINGING 'YANKEE DOODLE'? 'YANKEE DOODLE DANDY'? I'LL F—— KILL YOU!"

Niko joined in and that guy, I am here to tell you, is entirely tone deaf.

But the little kids kind of snapped to. We caught their attention.

"Yankee Doodle went to town a riding on a pony. I am a Yankee Doodle guy."

And the kids started marching and I led the parade, the saddest parade in the history of the world, away from the front of the store, away from the monster outside, and right to the stupid cookie and cracker aisle. We ate fudge-covered graham crackers for a good long while.

DAY 2

CHAPTER SEVEN

BLOOD TYPES

THE KIDS FELL ASLEEP, AFTER A WHILE. IT WAS MAYBE THREE IN the afternoon—hard to tell inside because the lighting was the same all day long. I don't know what time it was, but Astrid had told them it was time for a nap and the kids dropped into their sleeping bags like the walking dead.

The twins slept together, and Max and Ulysses moved their bags next to each other. Chloe and Batiste were sort of the odd men out. Batiste tried to snuggle up to Chloe, but she wouldn't have it.

"Quit it, Batiste," she said. "You smell."

She pushed him away.

"It's a sin to push," Batiste mumbled.

"Yeah, well. It's also a sin to try to hug someone who doesn't want to be hugged!"

"No, it's not!" Batiste protested.

"Yes, it is!"

"No!"

"Yes!"

"No."

"Yes!"

"Come on, you guys," I said, trying to be sane.

"Hugging is not a sin!" Batiste yelled.

"It is too, if the girl getting hugged doesn't want it!" Chloe countered.

"Hey!" Astrid hollered. "Shut up!"

Then Chloe hit Batiste in the stomach, which I admit was not entirely displeasing to me, because that Batiste was an aggravating kid.

Then Batiste said it was a sin to punch someone in the stomach.

He cried for a while, and gradually his cries gave way to the shallow rhythm of sleep breath.

It was a relief to have them asleep. Astrid and I sort of looked at each other and smiled. The moment had a weird feeling of middle-aged family life, with the two of us cast just where I'd like us to be, in about twenty years, but, of course, with about five too many kids.

"You're good with kids," she said to me.

"Not really," I said. "You're good with them."

Good conversation, right? I was really connecting with her.

"Counselor of the year, Indian Brook Day Camp. Three years running," she said, brushing a loose tendril of blond hair behind her ear.

"That's really something," I said. Again, with the skills.

She shrugged and walked away, over to the broken television, where the rest of the big kids were sitting and listening.

Everyone looked up when we came over, except for Josie. She was sitting with everyone, but was just staring ahead. There but not entirely "there."

DAY 2

"He's talking about the compounds," Alex told me in a whisper.

Whoever the anchor was, he had a very deep, reassuring voice. Nevertheless, what he told us was terrifying.

"Residents of the southwestern region of the United States," he told us. "Please be advised: There has been a breach of the chemical-weapons storage units located at NORAD in Colorado Springs, Colorado.

"The compounds attack based on blood type. People with blood type A will develop severe blisters on all exposed skin. After prolonged exposure, the internal organs will begin to hemorrhage, leading to organ failure and death."

I looked at Niko. He was type A. Personality and blood type, apparently.

"People who have type AB blood suffer from paranoid delusions and possible hallucinations."

Brayden buried his head in his hands.

"There is confusion as to the effects on people with type B blood. It is possible they will suffer from long-term reproductive difficulties and sterility. But there is hope that people with type B blood suffer no consequences from exposure."

Alex and Sahalia had been on the roof and showed no symptoms at all. They were type B. Jake, too, as he had been exposed in the storeroom and showed no signs.

My brother would be okay. That was some comfort to me.

"People with type O blood, which is the most common blood type, will become deranged and violent. Avoid these people at all costs. Containing them in a closet or basement is advised, if possible."

I felt everyone look at me.

My face went hot.

I was type O. Me and the gate rattler.

Awesome.

"Fortunately, the compounds wear off very quickly. If you are exposed, get to a safe place and flush your skin and mucus membranes with clean water. The effects subside within ten to twenty minutes. Prolonged exposure will lead to irreparable damage to all blood types except for type B."

The voice went on to advise us to stay indoors and await help.

"Like we have a choice," Brayden scoffed.

And then for the good news. Ha.

The anchor told us it was thought that the chemicals would disperse in between three to six months.

"Six *months*!" Astrid exclaimed.

He then reassured us that government operatives were hard at work deactivating the blackout cloud that now enveloped the area within an eight-hundred-mile radius of Colorado Springs. It was a magnetic cloud and would hover above the detonation site unaffected by rain or wind.

And then the anchor said this: "Good citizens of the United States of America, we are in the midst of the greatest crisis our country has ever known. But if we have courage and patience, if we persevere despite the great odds against us, we will come through this calamity. Good night, stay safe, and God bless you."

Then the whole report started again on a loop.

Somebody (probably Niko) had dragged beanbag chairs into the Media Department, so that's what we were sitting on. It was me, Jake, Brayden, Astrid, Niko, Alex, and Sahalia. Niko, who, I was beginning to realize, had a hard time sitting still, was starting to clean some of the earthquake mess up, but only in our area.

DAY 2

We were all just kind of sitting there together, taking in all we had heard. Everything that had happened.

I was wondering what blood type my parents were.

Praying for B.

Reproductive failure and sterility. Yes, let them both be type B.

"Hey, Niko," Jake drawled. "What do you think about the air in here? You think it's safe enough?"

"Yeah, we don't even know what type the little kids are. It'd suck to wake up in the middle of the night surrounded by blood-thirsty kindergarteners," Brayden said.

"We definitely need to keep our air supply shut off from the outside," Niko said.

"Hey," Sahalia said, "are we going to, like, suffocate if we're cut off from the outside?"

"Not with this quantity of air," Alex said. "The volume of air in a space this size is substantial."

"Maybe we could like set some air filters," Jake said. "In case some of that outside air is coming in . . ."

"I wonder if there are any plants inside," I said. "Or maybe some seeds. If we had plants, they would filter the air and give us oxygen."

"I'm more worried about power," Niko said. "I'm worried the blackout cloud is going to affect the solar harvest system on the roof."

"Great," moaned Brayden. "That's all we need. To be shut up here in the dark!"

"I've been thinking about it," Alex said, standing up. "The blackout cloud is what will determine how the power goes. Right before my brother attacked me up on the roof, did you see how the light went green?"

How screwed up is it that; me trying to kill Alex had now become a common reference point in all of our lives.

"If the light really did go green," Alex continued, "or even yellowish, then the blackout cloud is designed to block blue and red spectrums, which are the ones that allow for plant life. The solar panels will take any spectrum. So if only yellow gets through, that's okay. They can still run."

He was pacing now. Something he does when he gets really excited.

"God, you're a geek—" Sahalia moaned.

She looked so much older than my brother. It was hard to believe they were both thirteen.

"I've been thinking about food," I said, cutting her off. "There's a lot of fresh stuff we should eat before it goes bad."

"What we really need to do is clean up," Niko added. "We need to put everything back on the shelves and throw away the broken things, so we can fully take stock and prepare our—"

"Nobody's thinking about getting out of here?" Astrid interrupted. "We're just going to live here now? All one big happy family, like for the rest of our lives?"

We stopped talking.

Astrid was slung on a beanbag chair, one foot rhythmically tapping an overturned display case.

"Not for the rest of our lives. Just until things kind of get somewhat normal out there," Jake answered.

"What about our parents?" Astrid asked.

There was a long quiet. I studied my hands. The skin was dry and I had some cuts I hadn't even noticed. My hands looked rough.

"They're dead? We just assume they're dead, now?" There was an edge in Astrid's voice. An unhinged feeling.

DAY 2

"We'll just hide in here and eat candy when they could be dying outside. My mom could be getting attacked by a monster like the guy out front. Or my dad is paranoid and hiding comfortably under our kitchen sink.

"Or maybe my dad has my mom locked in the basement, because maybe she's type O and she went after him with her favorite chef's knife. Or maybe she's got him locked in the basement. No, wait. We don't have a basement. I guess they're dead. I guess they've clawed each other to death by now. And my brothers . . ."

Her voice caught in a sob.

"Eric's only two and a half. Probably don't need to worry about him. He's probably dead already . . ."

Jake stood up and walked over to her. He put a hand on her shoulder.

"It's okay, Astrid," he said.

She melted into his arms.

"Don't you care?" she choked out. "Isn't it driving you crazy to think of what is going on out there?!"

He held her in his big football-player arms and she wept.

I was up on my feet. I had propelled myself to my feet and I started walking to the Home Improvement aisle, without even knowing where I was going.

Alex followed me.

I stormed off into the Pet aisle, kicking some fallen doggie treat boxes out of my way.

"Dean?" Alex asked. "Do you know what type Mom and Dad are, by chance?"

I shook my head.

"I'm sorry that I have B and you got O," he said.

"That's stupid," I said. "I'm glad you are type B. It's the least scary of them all."

"Sterility is definitely the best one," he replied. "Because it's highly unlikely that I would be a father, anyway. It's highly unlikely I would ever want to, even if I could, after all of this."

I looked at him. Sometimes the way his brain worked just amazed me. He could deal with anything, as long as he could look at it scientifically.

"Anyway, I just wanted to say I'm sorry you got the worst type."

And satisfied with our discussion, he walked away.

Alex, I will tell you, was just like our dad. Looked like him, thought like him, hiked up his pants the same way.

Our dad was an engineer and a land surveyor, employed almost exclusively by Richardson Hearth Homes. He loved his work but hated the developments he helped build. All the houses with their customizable elements—countertops, appliances, façade colors—he said they were for people who were mall-minded. It was a phrase of his. Similar to small-minded, but *mall*-minded.

Mall-minded people were people who'd grown up working at one national chain store to earn a paycheck they'd spend on crappy products and bad food from other national chain stores.

It was kind of revealing about my dad. He looked down on his neighbors, but built the very homes they lived in. A weird paradox. And we lived, always, in one of his developments. Apparently we couldn't afford not to—they gave my parents such a steep discount.

What my dad did love was the technical aspect of his work. Surveying, measuring, working with machines and computers— all that stuff he was great at.

Alex was like that, too. He thought in terms of numbers and figures and trends.

DAY 2

When he was a little kid he was scared of everything. Dogs, trucks, the dark, Halloween; you name it, he was scared of it.

Our dad had taught him to analyze the things he feared.

So going trick-or-treating with him, when he was little, was like listening to a technical debriefing:

"That's not a real witch, it's a plastic figurine with LED lights for eyes and a prerecorded screech track. Those are not real gravestones; they are PVC molded into the shape of tombstones, with creepy sayings on them that were written by a gag writer. Those are not real demons coming down the street, those are the high school kids dressed in costumes they got at Walgreens or possibly ordered online . . ."

And all the while Alex'd be squeezing my hand like it offered his last link to sanity.

I had liked being his protector—the one who made him feel safe. Which was why I felt even worse about having attacked him.

Before, we had always made a good team—he was supersmart. I was super-stable. Kind of like our parents, actually.

Where our dad was brilliant and angsty, our mom was grounded and optimistic.

She loved books. That was one thing she and I really shared. Our house was full of old books. She'd buy them by the boxful, especially as people started using their tabs more and more for reading books.

Our mom had started buying books with a mania, as if she was afraid people would stop printing them at all.

She had multiple copies of her favorite books. I think she had eight copies of *A Room of One's Own* (sort of indecipherable to me) and five *Hitchhiker's Guide to the Galaxy* (a great read).

Mom was always telling me about her ideas for novels but never started writing any of them.

Once I asked her why she never wrote the books she told me about.

"Oh, sweetie," she had said. "I try. But, somehow, after I tell you about the idea, it's like the air is out of the balloon and I don't need to write it anymore."

So instead of being a writer, she took care of us.

And worked retail during the holidays.

Alex and I foraged for some snacks and eventually went back to the Media Department.

Little Caroline woke up crying and Astrid went to her. She picked her up and hugged her.

"I had a nightmare," Caroline sobbed. "I want my mommy."

"I know, I know," Astrid said, holding her close.

"Hey, thanks for waking me up, Cryoline," Chloe teased. "Now I need to go pee. Who's going to take me?"

"Saying Cryoline is name calling, Chloe," Batiste noted. "That's a you-know-what."

"No, it's not!" Chloe countered.

"Yes, it is too!" Batiste said.

"You know, Batiste, you're being very judgmental," Astrid noted. "I think being judgmental is a sin."

"That's not a sin!" Batiste said, offended. "I know all about sinning, and being judgmental is not a sin."

"I guess," Astrid said. "But do you really want to risk it?"

That gave him pause for thought.

I stifled a laugh at his perplexed expression.

Then Astrid said, "Okay, you guys, I'll take you to the bathroom. Everyone uses the bathroom and everyone washes hands. Then we'll go find something from the frozen foods aisle for dinner."

Little Henry asked, "Are we going to the ladies' room? I

DAY 2

don't want to use the ladies' room. I want to go in the men's room."

"My mom once took me in the ladies' room," Max volunteered. "And there was this lady in there crying and she had a ice cube and she was rubbing it on her eye and she said, 'If Harry hits me one more time, I don't know what I'll do,' and then this other lady came out of a stall and she said, 'If Harry hits you one more time, you give him the end of this to suck on!' And she puts a real, actual gun down on the sink. Made of metal, I am not even kidding. And then my momma turns to me and goes, 'Tell your daddy to bring you to the men's room.'"

I was getting the feeling that Max had lived a very, very interesting life. I took out my journal to write down what he'd said.

Astrid got the kids organized. She told Henry that they were all going to stick together and go in the ladies' room, which was good psychology, even if it elicited a round of groans from the boys.

CHAPTER EIGHT

WATER

I WAS MINDING MY OWN BUSINESS, WRITING SOME STUFF DOWN, when Brayden ambled over and kicked the beanbag chair I was sitting on.

"Jesus, Dean, are you a total reject? Are you from the Middle Ages?"

"Brayden . . . ," Jake said from his own beanbag, a "lay off" implicit in his tone.

"No, it's just, I knew that Geraldine was weird, I just didn't understand the total extremity of the situation."

"I write stuff down," I said. "I just like to write."

"Bet there's stuff about me in there," he said and he grabbed the journal from me.

"Come on!" I said, jumping to my feet.

He held it behind his back, an arm's length away.

When I tried to grab it, he'd switch it to the other hand.

It was a scene straight out of first grade.

"I bet there's stuff about all of us," Brayden taunted. "Especially Astrid."

I would've killed him if she'd overheard that. But she was off with the kids.

You know, you'd think that being locked in a Greenway during the end of the world would bring out the best in everyone, but—surprise!—Brayden was still an a-hole and a bully.

Brayden tore a page out and squinted at it, keeping the rest held above his head and out of my reach.

"Jeez, man, this stuff is dark," he said, reading to himself.

"You're such a jerk, Brayden!" I shouted. "How can you still be this immature?"

"Brayden, drop it," Jake commanded.

"Don't you want to know what it says about you, Simonsen?"

"I SAID DROP IT!" Jake shouted.

Brayden jumped. We all did.

Jake was standing, squared off to Brayden, with his hands in fists. His good-natured smile was gone. He was pissed.

"Whatever," Brayden said and tossed the notebook to the end of the aisle.

"You gotta learn when to lay off, man," Jake said with a rumble.

"Dude, I apologize," Brayden said to Jake, palms turned up in an appeal. He shrugged. "For real. Sorry."

Did I call Brayden a dick under my breath as I scrambled over the fallen books to retrieve my journal?

Of course I did.

And then there came this thin, tinny sound. Like a fire alarm or a siren. But it was coming from inside and it was getting louder.

It was Ulysses.

He was screaming and running for us.

We ran toward him and then we could hear the melee from the bathroom. Shrieking and screaming and inhuman sounds.

Niko pushed the door open.

The little children had gone crazy.

The McKinley twins were hiding under the sinks.

Chloe was sitting on Max and had her teeth sunk into his scalp. There was blood on the ground.

They were screaming and crying and attacking each other. But Astrid.

She had Batiste by the throat, up against the wall.

Her face was red. The veins in her throat were throbbing, huge. She looked like a bull.

And Batiste was getting killed. He was getting strangled to death and I hope you never see it because it is a horrible thing to see. His face was blue and his eyes were big and his legs were limp.

Niko and Jake were on her in a flash and they pulled her off him. She fought and thrashed and bit and punched and I wanted to watch and I wanted to join in and I could feel my blood rising, hard, when I was jerked out of there by a set of hands.

Sahalia, if you can believe it.

"You stay out of there, rage boy," she told me.

And I would have ripped her head off, but I had had only a little whiff of the stuff, so I forced myself to walk away. I walked off down an aisle and got myself to breathe.

Niko came out, holding a screaming, writhing Chloe.

"It's the water," Niko said. "The chemicals are coming in through the water."

He was starting to blister up.

"I'm okay," I told him through my teeth. "I can help." I

DAY 2

took Chloe's hands. She was trying to claw me. She struggled and cried and tried to bite me. But I was much stronger—stronger than I normally am. The whiffs of compound coming off her were sweet to me. And the fury in her was met with my own fury.

Chloe was such an annoying kid anyway, it was a pleasure to restrain her. I'm ashamed to write that, but it is the truth. I held her fat little wrists with a big, mean smile on my face.

Niko was starting to blister again.

"Go get Benadryl," I told him.

He ran, tripping, down the aisle.

"Be right back," he shouted.

Sahalia came out with the McKinley twins, who were clearly hallucinating and freaking out. You couldn't make out their words—they were just clutching each other and screaming.

Max came behind next, sobbing and pressing his hands onto his bleeding scalp.

"The water's off," Sahalia huffed.

Jake burst through the doors with Batiste in his arms. Batiste's head lolled on his shoulders.

"Clear some space," Jake said. "He's not breathing."

Brayden came forward. I hadn't realized he was not in the bathroom. He'd been somewhere behind us in the aisles.

A coward.

"I know CPR," Brayden said and he knelt down beside Batiste. But then he looked up, suddenly clammy and afraid. Maybe the compounds were taking effect. I guess I can give him the benefit of the doubt.

"So do I," Niko said. He moved into Brayden's space as Brayden gratefully slid aside.

Niko put his mouth over Batiste's blue lips and huffed into

him, like Batiste was a dying campfire. It didn't take long, thank God. I don't think Niko could have done it for long.

As it was, Niko started coughing and it was a wet sound.

A couple of long breaths, a couple of gentle but confident pushes on Batiste's skinny rib cage, and his eyes fluttered. He took a jagged breath. And then another.

I watched Brayden, watching Niko. It was jealousy on his face, mixed with regret. Maybe fear, too. But mostly jealousy.

Meanwhile, Jake wrestled Astrid out of the bathroom.

Her shirt was torn and she was bleeding from the ear.

"I need like rope or something!" Jake shouted. Astrid bucked and screamed. She elbowed Jake in the side of the head and he lost his grip.

She broke away and lurched from him. She slipped, but regained her balance and ran off into one of the dark aisles.

Astrid cast one last look at us and I read horror in her eyes.

We had five weeping grammar school kids, contaminated to some degree with chemical warfare compounds.

Now, anyway, we knew who was which blood type.

In addition to the beating he'd received from Chloe, Max was also starting to blister up (type A). The McKinley twins were hiding from us—they clearly had the paranoia (type AB). Ulysses was chattering to himself in Spanish, a rapid-fire monologue that made me pretty sure he had the paranoid type—type AB—as well as the twins.

Batiste had type B, the blood type that exhibited no symptoms, as did Alex, Jake, and Sahalia (sterility and reproductive failure—hooray!).

"We have to get them clean," Brayden said.

"You think?" I sort of shouted at him (type O).

DAY 2

"Screw you," Brayden said to me.

Ah, I wanted to slaughter him. I really did. I wanted to tear him limb from limb.

Niko looked at me.

"Dean, go," he said. "This stuff is too strong. It's affecting you."

"Yeah, go find Astrid," Brayden taunted. "You two are perfect for each other."

Apparently, I bit him.

I have no memory of it.

I woke up a while later, tied up, and lying facedown on a beanbag.

I struggled to sit up, but couldn't.

I rolled sort of onto my side.

There I saw Chloe, freshly bathed, wrapped in a towel, eating fun-size Butterfingers one after another like a chain smoker and watching me like I was her soap opera.

For the record, they washed the kids with bottled spring water in a big kiddy pool. Then they put the contaminated clothes in the pool and covered the whole thing with plastic sheeting. Vicious, psychedelically destructive, blister-inducing water, all sealed up in a kiddy pool. Pretty brilliant, actually.

My brother's idea.

They pushed the pool into the baby stroller aisle. That aisle was to become known to us later as the Dump.

"Chloe," I said as calmly as I could. "Please go tell Alex that I'm okay now and I'd like to be untied."

She shrugged.

"Chloe, go get Alex."

"Why should I?" she asked me in a snotty voice.

"Because I'm asking you to," I replied.

She ignored me, eating the chocolate coating off a Butterfinger bit by bit.

"Chloe!" I said.

"What'll you give me?"

"Are you kidding me?!"

She yawned.

"Go get Alex."

"I don't have to do what you say. You're not the boss of me."

"I'm asking you. Please."

"You're not asking, you're telling. No one likes a bossy bear, you know."

If my wrists hadn't been getting rubbed bloody by the nylon ropes, I probably would have found this conversation amusing.

"Chloe, fair Chloe, princess of all that is good and kind in this world, wouldst thou, couldst thou take a message to my brother yonder?"

She giggled.

"Say please," she baited.

"Oh, the prettiest of pleases for the prettiest of fair young maidens . . ."

"Oh-kay . . . ," she said and dragged herself off toward the other kids.

It was only then that I noticed that Batiste was in his sleeping bag, just beyond where Chloe had been sitting. He was just lying there, staring up at the ceiling.

"Hey, Batiste," I said. "Are you okay?"

He didn't answer.

* * *

DAY 2

Alex hurried over and picked the tight knots apart.

"You bit Brayden on the scalp," he told me with his eyes twinkling. He whispered, "It was awesome!"

"Where is everyone?" I asked, rubbing life back into my wrists.

"We're still washing the twins," he answered.

He turned to go back. I didn't follow.

"See you when we're done?" he asked.

"I'm not going anywhere," I said.

I heard mild snoring from a sleeping bag farther back in the aisle. I guess they had dosed Max to the gills with Benadryl, 'cause he was way conked out. His blisters looked three shades less angry, so it seemed to be working.

I went over to Batiste. He was naked, just wrapped in a towel inside his sleeping bag. He seemed subdued and cold.

"You okay, little guy?" I asked him.

His hands were like ice.

"I'm gonna get you all set up," I told him.

I went to the boys' clothing section and got some warm clothes for him. I even picked out a pair of those dumb chenille slipper socks. I figured he deserved something absurdly soft and warm.

"Hey, Batiste," I said, holding up the clothes. "Check out your new look."

But Batiste didn't move a muscle. So I just dressed him, I don't know, like you would a baby. Once I had all his clothes on, and the dumb socks, I rubbed his back.

Yes, I did. Be assured that I felt as uncomfortable actually doing it as I do writing about it.

But I could feel his skinny ribs relaxing a little so I kept at it.

I took it as a good sign when, a few minutes later, he croaked, "My throat hurts."

I went and got some children's Advil and a Popsicle for him. On my way back, I ran into Brayden. He was carrying Henry wrapped up in a towel.

Brayden pointed at me and said, "You're an a-hole."

Why that made me feel so happy, I can't quite say.

No one seemed to be thinking about dinner and the kids were getting hungry, so I grabbed some freezer foods: dinosaur-shaped chicken nuggets, frozen green beans, and two bags of Tater Tots.

Then I had to figure out how to actually cook the stuff.

In the Pizza Shack, there were only these industrial toaster ovens and a microwave. There was no stovetop so I didn't know what to do with the green beans at all. I just put them on one of the pizza trays and put them in an oven. They came out like straws made of charcoal. That's my best attempt at describing them. Desiccated, black straws of carbon.

The Tater Tots came out exactly perfect.

The chicken nuggets, on the other hand, were cold inside. The little kids didn't seem to mind. But Jake put some back in the oven for the older kids. And those dino nuggets joined my green beans in charcoal heaven.

We had mostly Tater Tots for dinner.

After everyone had eaten, I brought dinner to Josie and sat with her while she ate.

I had gotten into the habit of chatting with her. "At her" might be more like it.

Our conversations went something like this:

Me: How you doing, Josie?

Josie: ———

Me: Oh, I'm fine, thanks for asking. I mean, I'm a little depressed, what with the end of life as we know it. But I'm holding it together. How about you?

DAY 2

Josie: ———

Me: Yeah, that's what I thought. You seem to be having a pretty tough time. Hey, you know, I've been thinking. We have plenty of clean clothes. And we can't use the water anymore, but we've been using baby wipes to clean ourselves when we get dirty. They work pretty good. You want me to bring some over? You could sort of use a little cleaning off, if you don't mind me saying so. And the bandage on your head, it definitely needs to be changed.

Josie: ———

Me: Sure, I could bring over a new one. No problem. I'll bring over the baby wipes, too. I'd be lying if I said we weren't worried about you. You know you haven't said a single word since the bus . . .

Josie: ———

Me: Well, I'm here, if you need anything. Just say the word. Any word, actually . . .

Stuff like that.

Dessert was impossible to screw up: Popsicles.

"Niko," Alex said, with his mouth dyed purple. "I'm going to take a survey of the utilities in the store tomorrow. Dean and I think we should clean up the Grocery section right away. We should be eating the fresh produce—"

"Whoa, whoa, whoa!" Brayden interrupted. "Jake is on it. He's got a plan for all that."

"Yeah," Jake said, "tomorrow we're going to break into teams and start getting this place in shape."

Niko nodded at Alex. "Sounds like a good plan," Niko said.

"We can help clean," said little Henry. "Me and Caroline are good helpers."

"I'm a good cleaner, too," volunteered Max. "I'm good at

mopping. I've mopped up stuff you wouldn't believe if I told you!"

I could only imagine.

"Sure." Jake nodded. "Tomorrow we clean up."

The problem of toilets came up just after we all laid down in our sleeping bags for the night.

"Ulysses has to go pee," Max said.

"How do you know?" Jake asked.

"He's my friend. I understand him," Max answered.

"Tell him to pee in the corner," Jake mumbled. "That's what I did."

I couldn't judge. I'd done the same.

"That's unsanitary," Alex said.

"He's scared. He's not going out there alone. And neither am I."

"And I need to make," Chloe added.

"Awesome," Jake groaned.

This was a moment Astrid would have probably handled, but since she had gone AWOL, we had to figure it out.

Henry and Caroline started whispering to each other furiously. After a moment's debate, Henry raised his hand.

Jake didn't see him. But I did, so I said, "What is it, Henry?"

"Well, sometimes me and Caroline, like, if we're going to a sleepover, we wear pull-ups. So since this was like a sleepover, we got some pull-ups."

And he pulled out an opened package of size 6 pull-ups.

"So you think we should crap in a diaper?" Brayden asked.

Henry shrunk a bit.

Niko spoke up. "It's not a bad idea. We could lay a pull-ups or a diaper on the ground and do what we need to do. Then we just close it up and put it in a trash bag. It could work."

So that's what we did.

DAY 2

The little kids put them on outright. They didn't want to be getting up in the night, alone. I'm sure they didn't even want to think about the bathrooms, given what had happened the last time they went there.

They just started wearing pull-ups.

A little bit of regression, anyone?

(The next day, Niko set up latrines for us in the baby stroller aisle. They were weird things made of a toilet seat on top of a heavy-duty plastic basin, the kind they use at construction sites, which was lined with a plastic bag. Every so often, the bag got knotted up and thrown in a plastic storage tub. Just so you know.)

Around ten, the lights in the store dimmed automatically. This made it feel like night. The sleeping bag didn't do much cushioning against the hard floor. I made up my mind to drag over a lawn chair or something in the morning.

I ached and ached until I fell asleep.

I woke up to a little voice.

It was one of the kids sleep-talking. I couldn't tell which kid.

It was a one-word conversation.

One word repeated over and over, with different intonations, with different meanings.

The word was *mommy*.

Pleading, entreating. Calling, demanding. Beseeching, begging.

I thought maybe I was dreaming until Brayden said, "Shut up. SHUT UP!"

And the calls for mommy stopped.

CHAPTER NINE

AIR HORN

THE NEXT MORNING THE LITTLE KIDS WOKE UP FIRST. THEY THEN tried to wake Jake up, but he was deep in his snores, so they got me up. Niko was already up and probably off doing something industrious.

Alex was sleeping, too. I didn't want to wake him up.

So it was up to me to get breakfast.

I really, really did not want to become the cook of this operation, but that's what seemed to be happening.

I was beating eggs by hand when Batiste came over.

"Why don't you do that in a blender?" he asked.

"We don't have one," I answered. "That's part of what's so hard about cooking here. I only have these two industrial ovens and this big microwave."

"Why don't you just get one?" Batiste said, looking at me with his head cocked to the side like a little poodle.

I guess I looked as slow as I felt because he added, "From the shelves."

I started to laugh. We had been in the store for three days and it had not occurred to me that we had every single appliance right here. Just two aisles over.

"Of course," I said. "You want to help me?"

"Sure!" he said.

"Let's go."

Batiste and I outfitted the kitchen with the aforementioned blender, an electric griddle, a family-size George Foreman grill, a six-slice toaster, a toaster oven, an electric teakettle, a rice maker, a KitchenAid mixer, and every kind of pan, mixing bowl, whisk, spatula, cheese grater. Basically one of everything from the Kitchen aisle.

While we "shopped," Batiste told me about his parents and his church group and their preacher Reverend Grand and his dog, Blackie.

It made me feel like he was starting to recover from his experience with Astrid.

When we got back with all the supplies, the kids helped us unpack everything and they were pretty content for a while as I made the eggs and bacon (on a griddle pan, thank you!), but soon they started picking on one another and generally driving me crazy.

I had this messy kitchen I felt like I should deal with.

"Go find Jake," I told them. "Ask him what the plan is."

They went off, kicking boxes and roughhousing and whining and chatting.

I wrapped up a plate of eggs and bacon in tinfoil, wrote a little note on paper from my notebook, and left it on top of the plate. It said something like:

Astrid,
Here's some eggs for you. They turned out pretty
horrible, but they're for you if you want them.

I know you must be feeling lousy. I really do understand how you feel, so come find me if you want to talk.

From Dean

Alex came over eventually. I offered him eggs, but he took a Pop-Tart instead.

"Dean," he said. "What do you think is happening out there? Really."

I felt so tired. My eyes ached. Head ached. I didn't really want to talk about it, but truthfully I was relieved Alex was talking to me at all.

I took off my glasses and rubbed my eyes.

"I think that the type Os are killing and marauding through our town. Lots of people are hiding. Some people are blistering up and dying from it."

Alex nodded.

He took out several sheets of lined paper.

"I've been running the numbers," he said.

I looked at the sheet.

At the top it read **PRE-CRISIS POPULATION OF MONUMENT, CO: 7,000.**

Then lots of numbers and figures.

And at the bottom: **CURRENT ESTIMATED POPU-LATION: 2,200.**

I looked at the paper. At the horrors it speculated about.

I knew how my brother operated. Numbers and figures were therapeutic to him. Fear of things unknown and unquantifiable was what turned my little brother inside out.

"Do you want me to take you through it?" he asked brightly.

"No," I said. "No. I want you to hide that. Don't show it to people."

DAY 3

"It's just math," he said. He seemed offended.

"It's not just math," I told him. "It's people."

We got the kitchen cleaned up. Having no running water, this took some figuring out. The solution was Clorox wipes. Lots and lots of Clorox wipes.

We went back to the Media Department to find everyone screwing off.

Jake and Brayden were playing air hockey. They had busted out a deluxe air hockey table and were going at it. I could see they'd already played Ping-Pong and had a packaged dart board standing at the ready.

"What's going on, Jake?" I asked.

"BAM! VICTORY!" Jake shouted.

Sahalia cheered. She was watching them play.

"Next game I will own you, Simonsen!" Brayden answered.

Sahalia had changed her clothes and was wearing a really, really short skirt. I don't know, maybe it was just a scarf tied around her hips. She had on ripped fishnets and absurdly high-heeled boots. Some kind of a tank top over a paper-thin T. She looked like a twenty-year-old fashion model.

She had obviously decided to help herself to whatever she wanted from the store.

And so had the others.

Max and Ulysses were drinking from two-liter bottles of Coke and polishing off one of those five-pound boxes of fancy chocolates. They were joking and laughing, though I still didn't quite get how they understood each other at all.

Batiste had out a huge set of magic markers and was coloring in a "Bible Stories" coloring book.

Chloe, meanwhile, was in Barbie Heaven. She had one or two of every available Barbie out and ready. She also had a

Barbie house and a Barbie sports car and a Barbie pool and a Barbie Jeep and, I don't know, a Barbie wind farm and a Barbie shoe store and a Barbie NORAD. There were some Bratz thrown in for spice, but in general, it was a Barbie orgy.

Everyone was taking advantage of being locked in a Greenway. Kind of binging.

"Where are the twins?" I asked.

Jake and Brayden didn't seem to hear.

"Have you guys seen the twins?" I raised my voice.

"No," Jake said.

That was it. Just no.

"We're here," came Henry's little voice.

In the next aisle they had built a little house out of toy boxes. It was just big enough for them to get inside. I peeked in. They were curled up in there on a blanket, sucking their thumbs and talking to each other.

"I like how her face is when she smiles," Caroline said.

"Yeah, and I like her brown pants. The soft ones," Henry answered.

"And her hair."

"It's brown," Henry said. Caroline nodded, dreamy.

They were talking about their mother.

"So there's no plan?" I asked Jake.

"In a while," he answered. "We're starting with a little structured downtime. BAM! BULL'S-EYE!"

I walked away and Alex followed me.

I kicked a box of diapers.

"This is screwed," I said. "There's so much work to do.

Every single aisle is a freaking disaster zone. Are we supposed to do it all by ourselves?"

Alex put his hand on my arm.

"It's going to be okay," he said.

"It's not," I said.

All of a sudden I wanted to cry. I felt my face getting red and my breath felt like it was stuck in my throat.

"It will never be okay again," I said.

I walked off down an aisle, kicking the broken stuff away as I went.

I looked back.

Alex was just standing there, his shoulders sagging. His thin frame bowed over with the weight of the world.

I had to pull it together. I had to take care of my brother.

I wiped my eyes on the back of my hand.

Then I walked back to him.

"I have an idea," I said.

"What?"

"Monopoly marathon."

"Yes," he said simply.

Every summer our family got a house in Cape May, New Jersey (don't think about Cape May being gone), for a week. My mom grew up there so we'd eat like kings at all the local restaurants (don't think about Jaime's Waffle Stop being gone) since she knew all the locals (don't think about Jaime). But since my brother and I weren't really beach types, we'd mostly play Monopoly (Monopoly, safe to think about).

We spent maybe an hour making our own little game-room area. We pushed aside the fallen boxes to clear a space. Then we brought over a card table from the Home Department. We took a mini-fridge and stocked it with sodas. We got a bunch of chips and snacks and what have you. We even draped some beach towels over the aisle dividers to give our game room a beachy feel.

Somewhere around early afternoon, Niko came and found us. He didn't say anything, just took a look at what we were doing. We stopped and looked at him. His eyes revealed nothing, which was no surprise. After a moment, he turned and walked away.

It's hard to believe you can spend a whole day playing Monopoly, but of course, you can.

My brother and I had very different strategies. I bought everything I could. My brother only ever bought the railroads, the utilities, and the light-blue properties (Vermont, Connecticut, and Oriental Avenues).

The problems with his strategy, in my opinion, were many. First of all, it was incredibly annoying to play against him. Second, it seemed like it had to be insanely boring for him. Third, it felt like his strategy to only buy the light-blue properties was really shortsighted and somewhat stupid but he would always land on them. I mean, of the maybe fifty games we'd play each summer, I'd only get the chance to buy a light blue maybe three times. But the biggest problem about his inane strategy was that he'd often win.

For example, he won the first game.

. I got him on the second, however, when he hit my hotel on New York.

Game three, our big tiebreaker, was ended prematurely by the smell of pizza.

It smelled delicious and I sort of jumped up.

It had occurred to me that maybe Astrid was feeling better and had made us all lunch.

DAY 3

"When we come back, I'm going to destroy you," Alex said.

"Yes, sir, Mr. Water Works."

It was only Niko, though. He had figured out how to run the Pizza Shack ovens. He had cooked a bunch of pizzas and lined them all up on the counter.

The smells had not only drawn us—all of the little kids were there, and so were Jake, Brayden, and Sahalia.

Jake, Brayden, and Sahalia were sprawled out in one of the bigger booths. There was something in the way they were slouching and the way the little kids were looking at them that made me know immediately what was wrong.

They were drunk.

They had three big slushies in front of them and, as I watched, Jake took out a hip flask of some kind of alcohol and poured a shot into his cup.

Sahalia giggled and leaned across Brayden, putting her straw into Jake's cup.

"Hey, girl, keep your straw to yourself!" Jake half shouted, smiling.

"It's just a little sip," she crooned.

"No, no," Jake said. "It's the last straw!"

They thought this was hilarious.

Max and Ulysses also laughed, in that dumb way kids laugh when grown-ups do, just to be in on it.

Niko looked at me and Alex pointedly.

"Dinner's up," Niko said. "Everyone come up and help yourselves."

"You heard him!" Jake said with a grin. "Chop, chop! Everyone get up there!"

"Brave Hunter Man has spoken," Brayden said.

"You're not the boss, you know," Sahalia said to Niko with a roll of her eyes.

"Can it, Sasha," Jake said.

A nickname. Awesome. The senior had given the sexy thirteen-year-old a pet name.

"Come on, guys." I tried to break it up. "The pizza's hot. Let's eat."

Everyone sort of ambled up into a line for the food.

"I'm not eating sausage," Max protested. "My mom says sausage is made of pig bottoms."

"Your mom, your mom, your mom," Sahalia mocked. "You little kids are always talking about your moms! Enough already with the moms. They're not here and they're not coming anytime soon!"

This was a dumb thing to say and she didn't even notice.

The twins started to cry and Ulysses was right behind them with his jelly-bean tears.

Niko stepped in front of the counter and addressed the group, trying to get things back on line.

"I've been thinking," he said. "With Jake's permission, I have a plan for us to get some structure in place here."

" 'With Jake's permission,' that's bull," Brayden said, his voice too loud. "You want to take over."

"I don't want to take over. But I do think we need some clear plans—"

"You know what, Niko?" Jake said. "I know you have good intentions, but we just, like, went through a terrible thing, you know? The world outside is a total disaster and we don't know what's going to happen. I think we deserve a little break. A little chance to just like, relax and, like, chill out and even enjoy what we got here. Let's hang for a while. I mean, truly, honestly, what's the harm?"

DAY 3

"We're going to fall apart," Niko said calmly.

Jake threw up his hands and took an unsteady step back as Brayden pushed forward.

"Screw you, Niko!" Brayden said. "We don't want be told what to do by some freakish outcast!"

Brayden pushed Niko and Niko stepped back.

"I don't want to fight," Niko said.

"No, you just want us to take your orders. Like you even know what you're doing!"

Brayden pushed Niko again. Now Niko was backed against the counter. Niko tried to step away but slipped on a paper plate someone left on the ground and fell.

Niko scrambled to his feet but Brayden pushed him down again.

"Stop it!" Alex shouted.

The kids started to totally lose it, screaming and screeching in alarm, like a pack of monkeys.

"Cut it out, Brayden," Jake said.

Brayden was standing over Niko.

"What? You don't fight? You too 'Zen master'? You too 'Brave Hunter Man'? What is it with you?"

"I just want to be prepared," Niko said. "So that—"

"Oh my God!" Brayden yelled. "Oh my G-A-double dog-D, I just got it." He looked triumphant. Menacing and victorious. "You're a Boy Scout! A Boy Scout! Aren't you?"

Niko shrugged. Brushed his hair out of his eyes.

"Yes. I am a Boy Scout," Niko said.

Brayden doubled over in violent laughter.

Jake chuckled, too, and the little kids started laughing, mostly, I think, to relieve the tension that was building.

"'Be prepared,' that's your motto. A friggin' Boy Scout. He wants us to take direction from a friggin' Boy Scout."

"I don't know what's so funny about it," Niko said.

The little kids were laughing on, oblivious, as Niko went red around the ears.

"I'm glad Niko has Scout training," I said loudly. "If he didn't, I'd have died on the bus. He pulled me out of there. I'm glad he's a Scout."

"No one cares what you think, Geraldine," Brayden snarled.

"I'm glad Niko is a Scout, too," Alex offered. "He knows how to get stuff done."

"Okay, you guys, shut up," Brayden spat at me and Alex.

"Brayden, settle down," Jake said.

"Unless maybe . . . Oh, I see. I get it." He motioned at me and Alex. "You and your brother want in on Niko's little gay Scout thing. You guys wish you could be up in the woods, huffing on each other's campfires . . ."

Brayden started making a humping motion.

He was facing me so he didn't see Niko launch at him. Niko drove his head into Brayden's side.

Jake was on them in an instant, trying to separate them, but Niko reared back, slamming Jake's head into the metal cabinet, by accident I'm sure, but it sent Jake over the edge.

Jake started whaling on Niko. Punching.

Brayden already whaling on him, too.

The kids went totally berserk. Batiste ran off. Max was screeching. The twins, wailing and clutching at each other. Chloe, screaming and clawing at her head. It was insanity.

Niko was doing his best to fight back, but he was outmanned and overpowered. I stupidly scrambled over and tried to pull Jake and Brayden off Niko.

Brayden turned and smiled, like he was happy to see me, then he punched me in the side of my head.

I meant to just try to pull him off Niko but instead I started

DAY 3

punching him. He had my head in a one-armed grip but that didn't stop me from landing punches to his side and then—

BWRAAAAAAAAAAAAAAM!

An air horn.

So loud.

BWRAAAAAAAAAAAAAAM!

Everyone stopped fighting.

We looked up.

Josie had the air horn held high. She was standing on the counter.

She was in her grimy, stained clothes. Blood still crusted behind her ears, where Mrs. Wooly had missed. The cruddy gauze bandage stuck to her forehead by gore alone.

She looked like she had risen from the dead.

And she was totally in command.

"This fight is over," Josie said.

Her voice was quiet, but you could have heard it a mile away.

"Tomorrow we are going to have a ceremony to honor the dead."

We took that in.

"And then we'll have an election to pick someone, just until Mrs. Wooly gets back, to be our leader."

And that was that.

We had a plan.

CHAPTER TEN

MAMA DUCK

AFTER DINNER, WHICH WE ATE WITH HARDLY ANY FUSS AND hardly any talking, really, Josie got up and put her plate in the trash.

Then Chloe, Max, Ulysses, Batiste, Henry, and Caroline got up and put their plates in the trash.

Then Josie walked out of the Pizza Shack area.

And Chloe, Max, Ulysses, Batiste, Henry, and Caroline walked out of the Pizza Shack area.

Josie walked to the Children's Clothing section.

Chloe, Max, Ulysses, Batiste, Henry, and Caroline followed.

She asked them their sizes and picked out pajamas for them.

She handed each child a new pair of pajamas and they hugged the pajamas to them like they were a precious treasure. Like the pajamas were a dream come true.

Then Josie walked back toward the Media Department and they followed her. In a single file line.

It was astounding.

DAY 3

"I think I'm gonna puke," Sahalia said, breaking the calm Josie had left in her wake.

Alex won the last game of Monopoly, with his darn railroads and utilities and hotels on Connecticut, Vermont, and Oriental.

And when we went back to the Media Department, here's what I saw:

Six little kids in new sleeping bags on new air mattresses with new pillows in new pillowcases. All in a circle around Josie, who was sitting on the floor. Josie had a candle in front of her, and it cast a warm, golden circle of light on their clean, scrubbed faces.

Why hadn't I thought of an air mattress?

Josie had also (finally) cleaned herself up. She was wearing white pajamas and a pink robe and slippers. And her hair was back in its customary giraffe knots on top of her head. Her brown skin looked soft and glowing in the candlelight. The only thing that broke the spell was the big square of gauze taped over the gash on her forehead. But at least it was fresh gauze.

Josie was weaving an outrageous, preposterous, totally absurdist fairy tale. It went like this:

"When Mrs. Wooly comes, she's going to have a big, new yellow school bus. And she's going to open up the door and say, 'Come on in, guys, time to go home!' Henry and Caroline will get on first, of course, because they are the youngest."

"I'm older by fourteen minutes," Henry volunteered.

"Yes. Caroline will be first, then Henry. Then Max, then Ulysses, Batiste, and then Chloe, because she is the oldest of all of you. And then Mrs. Wooly will drive down the road. The sky will be so blue and the sun shining. She will drive on down the road to your house. Yes. And your parents will be there waiting.

"Oh! Imagine how worried they have been. No matter.

Now you are safe. Now you are home. And Mrs. Wooly will take you by the hand and lead you up the front walk and in you will go."

"And will you be in the bus?" Chloe wanted to know.

"Of course!" Josie said. "It's my job, too, to make sure you get home safely."

"And will you come in?" asked Caroline.

"Yes. If your parents invite me, then I will stay for dinner. Won't that be nice? I wonder what we will have."

"My nana makes a lasagna that's out of this world!" Chloe proclaimed loudly. "Everyone says so."

"If we go to my mom's, she'll gets us Popeyes," Max conceded. "If we go to my dad's, he'll get Mickey D's. Wendy's is his favorite, but he don't go there anymore because one time, my dad, he went through the drive-through at Wendy's in the middle of the night and you'll never guess what happened because this lady was working there and he says to her, 'You're too pretty to work the graveyard shift,' and she goes, 'You bet your sweet ass I am,' and he puts his arm out and she grabs on and he pulls her right outta the window, through the opening and she gets in his truck. And now she's my auntie Jean. She sleeps over. And she has a gold tooth."

"My goodness," Josie said.

Then there was a pause.

I imagine Josie was trying to compose herself.

"Is it real gold?" Chloe wanted to know.

"Yep," Max answered. "But it doesn't come out. Anyways, I like Popeyes better, anyway."

"Whether it's Popeyes or McDonald's, I think it will be a great feast," Josie said, smoothing down Max's unruly hair. "We will all be so happy, when Mrs. Wooly comes to take us home. And now it is time for rest and sweet dreams."

DAY 3

Josie tucked Henry's sleeping bag in around his shoulders and kissed Caroline on the forehead.

Josie was a natural.

Where Astrid had that kick-ass camp counselor thing, Josie was a mom. A sixteen-year-old, middle-aged mom.

Her story just about put me to sleep, too.

Alex was snoring.

We had followed Josie's example and gotten ourselves those self-inflating air mattresses.

The difference was mighty. Mighty comfortable. Settling onto it, I realized how sore and tired my bones felt. The adrenaline and the shock of, well, everything had had me flying high.

Now I was starting to feel my body again. And it was a wreck. Also I had a bitch of a headache from Brayden's punch.

Josie came over and knelt down next to my bed.

"Can you write something to say tomorrow?" she asked me.

"At the ceremony?"

She nodded.

"I don't know."

"You're a good writer."

"How do you know?" I said.

She rolled her eyes.

"It's just . . . I'm not a *public* writer. What I write is just a record. For me," I told her.

Josie sighed. The endless patience and gentleness she had seemed to have with the kids was gone. She rubbed her eyes agitatedly.

"We need a ceremony, okay? They need it. And it needs to feel like it's coming from everybody. Not just me. Do you see what I mean? It can't just be some dumb thing that I'm making everybody do. If it's going to work, to actually help us, it's got to come from us all."

"Okay, okay." I gave in. "You're right, Josie. I'll write something. I'll do it."

I had some thoughts already, to tell the truth.

"And thanks for organizing it," I said. "We do need to do something. For them."

She got up and stepped away from me, then turned back.

"No," she said. "It's me who should say thanks. So . . . thanks."

For the company, I guess.

"Hey, Dean, can I ask you something else?"

"Sure," I answered.

Josie looked down, as if she were inspecting her slippers.

"What day is it?" She laughed self-consciously. "I mean . . . I lost some time there. Everything was sort of fuzzy. It feels like we've been here for a long time, but I don't think so."

"It's Thursday." I said. "And we got here on Tuesday."

"Three days?" she said in shock. She started to laugh. "Three days?! That's totally insane."

"What's insane?" Niko said, approaching us silently, as usual. His left eye was swollen shut and though he was tidy in general, I could see the faint outline of nose-blood crusted in his nostrils.

"Wow. You okay?" Josie asked him.

"I'm fine," he said. The stoic Niko. Brave Hunter Man. "But thanks for asking." Polite, too.

"Did you know it's Thursday!" Josie said. "We've only been here for three days. Doesn't it seem like a lifetime?"

"It really does," Niko said.

I agreed. I thought of all that had happened—the bus crash,

DAY 3

learning about the megatsunami, the earthquake, the compounds, me attacking Alex, the guy at the gate, Astrid attacking Batiste . . .

Three days.

"I'm glad you're feeling better, Josie," Niko said.

"Yeah," I agreed. I rolled onto my back. I was sleepy and ready to go to sleep.

Niko stood watching Josie, who was lost in thought.

There was something going on with Niko that I'd never seen before. His usual detached, intelligent gaze was softened. He seemed more open.

Like he really was glad Josie was feeling better, not just because she was an asset to our group, but because he cared about her.

"Three days!" Josie said quietly, shaking her head.

CHAPTER ELEVEN

CEREMONY

ONE WEEK BEFORE THE CEREMONY, I'D SAY I WOULD HAVE BEEN about as likely to read an original poem in front of my classmates as I would have been to stand under Astrid's window and serenade her with a mariachi band.

But a week can change everything and now I was going to read a poem.

The poem had come to me in the middle of the night. I groped for my journal. I wrote furiously, trying to get the poem down on paper. My pen scratching on the paper was the only sound in the dark, quiet store besides the distant hum of the refrigerators.

I fell back asleep, convinced I had written the most beautiful poem in the world. In my sleepy state, I was sure it would heal the world—this poem of mine.

Then I woke up in the morning to hear Batiste repeating everything Chloe said.

When I opened my journal to bask in my brilliance, it was,

DAY 4

of course, total scribble scrabble. I could only make out a couple words. The pen drifted all over the page and the funny thing is that I had underlined, very emphatically, in several places, but there were no words above the underlines. Just lines with exclamation points after them.

So I pretty much had to start from scratch.

Hey, guess who cooked breakfast? Me and Alex. You would think everyone would have been tired of my half burnt–half raw delicacies, but they ate my cold yet crispy frozen waffles and blackened hash browns right up. At breakfast Josie told us the ceremony would be in the Bed and Bath area in one hour. She asked us not to go near there so she could finish setting it up.

"Do we get to dress up?" Caroline asked.

Max groaned and rolled his eyes.

"What? It's a ceremony, right? Like church?" she asked.

"That's a good idea, Caroline. Everyone get dressed up," Josie said.

"Can I just wear this?" Brayden asked. He had on jeans and a sweatshirt.

Josie looked pointedly to Jake. She waited.

Jake cleared his throat.

"I think we should all dress up," Jake said to Brayden. "You know, show respect."

I gave myself a good once-over with baby wipes and put on fresh clothes. I retrieved my journal from where I'd left it in my sleeping bag. I was looking over my poem, fretting about some word or comma or something, when I heard wind chimes.

"What's that sound?" came little Henry's voice.

He climbed out of the toy-box playhouse that he and his sister had made. Caroline came right behind him.

"Um, wind chimes," I said. "I think Josie is making that sound to tell us it's time to go to the ceremony."

"Our mom loves those things," Henry told me, taking my hand. "She has like five of them and they hang in the garden out back. They get all tangled up in the winter but she always goes and straightens them out. She just loves the sound of 'em."

"I know," I said. "We can hear them from our yard."

My mom called their mom a hippie because of all her wind chimes, but I wasn't about to say that.

"Our mommy says they sound like fairy music," Caroline added.

"Hey!" Henry said. "Do you think we could get some for her? Take them with us when it's time to go?"

"That's a good present," Caroline added, nodding.

"Sure," I said. "You can take her *two* wind chimes, if you want. One from each of you."

The twins grinned at each other.

They had chosen matching dress-up clothes for themselves. Henry in black pants, a plaid shirt, and a sweater vest. Caroline in a little plaid dress that matched Henry's shirt and tights and shiny black shoes.

They had washed their freckled faces and combed their hair.

I thought, Who are these kids?

And what do they think is going on here?

He certainly didn't ask to be picked up, but I hoisted up that little Henry anyway. He put his arms around my neck and it felt good. Caroline clung to my hand.

"I'm glad you're here, Dean," she said to me. "Because you're our neighbor and we knew you from before."

"Me, too," I told her.

* * *

DAY 4

Josie had cleared a big space by pushing an aisle out of the way. This would have involved unbolting it from the ground, so I suspect Niko had a hand in the preparations.

She had tacked up some gold and orange ladies scarves over the fluorescent lights on the ceiling and that made a big difference. The light was soft and peachy and calming. There were a bunch of area rugs overlapping, covering the floor. A wide circle of pillows for us to sit on went around the edge of the space. In front of each pillow there was an unlit pillar candle. In the center there was this sort of decorated place with a big wall mirror lying flat, and some Christmas tree lights spread out and some kind of decorative crystal balls scattered among the lights.

It looked nice. Pretty.

"Please be seated," Josie told me, Henry, and Caroline. We each sat on a pillow.

Chloe was sitting next to Josie and behind them the wind chimes were hung on the edge of the aisle divider. Every so often Josie would nod to Chloe and Chloe would stroke the wind chimes with a little mallet.

Jake and Brayden ambled over. They both bore some signs of the fistfight they'd had with Niko the day before. A little bruising here, some scrape marks there. Jake looked a little queasy and I noticed they both shielded their eyes from the Christmas tree lights.

You know you have a hangover when *Christmas tree lights* hurt your eyes.

Brayden looked at the setup and made a sarcastic grimace. To his credit, he didn't snort or say anything derisive. I'm sure it was a challenge not to be a dick.

Niko entered the circle. I hadn't heard him coming. You

never heard him coming. Must have been a Boy Scout thing. He looked slightly better than he did the night before. But maybe it was just the candlelight making him glowy.

Niko sat down across the circle from Jake and Brayden. I saw them meet one another's eyes and look away. An uneasy look, an appraising look.

Sahalia came carrying a guitar, of all things. She was wearing white jeans and several white shirts, all flowing over each other. She looked beautiful and very pure. No makeup. Respectful.

I tell you, just when you think you know someone, she shows up looking pretty and carrying a guitar.

She sat cross-legged and put the guitar behind her, darting her eyes over to Jake and Brayden, to see if they were going to make fun of her for the guitar. Jake didn't look at her. Brayden smirked at her, half mocking, half (I don't know) flirting?

Chloe kept jangling the wind chimes until everyone had arrived and there was only one empty space: Astrid's.

"Where's Astrid?" Max asked. "Isn't she coming?"

And the kids started joining in, asking for her.

"Let's call her," Josie suggested. "Maybe she'll come."

And the kids started yelling. "Astrid! Astrid!"

Chloe turned and started whacking the wind chimes real loud.

Astrid didn't come.

I was really hoping she would. She had been gone for about twenty-four hours, at that point.

I knew Astrid was safe. There was nowhere she could go. But I also knew she must be beating herself up about what had happened in the bathroom with Batiste.

And she was going to have to get over it. She'd just have to.

DAY 4

Batiste sat there, still and pale. The bruises around his neck were blue and brown. It looked like he was dirty at the neck, which he probably was, anyway.

Batiste didn't call for Astrid. He hadn't gotten over what had happened either. But he could. I assumed he could, anyway. After all, Alex had forgiven me. For the most part, anyway.

"I think she must be napping," Josie said finally. "Let's start and maybe she will join in."

Chloe turned and struck the wind chimes again.

"Chloe, enough with the wind chimes," Josie said.

"Sor-ry," Chloe said under her breath.

Josie closed her eyes and took a long, slow breath. She opened her eyes and began.

"We are here to honor those who have died. We don't know how many have gone. We don't really even know what is going on outside. But we can pray for those who have passed and hold them in our hearts and help them go on up to Heaven.

"They don't talk about Heaven very much at my church. It's a UU church—that's Unitarian Universalist—and the UU's sort of believe in the ideas from a lot of religions, but don't talk about Heaven and Hell and sins and all that.

"But *I* believe in Heaven. And that is where I see all the beautiful souls going. People from other religions believe other things. And that's good. Whatever they believe about what happens after death, that's what's happening to them.

"We each make our own Heaven, that's what I think."

The little kids were starting to shift around and fidget.

Josie nodded to Sahalia.

Sahalia took out the guitar and strummed a few chords.

"This is one of my favorite songs," Sahalia said. "It's by Insect of Zero. I don't know if you know it, but anyway, here it is."

I didn't know the song. I didn't even know the band.

Sahalia started to sing and her voice was very gravelly and raspy. A satisfying voice. Like you had an itch in your ear and her voice could scratch it.

Here's what she sang:

Birdies in the sky, go fly away from me.
Kitties on the couch, you cats just leave me be.

I'm in a biting mood, a fighting mood, a car-tire-lighting mood.
I need to sit here quietly.
If you know what is good,
you'll stay away
And leave me be.

Fishies in the brook, don't bite my hook today.
Doggies on the street, just go the other way.

I'm in a biting mood, a fighting mood, a car-tire-lighting mood.
I need to sit here quietly.
If you know what is good,
you'll stay away
And leave me be.
Dear God, just leave me be.

Looking at the words, they seem pretty antisocial. But the melody was beautiful and mournful. Like a funeral song.

I don't know. It was pretty perfect.

When the song was finished, Josie nodded to me.

"Now Dean has something to read."

Alex looked at me in surprise. I shrugged and opened my journal.

I will tell you that not only did I *not* feel intimidated by Brayden and Jake, or nervous to expose my feelings, I *wanted* to do it.

And I hoped that Astrid was lurking near. I was pretty sure

DAY 4

she was. I wanted her to hear me and know my thoughts. And I hoped that my dumb poem might help her feel better.

Here was my poem:

Night came and fell hard.
Not like God drawing a blanket over our land
But like someone snuffing a candle.
Sudden and total.
Out—just like that.

Now we are waiting.
Waiting in the dark
To see if someone
Will switch on the light.

We can cower,
We can fear,
We can get lost together or
Get lost alone.

But the truth is:
I am the light. You are the light.
We are lit up together.
We are silhouettes of sunlight
cast against the night.

Shining now, let us
Shining, hold the light,
Shining, so that our families
Can find us.

Shining.

I know. A poem. Gay. What can I say?

Josie got up. We hadn't planned a thing, but darn if she

didn't strike a match and hold it up. She took her candle and lit it. It was as if we had choreographed it—my poem would be about light and then we'd light candles. But we hadn't.

Josie turned to Ulysses, who was sitting to her left, and held out her candle toward him. He knew what to do; he grabbed his pillar and lit it from Josie's. Then he turned to Max, sitting next to him, and lit Max's candle. When it got to Astrid's empty space, Jake just reached over and lit it.

I was glad he had done that. I wished I had done it.

When the flame went all the way around the circle, Josie reached forward and put her candle on the mirrors she had set in the center of the circle. She nodded for us all to do the same.

Fourteen lights stood there flickering together. The crystals and the mirror reflected the light, making it sparkle out all over the place.

The little kids were mesmerized.

Josie got up. She had a basket and in it were slips of paper and cardboard. They were photographs of people. Not famous people, just regular people. She had cut them out of magazines, off product packaging, out of book covers.

"These are just some pictures of people we don't know," Josie said. We each took a slip out of the basket.

"I want you to take one photograph and look at that person and just send them love. See them in a circle of light and wish them peace."

Ulysses waved his hand at Josie. He whispered something in Spanish, as he held out his photo. This was maybe the third time I'd ever heard him speak. It was serious, whatever it was he was saying, and he started to cry.

He pushed his picture back into Josie's hands.

"What's he saying?" I asked Max. But Josie got it. She quickly

DAY 4

looked through the photographs and gave Ulysses one of a fat Chinese man eating an apple.

"This one okay?" she asked.

Ulysses nodded.

I saw Josie look at the photo Ulysses had had. It was a photo of a smiling Latina grandmother making cookies. It probably looked too much like Ulysses's own grandmother.

Ulysses wiped his nose on his sleeve. This sweet, Spanish-speaking kid, alone with a bunch of Anglos. His spirit not crushed. Just doing the best he could. I really loved that kid.

I looked at the scrap of cardboard in my hand.

It was a baby crawling around in nothing but a diaper.

It made my heart hurt to think of the baby. Most likely dead now. A baby.

I started to think this was not a good idea. The whole ceremony. What were we trying to do, anyway?

I started to really protest, in my mind. This was a waste of time. The little kids were just going to get upset, or confused. This was a stupid idea and who did Josie think she was, anyway? It wasn't her place to lead us into some terrible ordeal where we thought about the dead babies and got all torn to pieces.

Who did she think she was, anyway?

Josie held her stupid photo to her chest and started to sing.

Peace upon you, peace around you,
Go now in peace.
Peace within you, peace surround you,
Go now in peace.

It was a very simple song, and after she had sung it a couple of times, the other kids joined in as best they could.

Sahalia played the chords on her guitar.

I didn't want to sing the stupid song.

I looked at the baby on my scrap of cardboard.

I felt so bad for that baby.

"Everyone sing," Josie commanded.

I glared at her.

"Sing, Dean," she insisted.

I couldn't do it.

"Sing."

Alex was on my left and he put his hand on my shoulder.

I felt so glad to have him. So lucky to be with my brother and guilty that I had family, when so many people didn't.

Everything was too much for me.

So I looked at my piece of cardboard and just focused narrower and narrower until that baby was the only thing I could see.

And I opened my mouth and whisper-sang, "Go now in peace," to the baby.

I didn't think about *all* the babies. All the people. All the everyone who was lost now. I just sang about the one curly-haired baby, singing him to peace and to rest.

I could sing the baby up to Heaven. The one baby.

I could sing for him and him alone.

Eventually Josie said, "Amen."

And I realized I had tears running down my face. They'd soaked the collar of my button-down shirt and were somehow also in my ears, which had never happened to me before.

"That's it," Josie said. "Our ceremony is over."

"Wait," said Batiste. "Can I say a prayer?"

"Of course," Josie said.

Batiste stood up and recited.

"Our Father, who art in Heaven, Halloween Thy Name. Thy kingdom come, Thy will be done, on earth as it is in heaven. Give us this day our daily bread, and forgive the breast

DAY 4

passers, and forgive the breast passes against us and lead us not into temptation, but deliver us from evil. Amen."

"Amen," we echoed.

I was quite sure that Halloween was not the name of God, and I didn't know what on earth a "breast passer" was, though I enjoyed imagining it to a degree, but it was nice Batiste wanted to make a contribution. And he had a beaming look on his face. Pride and happiness. He had given us something. For all his sanctimoniousness, he was growing on me.

Alex leaned against me and I put my arm around him and gave him a half hug.

Caroline and Henry were huddled peacefully together. Ulysses was up on Josie's lap while Max cuddled into her side. She was smoothing Max's cowlick. The most persistent cowlick in the world. It just sprung up anew after her every stroke.

Chloe had scooted over to Niko and was sidled up against him.

Niko didn't seem to mind. Too much.

Brayden was looking at the floor with a studied concentration that made me think he'd been upset, too, and didn't want us to see. Jake pulled up the bottom of his T-shirt, revealing (of course) his perfect six-pack abs. Then he blew his nose on the bottom of his shirt and laughed with a self-deprecating snort.

I took a long breath and let it out.

"Jeez Louise," said Chloe. "Let's eat. I'm starving."

We laughed.

It was the first easy laugh I had had in the last three days.

CHAPTER TWELVE

ELECTIONS

LUNCH: PIZZA.

    Cook: me.

    Excited about it: no.

"Oh man," Chloe moaned as she pushed her tray down the counter. "I never thought I'd get tired of eating pizza but you know what? I am."

"We're all tired of it," I snapped. "But I'm doing the best I can and I'm not getting much help."

"We can help!" Caroline said. "Me and Henry are real good helpers."

"Yeah," Henry added. "We help our mommy all the time. We can do the shopping, the chopping, AND the mopping!"

He and Caroline giggled at that, what had to be old family joke.

"I'm a great cook, too," added Chloe. "You should let me help. I can make pasta with butter so good."

DAY 4

"Okay," I said. "I tell you what. Every day I'll pick a helper and that helper will pick out what we're going to eat, and somehow, we'll figure out how to cook it together."

"Yay! Yay!" the little kids cheered, jumping up and down.

Then it was a chorus of "Pick me! Pick me!"

"Okay," I said, thinking it over. "Today's helper will be Chloe. And tomorrow will be Ulysses."

I figured I'd get the most annoying kid over with first. After all I had already cooked two out of the three meals for the day.

We ate our pizza and we waited for Jake and Brayden to show up.

It was election time.

Niko was there, looking over his notes. He looked nervous, but eager.

Jake and Brayden had skipped lunch and were nowhere to be seen.

Josie paced up near the counter.

"All right, hmmm, Jake and Brayden must have forgotten what we're doing," she said, stalling. "I know, let's sing some songs. Who knows 'She'll Be Comin' Round the Mountain'?"

"She" had driven her six white horses and "She" had eaten chicken and dumplings and "She" was having to sleep with Grandma when, at last, Jake and Brayden showed up.

Apparently they'd been planning a splashy opening for his election speech.

We heard Jake's voice booming from a distance.

"Thirty-four, twenty-seven, hut, hut, HIKE!"

And then Brayden came running toward us, leaping and jumping over the fallen merchandise in his way.

He was wearing a football helmet and an oversize sweatshirt

stuffed with towels or something to look like pads. On the front he had written a giant "2" with a magic marker.

Brayden came running toward us and then turned, and *BAM*, a football flew into his hands.

"Touchdown!" he shouted, spiking the ball.

The kids looked half thrilled, half terrified.

Then Jake came jogging into the Pizza Shack. He gave Brayden a high five and Brayden handed him the football.

Jake, too, wore a football helmet and a sweatshirt made to look like a uniform. He took off his helmet and tossed it onto the table. His jersey read QB on the front and #1 on the back.

"Guys, I am the QB," he said. "That means quarterback! The quarterback is the guy on the team who calls the shots and makes sure everyone plays their best. And I'm gonna be a great QB for this team. Us. That's why you should elect me the leader!"

The kids started clapping and cheering like crazy.

Niko looked at Josie and then back at his notes.

Jake's stunt was charming and silly and totally cool, too.

It didn't look good for Niko.

Josie tried to get a word in, but Jake continued.

"I say there is no reason in the world why we can't have some fun here! We've got, like, every game in the world. We've got all the food we can eat. I think this could be like summer training camp—"

He was talking too fast. He seemed wired. High, almost.

And then I wondered, was he actually high?

He was acting really weird.

"I gotta say," Brayden said, "that Jake is a great leader. You guys are gonna love having him as the boss. I guarantee it."

Somehow looking at Brayden standing there with a big #2 on his chest made me very, very nervous.

DAY 4

"We all appreciate your enthusiasm, Brayden," Josie said, finally getting in there. "But really, this is just for the two candidates."

"Totally! Sorry. My apologies, everyone."

"Dude," Jake said. "She's right, sit down, bro. This is mano a mano. Me and Niko only."

Brayden went and sat down in a booth to the side.

"Now, just to be clear," Jake rambled on. "I don't see this as just a *football* training camp—though I think we got the makings of a great team here—but every kind of sport. I even think we can make the things like cleaning up and cooking and all that crap, that stuff can be fun, too! We can have teams and have contests and prizes. Stuff like that!"

He grinned at us all. Then gave a thumbs-up.

"Okay," Josie said. "Is there anything else you'd like to say?"

Jake thought about it for a moment.

"Vote for me and we'll par-tee!" he said.

I hope he was improvising because as a slogan, it pretty much sucked.

Jake just stood there with his thumb still up. The kids gave a deflated cheer for him. They were following his cues, but they didn't seem to buy it a hundred percent. I certainly didn't.

"All right," Josie said. "Then let's hear from Niko."

"Great!" Jake said.

Niko stood and walked over to stand next to Josie, but Jake didn't sit down. He was just kind of standing there, fidgeting, throwing the ball in the air.

"Jake, why don't you sit down while Niko talks," Josie said, showing Jake where to sit.

The little kids giggled.

Jake was acting really stoned.

I wondered if this would help him or hurt him at "the polls."

"Hey, guys," Niko began. "It was a really cool idea to come in costume. I wish I thought of it. Though I don't know how cool you would think it was if I came in my Scout uniform . . ."

He looked up at us.

Niko was trying to crack a joke, I realized too late.

Someone needed to work with him on his delivery.

"But, you know, maybe Boy Scouts isn't cool to some people, but the training I got as a Scout has really helped me here. And all of us. You know, I know first aid and I helped us to get out of the bus and stuff."

Brayden whispered, "Yo!" to Jake and held his hands out. Jake passed him the ball.

"If you pick me, it's not going to be all games and playing," Niko continued. "I think we need order and structure. Everyone's gonna have to work if we're going to make it. That's just what I think."

The kids were looking down at their laps. A couple were starting to fidget.

Niko's eyes glanced over to Josie and I saw her make a little motion with her hands, like, Give us more.

Niko took a deep breath. Then he seemed to pull himself together. He stood up straight. He looked out at all of us.

"I am not good at making speeches. I'm not the most popular kid at school."

Brayden snickered off to the right.

"But I know what needs to be done here," Niko continued. "I know how to organize and delegate. I know how to ration food, so we'll be able to stay well fed for as long as possible. I know how to keep my head in a crisis. I think you all know that about me already.

"I know how to survive and I'll teach you all how to survive. That's what we need to learn now. I think we are all a lot

DAY 4

luckier than pretty much everyone in this part of the country."

He looked out and his gaze traveled over each of us. His posture, his straightness, seemed to magnetize us somehow and we all sat up taller in our seats.

"We are going to honor those who have died by surviving. All of us. That's my promise to you. If you elect me, we're all getting out of here safe and sound."

Niko strode to the back of the tables and sat down, alone.

Josie passed out pens from a new box of ballpoints and little scraps of paper. Each one was numbered.

"All right," she told us. "Write the name of the boy who you want to be our group leader until Mrs. Wooly comes."

There was a moment of circular scribbling as everyone got the ballpoints to flow.

Then there was a pause, while people thought, and eventually they started writing.

I watched the kids writing. These stupid little kids. How could they know enough to make a good choice here?

If they chose Jake, we were in serious trouble.

Niko was the only rational choice, but he hadn't played to the kids. He hadn't promised them a good time.

What would the little kids pick? Good times or survival skills?

I wrote Niko, and I underlined it several times.

Then I rose and put my vote into the empty personal-size pizza box Alex had created as a ballot box.

Alex retired to the corner booth, where he counted and recounted dutifully.

He rose and walked to the front of the room.

I tried to catch his eye, but he kept his gaze on the floor.

Alex whispered the results to Josie.

She took a moment and then spoke.

"This was a really close race, and that speaks to the fact that both our candidates are such good guys. Let's not let there be any hard feelings, guys . . ."

She looked out at Jake and Niko.

"The winner is Niko."

There were some cheers and a couple of boos. Brayden pronounced the election bull— (such a vocabulary!), but Jake rose to shake Niko's hand.

"Congratulations," Jake said. "Let me know what I can do to help, all right, man?"

Jake was sort of dancing on the tips of his toes. He had that much energy.

"Yes. Thank you," said Niko.

Niko's straight hair fell into his eyes and he pushed it back. Everything about Niko was straight. His hair, his posture, his whole way of being. The kid was utterly straight and totally trustworthy.

"Come on, man," I heard Jake say to Brayden as they walked away, "let's go get drunk."

DAY 4

CHAPTER THIRTEEN

GREENWAY 2.0

WHAT WAS I DREAMING OF? PLUMES OF DEADLY INK? ASTRID'S wild wavy hair draping across my face? A murderer rattling a gate?

I don't know. When Niko nudged me awake, I sat up so fast I shook it all out of my head.

"What time is it?" I mumbled, squinting in the low light of the store.

"Seven," Niko said. "Seven-oh-eight. I need your help in the Kitchen."

"Are you kidding me?" I asked. "Come back in two hours."

I closed my eyes and rolled over on my air mattress.

Niko just stood over me. Hands on hips. Just waiting.

"Okay, okay," I said.

"Meet me in the Kitchen," he said.

* * *

He had two giant poster boards and a set of colored Sharpies. He was putting the finishing touches on a map of the store and this detailed daily schedule.

Niko had spent yesterday afternoon walking around the store with Alex, while I helped Josie with the kids. Dinner had been fairly uneventful, with Jake and Brayden off drunk and doing God knows what; Sahalia skulking around our perimeter, pissed off at everyone; and Josie being the loving mother to her large brood.

Yawning, I started a fresh pot of coffee.

"Why did I have to get up this early?" I asked him.

"You're the cook," he said. "I need you to get breakfast ready and then we'll wake everyone up and I'll give them their assignments for the day."

"Man, they're gonna love that," I said.

"Structure," Niko said. "Children need structure."

"You're not going to try to get Jake and Brayden to follow your plan, are you?"

Niko brushed his brown hair out of his eyes. He glanced at me.

"Not so much," he said.

"Good," I replied instantly.

It was funny and we laughed.

I think it was maybe the first time we'd ever laughed together.

I heard another voice join our laughter and turned to see Ulysses. He was wearing Batman pajamas, his round little belly showed under the top.

Trust Ulysses to join in laughing when he didn't even know what the joke was.

"*Soy tu* 'helper'!" he said. He pointed to his chest. "Ulysses help today."

DAY 5

"Yes, that's right," I said, tousling his hair. "What should we have?"

"Huevos rancheros!"

"Okay," I said. "You know how to make?"

"*Sí, sí!*" he chirped.

"Let's go get eggs," I said to him.

I nodded to Niko as we left. He was busy with his charts.

If huevos rancheros is scrambled eggs with salsa on top, then Ulysses did, indeed, know how to make huevos rancheros.

"Okay, team." Niko addressed us after everyone had assembled and eaten breakfast. "We are going to do two things today. We are going to begin restoring and cleaning up the Greenway. And we are going to assess our resources."

Chloe groaned, "Awww," as if assessing resources was a chore her parents made her do every Sunday morning.

"Alex, you and I will take an inventory of our power and security. The rest of you will begin Operation Restock."

Niko took the top poster board away and he showed us all the map of the store. Each kid's name was on a sticky note and was placed in an area.

Sahalia—Media Department.

Chloe—Pharmacy.

Max and Ulysses—Automotive.

Batiste—Toys.

The McKinley Twins—Home Improvement.

Me—(surprise, surprise) Food and Drinks.

"Why doesn't Josie have an aisle?" Chloe asked.

"I have a secret project," Josie told us.

"Oooh, what is it? What is it?" the kids demanded.

"You'll see," she answered with a wink.

Niko went on with our assignments—we were to restore each aisle exactly to how it had been before the earthquake.

Niko stood up and gestured over to the cart corral right next to our dead school bus.

There were six stocked shopping carts lined up. Each cart held a mop, a broom, a dust pan, 409 spray, Pine-Sol, paper towels, rags, and trash bags—lots of trash bags.

First, Niko told us, we should load up carts with everything broken and damaged, then haul it over to the stroller aisle—now dubbed the Dump. Then we were to go back to our aisles, replace the remaining items on the shelves, and clean up.

This was for nine a.m. to noon. Then we'd have lunch. Then rest time.

Josie nodded. It was clear she'd been consulted in this plan of Niko's.

And then another three-hour work shift on Operation Restock.

Then the kids had free play until dinner.

I expected total rebellion from the kids. But they took their carts willingly.

Okay, everyone except for Sahalia. She took hers unwillingly and crashed off, spitting curses under her breath.

The little kids seemed pretty psyched to have a job to do.

"I'm gonna clean my aisles the fastest," boasted Chloe.

"Nuh-uh," answered Max. "Me and Ulysses are the team to beat!"

Jake and Brayden, of course, did not participate.

They had made themselves a little bunker in the Sports aisle and were busy drinking beer and playing laser tag. It was as if they had decided not to recognize Niko's leadership.

Throughout the day we heard them shouting and cursing

DAY 5

as they tromped around. It sounded like they were breaking stuff, in the course of their game.

Which was just what we needed—more to clean.

It also sounded like they were having fun.

But restocking the aisles was sort of fun, too, in its own way.

Niko taught everyone how to read the labels on the shelving units, so each Polly Pocket set went to the right space; and how to face the products out, so you could find said Polly Pocket set with ease. He was a perfectionist and asked for nothing less than total commitment to detail from each of us.

"Caroline, I see that you have these sheer drapes organized, but I noticed that the cream sixty-inch drapes are in with the white forty-eight-inch ones," Niko would say.

"We were wondering about that!" Caroline would chirp from atop her step stool.

And then they would take out the cream ones and find where they went and put them there and it was better.

"Hey, Chloe, see how these Advil have this child-safety lid? They go right here. These other ones, with the easy-off lid, they go over here."

"Whatever," Chloe would groan.

But she would stomp over and take them and put them in the right place.

It was very calming to have this repetitious work to do. I could have gone on inventorying forever.

After serving the cheese enchiladas Ulysses and I made for dinner and cleaning up, I was nearly asleep on my feet but I wanted to look for Astrid. I took a plate of enchiladas, covered in foil.

"What are you doing with that?" Niko asked me.

"I'm leaving them out for Astrid," I said.

"Good idea," Niko said, yawning. "She's on my list."

Yeah, I thought to myself, she's on my list, too.

I had no doubt that she was still in the store—there was no way for her to leave, and why would she?

But where was she holed up? Even after a day of cleaning, the store was pretty messy, it's not like I could look for clues.

I set up a stool in the center of the main food aisle and just left the plate there.

No note. Too tired.

DAY 5

CHAPTER FOURTEEN

THE POWER OF PANCAKES

I WOKE UP TO THE *BEEP-BEEP-BEEP* OF MY PANASONIC TRAVEL alarm clock. Everyone else got to sleep until eight, but for me and my little kitchen helper, whoever it turned out to be that day, it was up at seven. We had to make breakfast for the troops.

"Batiste," I whispered to the sleeping boy. With his face softened by sleep, he looked less superior and judgmental. He looked sweet, curled onto his side, with his two hands placed under his cheek as if in prayer.

"Batiste." I nudged him with my sneaker. "We have to make breakfast."

He opened his eyes and looked straight at me.

"Stuffed pancakes with fresh berry syrup."

"What's that?" I asked.

"Breakfast. I already planned the menu."

"Okay," I said. "Do you know how to make that?"

"Duh," he answered.

Okay. I guess it was a stupid question. Still there's nothing like sarcasm from an eight-year-old to make you want to wring their neck. Especially at seven in the morning.

But he could cook, actually. He walked through the aisles like a pro, selecting Bisquick, a dozen noncrushed eggs, two bags of frozen berries, a brick of cream cheese, vanilla extract, and a box of confectioner's sugar.

We found Niko in the kitchen. This was why I didn't complain about having to get up at seven. Niko got up at six. Yep, six. *Seis*. Six a.m.

"Good morning," he said brightly. "Batiste, you're Dean's helper for today?"

"Yes and I have the whole day planned." Batiste turned to me. "We need the blender."

As for Batiste, he reprimanded me once for not washing my hands ("Cleanliness is next to Godliness, Dean!"), but besides that, he was a great helper. In fact, I sort of became his helper as he whipped up the cream cheese and sugar in the blender and then mixed pancake batter in the KitchenAid and then created these delicious pancakes in a cast-iron muffin pan.

Who knew eight-year-olds could cook?

"Wow!" said the kids as they filed in, led by Josie.

"Oh my God, that smells amazing," Sahalia moaned. She was still in her pajamas but everyone else was fully dressed and ready for work.

"Good morning, Josie," Niko said, crossing to Josie with a cup of coffee. "You want some coffee?"

"No, thanks, I drink tea," she said.

"Oh. Okay," Niko said. Then he just stood there.

DAY 6

"Chloe and Ulysses, please keep your places in line. You know where you are to stand. Yes, you do."

"That's so smart that you gave them, like, a set place in line," Niko said to Josie.

I felt for the guy. He was truly horrible with the small talk.

Josie didn't seem to notice Niko's awkward efforts. In fact, she didn't seem to notice Niko at all.

"Max," Josie said, moving away. "Everyone gets one to start, then you may have seconds if there is enough for everyone."

"I made enough for you all to have thirds," Batiste said proudly.

And we did have thirds. The only thing that diminished our pleasure in eating the pancakes was that every time someone said, "God, these are good!" Batiste reprimanded them for taking the Lord's name in vain.

I had hardly seen Alex for the last day and so I tried to grab him after breakfast.

"Hey, A," I said. "Think you could stick around for a few minutes after breakfast? I was hoping I could get you to look at these ovens. I can't get the temperature right . . ."

A machine that needed adjusting might grab his interest.

"Sorry, Dean. But Niko needs me," he said, hurrying off.

I was left there, wearing an apron, feeling like a middle-aged mother whose children have discovered the mall.

After breakfast I took a plate with three stuffed pancakes drowning in berry sauce and wandered around looking for Astrid.

Instead, I ran into Jake and Brayden.

They had cleared away a section of the Women's Department and set up a makeshift bowling alley with bottles of bubble bath and a heavy yoga ball.

"Dude! You shouldn't have!" Jake said when he saw me with the plate.

He ambled over. His eyes were bloodshot and he smelled like old beer.

"They're not for you, Jake," Brayden said. "They're for Astrid."

I felt the blood rush to my face.

"Aw, is that right?" Jake drawled.

"Well, I've been leaving food out for her. I want her to know, you know, that she's welcome to come back."

"That is so sweet," Brayden said. "And here we thought the food was for us."

"God, that smells good," Jake said. "Do you mind if we eat them? I really don't think Astrid would mind. I saw her yesterday, eating some trail mix. I think she's doing fine."

I shrugged. I didn't want them to eat her pancakes, but I didn't want to look like an idiot, either. Or like I cared.

Jake took the plate from me, and he and Brayden fell on the pancakes like they were starving to death.

"These are fantastic!" Brayden said, his mouth full. "These are the best pancakes I've ever had."

"It's all Batiste," I said. "Turns out he can cook."

"Jeez," Jake mumbled, wiping his mouth on his sleeve. "What's for lunch?"

And there they were at lunch, lined up with all the other kids. Sahalia was right behind Jake, trying to start a conversation with him. He ignored her but was pretty nice to the other kids, joking around and ruffling Max's hair.

Niko walked into the kitchen and saw Jake and Brayden there and paused in his stride. Then he just picked up a tray and got on line.

DAY 6

Lunch was less of an immediate hit. Curried tuna fish on toast. The curried tuna had slivered almonds and currants in it (who knew they sold currants at Greenway? Organic, no less).

Batiste told everyone they would like it and, true enough, once they started eating, they loved it.

"Where did you learn to cook?" Chloe asked him.

"Church camp," he answered.

While everyone was eating, I saw Niko approach Jake and Brayden's table.

"Hey, guys," Niko said.

"Niko." Jake nodded.

Brayden just kept eating.

"Jake, I was hoping you would take on an assignment—Head of Security," Niko said all in a rush. "I want someone strong and capable to check the store and make sure everything is safe."

The little kids prattled on, eating their curried tuna and slurping their juice boxes, but Josie and I shared a look: Would Jake fall in line? Would he help us or were he and Brayden going to be a problem?

"I'll think about it," Jake said.

Niko let out his breath.

"Good."

Niko took his tray over to Josie and sat with her.

As Batiste went around and gave out the dulce de leche cupcakes we had spent most of the morning on, I watched Jake relax. He walked over to Chloe and complimented her on her hair accessories, which were numerous. And he got Max and Ulysses excited about the idea of starting a little football team.

Brayden went along with Jake, but he seemed distracted. I watched him watching Niko.

Niko was trying, in his uneasy way, to flirt with Josie.

And, out of the corner of his eye, Brayden just watched.

The "secret" assignment Niko had given Josie to do, while the little kids were all busy doing their aisles, was to improve our living quarters.

She had gone through the store looking for the coziest, safest-feeling space in the store.

It turned out to be the dressing rooms. They stood in the northwest corner of the store, against the wall.

One of the things that made them feel homey is that the rest of the store had a cold, linoleum floor—but the dressing rooms had bamboo floors.

The ladies' and men's dressing rooms shared a common wall and shared the same layout. There was one big dressing room (measuring six by ten feet—handicapped accessible) when you first entered, then beyond it there were eight dressing rooms, four on each side of a fairly wide hallway. Each small dressing room was a paltry four feet by four feet.

I know this because that afternoon Josie asked me to help her take down some of the walls. Her idea was to have the little kids sleep together in the two big dressing rooms. For the bigger kids she wanted to make us each a eight-by-four sleeping berth by taking down a wall separating two of the smaller dressing rooms. There would be four of these berths in the ladies' room and four in the men's dressing room.

"I'm not really good with carpentry," I told her as we studied the spaces.

"Well, you're better than me," Josie said.

"I bet Niko would do a really good job at this," I said.

I don't know. I felt for the guy. It was clear, to me, anyway, that he had a thing for Josie. I thought I might as well set him up a bit.

DAY 6

Josie rolled her eyes.

"Niko is . . ."

"What?" I asked.

"He's so uptight and formal. He's exhausting," she answered.

"Yeah, I guess I could see that," I said.

"So maybe we cut this panel out here?" Josie said, tapping on the wall. "We each want privacy and also to be able to stretch out."

"Have you guys seen Jake?" came Brayden's voice.

We stepped out of the dressing rooms.

Brayden was standing there, his hands jammed in his pockets. His dark hair was falling in his eyes and he looked down at his feet.

"We haven't seen him," Josie said.

"Maybe he decided to start doing his job," I said, going back into the dressing rooms.

"What are you guys doing in there?" I heard Brayden ask Josie.

"We're taking down some walls to make sleeping areas for everyone."

"Want some help?" Brayden said. "I used to frame houses in the summer, so I know how to handle a hammer."

It was so alien to me, the concept that Brayden would want to help—be offering to help—that I actually had to peek back out to see if he was serious.

He was.

He was just standing there, with his head hung, like a sad puppy.

"I'd love your help, Brayden," Josie answered. "You know, I have to say, it would be really good for all of us if you and Jake came back and participated."

"Yeah," Brayden said. "I think you're right. So, put me to work . . ."

And he smiled. He had a movie star smile.

I don't know that I'd ever seen him smile before.

I'd seen him laugh. In a mean way. But this was something new. This, I realized, was the smile he gave girls.

"You guys don't need me then," I said.

"I guess not," Josie said.

She turned away from Brayden, breaking his gaze. Her eyes were twinkling, though. And she seemed flushed.

"Let me show you what I was thinking of doing, Brayden," she said, going into the dressing room.

I got the hell out of there.

DAY 6

CHAPTER FIFTEEN

MY FOOD AISLE AT NIGHT

JOSIE AND BRAYDEN WORKED HARD ALL AFTERNOON AND BY the evening free play period, they had new sleeping quarters for us all.

Josie led the little kids over. They rushed in to the dressing rooms. There was hooting and hollering from inside, but Niko and I stopped to look at the area right outside the dressing rooms.

Josie and Brayden had made it into a living room.

The floor was carpeted and they had laid down a bunch of throw rugs over it. They had brought over the beanbag chairs from the Media Department and added some more furniture. There were two futon couches, a fake-fur butterfly chair and two coffee tables and a desk. A lava lamp gently oozed on one of the coffee tables. There was a mini-fridge and a case of water bottles next to it. They had tricked it out to an absurd degree.

Right next to the furniture, there was a small clearing, with three card tables and seven folding chairs distributed among the tables. A table lamp stood on each table and two bookshelves had been stocked with what looked to me like one each of every book in the Book Department.

It was a kind of work area. Like a library.

"Downright homey," Niko said to me.

Was that a joke? I glanced at him. Couldn't tell.

So I just repeated him. "Downright homey."

The kids were going berserk, so I stepped inside to see what all the racket was about.

Brayden had neatly removed the wall between the men's and ladies' dressing rooms so it was now one big bunker, with a hallway running down the middle and berths off to either side.

Josie and Brayden had Sharpied the names of the kids on the doors.

Chloe grabbed my hand.

"I found your bedroom," she said. "I'll show you."

Chloe dragged me down the hall to one of the dressing rooms in what had been the men's side.

Sure enough, it read "Dean" on the door.

Inside it was smallish. Four by eight. A hammock had been slung end to end. A locker stood on the floor. On top of the locker, a small lamp.

Above the hammock, running along the wall, there was a shelf.

And on the shelf were books.

An assortment of the paperbacks from the Book Department. Some mysteries, some cyborg fiction, five cookbooks. I laughed at that.

"Do you like your room?" Josie came up behind me.

"I really do."

"You can, like, customize it any way you want. I just put some stuff here because I thought you'd like it."

"I like it," I said.

DAY 6

"If you don't like the hammock, you can stick with your air mattress, though I'm not sure it will fit in here."

"I like it just like this," I said.

From the hallway outside my door I heard Max and Ulysses speaking. Ulysses said something and Max laughed.

"What'd he say?" Chloe demanded.

"Ulysses says it's like a train!" Max announced.

"It is just like a train!" Chloe declared.

Our bedrooms, the dressing rooms at the Greenway, had just been given their new name: the Train.

The Train and its architects, Josie and Brayden, were all the talk at dinner.

Josie sat with Jake and Brayden, which was an entirely new arrangement. And the three laughed and palled around all during dinner.

At one point Brayden stretched and put his arm across the back of the booth. Oldest move in the book. And Josie leaned right back into him.

Niko took his tray and sat at the table next to them. He kept trying to get into the conversation.

"You know, once, in Scouts, we took a trip to Yosemite. It got so cold at night we had to build makeshift lean-tos. We were out there at three in the morning, scraping up pine needles and leaves for insulation."

"Wow," Brayden said dryly. "Great story."

And they laughed.

"But the funny thing was that then when we started the campfire, these pine needles kept falling in the fire and flaring up!"

"Oh man," Jake interrupted, turning to Brayden. "You remember when Fat Marty lit that grease bomb?!"

"It was so funny, Josie," Brayden said. "He saved, like, a month's worth of bacon grease. He wanted to show us how to make a grease bomb."

"And then he lit it and instead of exploding, it just gave off this horrible smoke."

"And his mom came in screaming and she grabbed this fire extinguisher and doused us all."

"It was crazy," Brayden said. "Took us like five hours to clean it up."

And Josie laughed. She was eating it up. Brayden's rough-guy, laid-back charm.

Niko sat there, trying so hard to be cool. Smiling, laughing at the right places.

But I could see that every time Brayden touched Josie or nudged her or said her name, it was like a knife in his gut.

There was another person who didn't seem to be so thrilled with the budding romance between Josie and Brayden: Sahalia.

She was acting extra-insolent and slouchy. She had nearly thrown down her tray with her food and now she just sat there with her arms crossed, staring daggers at Josie.

After we all settled down in our plush new accommodations, I realized I'd left my journal in the Kitchen.

The lights had already dimmed automatically, which meant it was after ten, but I could see, sort of, so I went to get my journal.

Approaching the Food aisle, I heard a voice.

More specifically, I heard hushed laugher. Astrid's.

I walked slowly, quietly. I didn't want to scare her off.

But she didn't hear me. She was with Jake.

She and Jake were sitting together near the iced tea. She was eating the plate of food I had left out for her. Barbecued

DAY 6

chicken and corn salad with buttermilk dressing—thank you, Chef Batiste.

Jake kept snatching little bits of food off the plate.

"Quit it," Astrid said. "You already ate."

Jake put his hand on her knee. She let it stay there and continued to eat.

"I know, but it's good."

"It's delicious," Astrid said.

I felt proud, which was kind of stupid, since it was mostly Batiste's cooking, anyway.

"You should come back," Jake said. "The little kids are always asking about you."

This wasn't true, actually. Now that motherly Josie had stepped in as mama duck, they actually seemed to have forgotten about rough-and-tumble Astrid.

I don't think it had anything to do with Astrid's personality. I just think it served them well to have a very short memory at this stage in their trauma.

"I don't want to," she sort of growled. "I told you."

"We miss you," Jake said. "Well, Brayden doesn't miss you, but Dean does."

I felt my face burn in the dark.

He knew I had a crush on Astrid and Astrid did, too.

"Please," she said. "He's harmless."

Harmless. Okay.

I tried to quiet my breathing. Now I really, really didn't want them to know I was there.

Astrid finished the food. She put her finger to the sauce on the plate and licked her finger clean.

She put her finger in the sauce again, but this time, before she could get it to her mouth, Jake licked it.

Kneeling in front of her, he took the plate from her.

She let him.

He put his hand on her neck and drew her toward him.

She let him.

He kissed her.

She started to cry.

"I miss my mom," she said. "I miss my brothers. And Alicia. And Jaden. And Rini."

"I know," Jake murmured, rubbing her neck.

"I'm scared. I'm scared sick."

"Baby, we're all scared," Jake said. "Brayden and Josie made a really nice bed for you. You have your own little room. You should come and see it."

"I told you I can't! I shake all the time. I'm too scared. I'm so scared I start to choke and I can't breathe and I throw up! I don't want to have to be around them!"

He took her into his arms. She clung to him, like he was a life raft and she was drowning.

"It's gonna be okay," Jake said.

"Aren't you scared?" she asked him.

"We're gonna be okay, Astrid."

"You're not scared?"

Jake responded by kissing her harder. Suddenly, they were all over each other.

I knew I should back away but I didn't.

Astrid pushed him off her for a moment and sat up.

Slowly, with Jake watching, and me watching, too, she unbuttoned her shirt.

It was so wrong of me to watch, but I couldn't, couldn't stop.

She brushed the tears away with her forearm as she unbuttoned. Astrid slid her shirt off her shoulders and unclasped her bra behind her back. She let the bra fall away and then she was naked from the waist up.

DAY 6

Astrid's body was so beautiful my throat closed up.

So smooth and wonderful and soft. She looked so soft. A sculpture of some Greek goddess awoken from cold stone into warm pulsing life.

Jake reached up and touched her breasts. He cupped them both.

"Which one's Cinderella again?" he asked her.

"Neither of my breasts is named Cinderella." She laughed, sort of unwillingly.

Obviously, this was some old joke between them.

"Hello, Cinderella," Jake said to one of her beautiful, perfect breasts.

He kissed it.

He nuzzled the other one. "Now, don't get jealous, Snow White. There's enough of me for both of you."

Somehow, hearing him say this—watching this weird, private joke—was even worse than seeing them make out.

Astrid just bent down and kissed him hard.

"Make me feel better," she told him. "Make me feel something."

He rolled her under him and I couldn't see anymore, which was good because I already knew I was going to feel absolutely terrible about what I'd witnessed.

I backed away and I was almost out of earshot when I heard Jake say, "Just forget it."

And I stopped to listen.

"Here," Astrid said.

"Forget it," Jake mumbled. "It's no good."

"Wait, Jake, come on."

"Leave me alone."

"It's just stress," Astrid said. "It's not like this has happened before."

"Just leave me alone, I said," he growled.

I heard the sounds of him pulling his pants on.

"Jake . . . please," Astrid said. "Don't go."

"There's a nice bed for you over at the Train. We're all waiting for you. If you're so scared, come back to us."

"I told you, I can't."

"See you, Astrid," he said.

I crouched down as Jake passed by. I held my breath.

After a moment, I went closer to Astrid.

She was sitting up, looking in the direction Jake had gone. She absentmindedly twirled her hair in her fingers, trying to get a knot out. Then she sniffed her armpit and made a face.

As I watched, Astrid slid the straps of her bra onto her shoulders and fitted the lacy cups around her breasts.

My whole body was on fire for Astrid.

I must have moved because suddenly she stopped.

"Jake?" she whispered. Then she listened.

She looked right my way and I was sure she couldn't see me, but I froze.

Each heartbeat pounding like a drum.

Finally she decided no one was there. She dressed quickly and then, much to my surprise, she climbed right up the iced tea shelves, using them as a ladder.

About halfway up, she reached up and moved aside one of the ceiling panels. I got a glimpse of a sleeping bag and some paperback books up there.

She balanced on the top support of the shelving unit and then crawled into her hiding space.

The ceiling tiles gave just the slightest bit.

Astrid was hiding in one of my food aisles. And I had seen her topless. I hated myself for it, but I had.

DAY 6

CHAPTER SIXTEEN

A LADY

THE NEXT MORNING, I COULD HARDLY LOOK JAKE IN THE EYE. Caroline and Henry were my helpers for the day, and their chirpy good cheer was an excellent distraction.

Scrambled eggs sandwiched between chocolate chip waffles. Wow.

Niko had a change in plans for us. He rapped on his tray, to get our attention.

"You all did an excellent job of restocking the shelves and taking inventory of our assets and I want to thank you," Niko said. "I know that you're not all completely finished with your assignments, but we're going to shift our routine a bit now.

"The big kids will work together on projects that we need to attend to and the little kids will be attending school."

A rising chorus of *awwww*s and *no way*s drowned out Niko's voice for a moment.

School. That was what the card tables and folding chairs in our new "living room" were about.

"Josie will tell you all about it." He gestured for Josie to rise and address us.

"Now, listen, you guys," she said. "It's not going to be a drag, like real school. We're going to learn fun things and do lots of art projects. Maybe Jake will even teach us some football, right, Jake?"

"Most probably, maybe," he said, toasting her with a half-eaten waffle sandwich.

Josie sat down and Brayden put his arm around her. He tried to nuzzle her neck, but she shook her head slightly. A not-in-front-of-the-kids shake.

Niko took back the floor. He seemed steely now. Cold and efficient.

"Another thing that's going to change is the way we are using electricity. Alex has worked hard to make an energy plan that conserves our resources as much as possible, and we need to put it into action right away."

Alex stood up.

"Yeah, um, so during the day, we'll have the lights on here in the kitchen and also in Living Room area—"

"The school," Josie corrected.

"And besides that," Alex continued, "the other parts of the store will be dark."

"Dark?" asked Caroline.

"Like how dark?" said Henry.

"It will be pretty dark, I think. But don't be scared because, remember, this store is completely sealed off from the outside. So nothing can get in here. Everything in the store is a known quantity," Alex said.

DAY 7

He was half talking to himself, I knew. Telling himself not to be scared.

"Plus we can each have a flashlight," Josie added.

Batiste, Ulysses, and Max seemed excited about having flashlights, but Henry and Caroline looked scared.

Chloe was just scratching her head. Scratching hard and with purpose.

Niko laid out the work plan for the day.

The big kids would be helping to consolidate the frozen food in the kitchen freezers, to save on power.

I could see the planning behind the big change in routine. We couldn't waste the energy to have the kids scattered all around the store working. Niko wanted them in one place so we'd only have to light a certain area of the store.

It made sense. But the whole thing made me irritated and what I realized was that I was pissed that Alex hadn't told me about it.

He knew the power was giving out and he didn't tell me. He told Niko instead.

Niko had him off and running the store while I was stuck in the Kitchen. He and Niko were becoming best buddies while I was stuck hanging out with the kindergarteners.

I didn't like Niko spending more time with Alex than I did. It didn't feel right to me. We were brothers. I should know everything he knew and vice versa.

Now that I was aware of not hanging around with my brother, it was all I could think about. At afternoon free period I tried to get him to play Monopoly. He had a game of Stratego going with Niko. And at dinner Alex asked Niko to go with him off to look at a set of video walkie-talkies he had found and was working on in our Living Room area. So I cleaned the Kitchen.

I went to my hammock in a huff, determined to talk to Alex the next day.

It felt like I'd only been asleep for a moment when I was shaken awake.

It was Jake.

"Get up!" he whispered. "There's a woman outside at the loading docks. She wants us to let her in."

Niko, Josie, Brayden, Jake, and I all stumbled into the common hallway of the Train. Jake motioned for us to be quiet and to follow him.

Once we were out of earshot of the kids, Niko turned to Josie.

"Josie, please stay here and make sure the kids stay safe."

"I want to come," she whispered. "They're asleep. They'll be fine."

"We need you here," Niko said.

"Come on, dude, she wants to come," Brayden argued.

Trying to win points with his new girlfriend.

"The answer is no. I need to know that the kids are safe and here," Niko said. "The rest of you come on."

Niko took off toward the storeroom, I followed with the other boys and Josie crossed her arms and stayed behind.

Niko had authority, there's no denying.

"You're so sexist," Josie hissed after him. He sort of was, I guess.

In the storeroom we heard an electronically transmitted voice. A woman.

"Hello? Are you back? Please! You have to hurry."

Jake pointed and we saw something we'd not seen before—there was a video intercom, right on the wall.

DAY 7

A woman's face, head wrapped in a shawl, face covered by layers of material, took up the frame.

"I was doing my rounds and I saw her," Jake said. "I didn't even know there was an intercom."

"Please let me in," she begged.

Niko pressed a button on the intercom.

"Hello. We see you. How many of you are there?"

"Just me! Just me!" she whispered. You could see she was craning her neck to look behind her.

Niko took his finger off the button. He turned to us.

"Listen," he said. "I want to let her in, but we can't. We physically can't. We don't know how to retract the security gate *and* we don't have keys to the door."

"I don't trust her anyway," Brayden said. "See how she's looking behind her all the time? She's got people with her. No question. It could be a trap."

"I think she's alone," Jake said. "But Niko's right. We couldn't get the door open if we wanted."

"Please!" she said, pleading. "Please hurry!"

She removed the material from around her face, maybe so we could see she was honest. There were dark circles under her eyes and they were rimmed red. She looked like someone's mom.

"Please! I am begging you!"

Niko grabbed his hair and pulled. He was in agony.

"What about the hatch?" I said. "We open the hatch and throw a ladder down!"

"Yes!" Niko said. "Yes!"

But then the woman screamed. And her face disappeared from the monitor.

And we heard a voice that was low and menacing. A voice that was familiar.

"You. Get. Away. From. My. Store."

He was talking to the woman and his speech was interrupted by heavy sounds. The sounds, I think, of him hitting her.

"This. Is. MY. STORE."

It was the monster from the front gate.

He was "guarding" our store.

Which explained why we hadn't had more people trying to get in, to get food and water.

I looked at the screen in shock, expecting at any moment to see the face of the monster, but it did not appear.

I guess he was too deranged to notice the camera.

We could hear what was going on outside, the last sounds of a scuffle, and then it was quiet. Then we heard what I imagined to be the sound of the man dragging the woman's body away.

After a few moments of inactivity, the intercom shut off automatically.

We were frozen in a moment of horror, I think is the best way to describe it.

There had been a woman there. Right outside the door. And now she was dead.

And then Niko roared.

He balled his hands into fists and started striking his own head. *Bam, bam, bam!*

"Niko, stop!" I shouted.

He turned to the nearest shelving unit and started pummeling the boxes.

I stepped forward to try to help him. To restrain him, somehow, so he wouldn't hurt himself.

"Let him be," Jake said. "He's just working stuff out."

Niko destroyed the aisle, ripping, punching, tearing, throwing, cursing, spitting, shouting. Crying.

DAY 7

Slowly, he started winding down.

"All right, man," came Jake's drawl. "It's gonna be okay."

"It's not okay," Niko shouted. "She's dead and if I'd just thought faster, I could have saved her!"

He drove his head into a heavy, wooden crate.

"You're pissed!" I shouted. "You're so angry you want to burst!"

My volume and intensity surprised him (and me), and he stopped what he was doing.

"We could've saved her and we failed! You could have saved her and you failed!" I shouted.

It seemed like he needed me to push back at him with the same weight of his own anger and despair.

"She'd dead! They're all dead and we can do nothing to save them!"

Niko crumpled to his knees and rested his forehead on the linoleum. Now I could stop yelling. He could hear me.

"It's not your fault, Niko," I said.

"But I could have helped her."

"It's not your fault," I repeated.

"You didn't cause the tsunami, man," Jake said quietly.

"It's not your fault."

"It's nobody's fault," Brayden said.

Niko's body relaxed.

Jake, Brayden, and I just watched him for a while as his chest heaved and he regained his usual composure.

Niko drew his sleeve across his face.

He sat up and looked around.

"Shoot," he said. "Look at this mess."

We laughed a little when he said that.

"Come on, man," Jake said. "Let's go get a drink."

Jake hauled Niko to his feet and we left the storeroom.

But I gave a backward glance at the monitor.

It was black and silent.

One more lady was dead. Add her to the millions dead outside and she figured pretty small. But to us, she was big.

DAY 7

CHAPTER SEVENTEEN

RUM

WE GATHERED IN THE KITCHEN. JAKE HAD A BOTTLE OF RUM AND was pouring liberal shots into Dixie cups.

Jake held his cup aloft. "To Niko, a really good guy, even if he is a Boy Scout."

"Here, here," I said, tapping my cup with them.

I took a sip. Straight rum. It burned. But it felt good to feel something strong besides failure.

Brayden knocked his down without a grimace.

"You know," Jake said, after he drained his cup. "I love Boy Scouts. You know why?"

"Why?" Niko asked.

"They give a real good hand job."

We cracked up.

"No, really. All that time up in the mountains with nothing to do. They always come prepared, too, with little lotion bottles."

"Ha-ha," Niko said. But he didn't seem mad at all. "We get a lot of those jokes. But back in Buffalo—"

"You're from Buffalo? New York?" Brayden interrupted him. "I have an aunt from there."

All this time we'd been surviving the end of the world together and I'd never even asked Niko where he was from.

"Yeah. Back in Buffalo there were ninety-eight guys in my troop. And you know why I joined? Because it was fun. I mean, I learned so much. But mostly I just did it because we were laughing all the time."

"You must have really missed them, when you moved here," I said. He shrugged.

"I will tell you guys something you're probably not going to believe, but back in Buffalo, I had a lot of friends. I really did," Niko continued. He brushed his hair out of his eyes. "I know it will strain your imaginations, but I even had a girlfriend."

"What's her name?" I asked.

"Is she hot?" Jake said at the same time.

"Lina and . . . yeah," Niko said.

We all laughed again.

"She's very pretty. She was a senior last year. Now she's at Sarah Lawrence."

"Wait a minute, you're telling me last year, when you were a sophomore, you were dating a senior?"

Niko shrugged. "Yeah."

After a moment, Jake said, "Cool."

Brayden squinted at Niko. I could tell he was thinking what I was thinking (and probably Jake, too): No. Way.

Niko was making up a girlfriend.

But after what he'd just been through, not a one of us, not even Brayden, called him on it.

DAY 7

"All right, I got a question for you boys," Brayden said. "Where's the craziest place you ever did it?"

"Oh God." Jake rolled his eyes. "Not this again."

"What?" Brayden protested.

"This is like his favorite question," Jake snorted. "And anyway, man, not all the present company can answer this one." He nodded toward me.

I don't think he was *trying* to be mean.

"Oh yeah," Brayden said. "No speakee the nookie, eh, Dean?"

I felt my stupid face going red.

"Why do you all assume that about me?" I said. Trying to play cool and failing, I'm sure.

Jake reached across the table and poured us all another big shot.

"Dude," Jake said. "We only assume it about you because it's true."

They laughed good-naturedly.

"You guys are a-holes," I said, playing it off.

"Hey, Brayden," Jake said. "Speaking of the nooks, how's Josie treating you?"

I shot a look at Niko. What was Jake thinking? Maybe he didn't know that Niko liked Josie. Was that possible?

Brayden took a swig from his drink. He avoided looking at Niko, but grinned.

"It's all right," he said. "Very nice girl."

"Ha!" Jake laughed. "That means she's not putting out."

Niko studied the cup in his hands.

"We do a lot of cuddling," Brayden said.

Niko looked so relieved, I had to laugh. Jake clapped me on the shoulder. I was really feeling the rum.

"Oh man, getting laid is so awesome," Jake said, scratching

his head. "It's just absolutely the best thing ever. Once you get it, all you can think of is getting it again. Sometimes I'm having sex and I'm worried about the next time I'm gonna have sex!"

I slugged back the rest of my rum.

I really hoped he'd shut up soon.

"You'll get there, in time, Dean. You'll discover for yourself the beautiful, beautiful world of the hot little clam."

It was so base. So vulgar.

He was talking about Astrid.

He didn't love her. He just wanted her for her body.

It wasn't fair.

"It must be so easy for you," I said. My face was hot.

"How so?"

"You come to our school, you're immediately popular. You're the best player on the football team. You get the hottest girl in school. The best girl, without lifting a finger."

I was loose. I felt big, like I could say what I really felt. I was drunk.

"And who are you, really?" I said to Jake, pouring myself another drink. "I mean, what do you have, besides charm and some muscle?"

"All right, settle down, Geraldine," Brayden said.

I drained my paper cup.

"That's a lot of rum for a lightweight like you," Jake said.

"You don't deserve her." I stood up. "She's so smart, so beautiful. She's wild and funny and kind, and you're just a dumb jock. You don't even love her. You just want her so you can get your rocks off."

Jake got up, sending his chair crashing down behind him. "You're out of line, Dean."

My blood was pounding and I laughed.

"Out of line! Yeah, I know. If I ever speak up. If I ever

DAY 7

stand up for myself or draw attention to myself, I'm out of line, right? Because I'm not as good as you? Is that it?"

Niko came toward me, hands out, like he was going to calm me down.

I pointed at Jake. "HE DOESN'T DESERVE HER. She's a goddess and he's named her body parts after Disney princesses!"

Jake roared at that, of course.

And launched himself at me, of course.

And started beating the crap out of me, of course.

After he got in some good punches, they pulled him off me.

I lay on the ground, panting. Blood was on my face and on the linoleum.

Jake gasped, trying to catch his breath, as they held him back.

"He's a sneak," Jake said, pointing to me. "He's a pervert."

"What is going on here?" Josie's voice came.

She rushed to my side.

"What happened?"

Niko and Brayden looked guilty. Jake stormed away.

"Brayden?" Josie said.

"Josie, it just got out of control," he said.

Josie shot Brayden and Niko an angry look.

"Well?" she said. "Is someone going to help me get him up?"

I curled on my side and puked.

CHAPTER EIGHTEEN

I MEET PAINKILLERS

MOTHER JOSIE GOT ME CLEANED UP AND PUT ME TO BED. I asked her to take the breakfast shift for me and she agreed.

"Sleep it off," she said. "You smell like a wino."

Then I lay there the rest of the night and had feverish dreams where Jake's fist met my face in different setups. He hit me in the library. He hit me on line for tickets at the Royal Cinemas. He hit me in my bed at home.

Through it all my head throbbed like it would split open.

In the morning I felt like I'd fallen off a ski lift, then fallen down a black diamond mogul field and been hit by a Snowcat.

Also, I had a headache.

But I knew what I had to do. I had to apologize to Jake. I couldn't have him as my enemy.

I was going to have to lie to him.

* * *

DAY 8

After the little kids woke up and got herded off to the Dump for their morning ablutions, I got to my feet in increments.

My nose pounded rhythmically with pain. It was crusted full of blood so I had to breathe out of my mouth, which tasted like the bottom of a garbage disposal.

I stumbled down the hall and knocked on Jake's door.

"Jake," I wheezed.

I was allowing myself to sound as pitiful as I felt.

I knocked again.

"Jake," I said. "I want to apologize."

The door to the berth creaked open a slit.

"What?" came his voice.

"Astrid told me that stuff in confidence," I said, sort of gasping as I spoke. "I had no right to tell the other guys. I'm sorry."

I had his attention.

The door opened a hand's width. I could see him in his hammock, looking at me through the gap.

"What are you talking about?" he said.

"Astrid talks to me sometimes," I explained. "When I get food, sometimes she comes down and talks to me. She told me, some stuff about you two . . ."

Jake watched me through the door.

A beat. A beat. A beat.

Would he buy it?

"Pretty private stuff," he grumbled. "What else did she say?"

"Nothing," I said. "Just about how you met and . . ."

Think. Think. Think.

"She really loves you," I said. "She said she feels scared and you're the only one who makes her feel safe."

He crossed his arms.

"I do love her," he said. "You were wrong to say that stuff."

He was buying it. I felt faint with relief or pain. Couldn't say which.

"I know," I said. "I'm sorry. You know, I never really drank that much before."

WHANG, WHANG, WHANG went the pulse of dagger-tip pain at the bridge of my nose.

"Yeah," he drawled. "I told you to slow down. Shoot, I thought you'd been spying on us. I didn't know you two were friendly."

"I think she gets lonely," I said. "And I guess you probably know I have this stupid crush on her."

I was giving him what I already knew he knew.

That's how you do it. You win confidence by telling your secrets. It seemed like he was buying it.

I really needed him to buy it.

"Well, shoot, booker," he said. "Then I'm sorry I beat you up so much."

"I deserved it," I said.

My nose was throbbing. It sent a constant stab of pain through the middle of my forehead.

"Hey, what does 'booker' mean, anyway?" I asked.

"Someone who reads a lot. Kind of a nerd, sorta," he said with a sheepish smile.

Fine. He could put me down. Whatever.

As long as he didn't slaughter me for spying on him.

I turned to leave and had to put out my hand to steady myself. Everything was getting electric at the edges of my field of vision. Little zapping fish swimming up and nearly taking me down with them.

Then Jake was up and supporting me, his shoulder under my arm. I leaned on him heavily, trying not to black out.

DAY 8

"I think I mighta broken your nose for you," he said apologetically. "Why don't you let me fix you up?"

Jake eased me down onto the futon sofa in the living room and then went and got the materials he needed to tape up my nose.

He came back with surgical tape, cotton balls, a pair of scissors, and a bottle of hydrogen peroxide.

"This happened to me once when we played Abilene Cooper. They had a linebacker, must have weighed three hundred pounds. Guy hit me like a bull on a rodeo clown."

He looked around.

"Aw, shoot, I forgot to get some kind of cloth."

He grabbed a chenille throw blanket.

"Josie'll be pissed, but who cares," he said. He doused a corner with hydrogen peroxide and then started swabbing my face.

I tried not to pull away, but it hurt like hell.

"Oh, wait," Jake said. "I forgot the best part."

From his back pocket he drew two foil packs of pills.

"Got you some pain meds. They're strong. Real fun." He popped one out and gave it to me. It melted in my mouth. Minty.

"Nice, huh? Works pretty fast." And he handed me the other one. "And these are demi-roids. Gonna help your body heal and you know what, dude, you should just keep taking them for a while. Help fill out your physique a bit, if you know what I mean . . ."

I pocketed the steroids to take later when I had water handy.

I was already starting to feel better. More warm and relaxed. I lay back on the futon.

"That's the way," Jake said. "Now close your eyes and mouth for me."

He poured the hydrogen peroxide into my nose.

I sat up, sputtering and frothing.

Jake pressed the throw blanket into my face.

"Good, good."

Next he felt my nose. And then he stuck cotton up into each nostril.

"You're lucky," he said. "Nice clean break. It'll make you look manly."

He put two pieces of tape across the bridge of my nose.

"You oughta thank me for breaking it. Girls love a broken nose."

I could barely talk, between the hangover, the pain pills, and the two cotton balls jammed up my nose.

"Franth, Janke," I managed to say.

He laughed.

"You're all right, booker."

He held out his hand.

"I'm sorry I jumped to conclusions."

I shook his hand—slowly. He was smiling at me, really asking for my forgiveness.

I felt like an a-hole. I *had* deserved a beating for what I had done. And now I had tricked a guy who, for all his faults, was pretty decent.

I shook his hand and said, "Itd wath my fault."

"Oh my God, what happened to you?" came Chloe's noisy, nosy voice.

The little kids were coming back from breakfast, preparing themselves for their school.

They saw me and gasped, gathering around.

"He got beat up," Max said, confident.

"Did you get beat up, Dean?" little Caroline asked, scratching her head.

"I fewl," I lied. "Off a shelf."

DAY 8

"No, he didn't," Max said. "He got beat up."

"Naw, Dean fell off a shelf, kids," Jake said. "I saw him fall myself."

"Maybe," Max conceded. He looked at me and then at Jake and then back at me. Each time he moved his head his blond cowlick bobbed like a feather on an old lady's hat.

"But all I can say is that my mom's sister, Raylene, who is my aunt but don't like to be called aunt because she says it makes her feel old so I call her Sissy Raylene. Anyways, she used to come over for poker and she'd look all busted up and my mom'd say, 'What happened?' and Sissy Raylene'd look over at her husband, Mack, and say, 'I fell off a ladder.' And my mom would say, 'Looks to me like you got beat up.' And Sissy Raylene's husband, Mack, would say, 'No. She fell off a ladder.' And then Mack would go in to play poker and Sissy Raylene would cry to my mom and say, 'Actually, Mack beat me up.'"

Max looked at me and Jake pointedly.

"That's all I'm saying."

Just then Josie came up.

"Hm. Nice to see you two up and about," she said.

She picked up the grisly, bloody throw blanket.

"Nice. Thanks for this," she said, regarding the blanket. "And I have good news. Have you noticed that everyone is scratching their head a lot?"

I had sort of noticed, and actually, at that very moment, several of the little kids were doing it.

"We have lice." She turned to the kids. "Kids, go put your bathing suits on."

The little kids cheered and jumped for joy. Sahalia slumped off behind them, looking put out, as usual.

Josie turned to us.

"You, too."

CHAPTER NINETEEN

LICE AND OTHER VERMIN

JOSIE TOLD US TO SUIT UP AND HEAD TO THE DUMP.

She wanted us all to wash our hair immediately. Actually, to be specific, she wanted to wash our hair for us.

Jake and I found suits, changed, and went over.

All the little kids were wearing bathing suits. It was really cute. They were shivering in the cold air of the store, so Niko handed out towels from a big stack Josie had brought.

Josie had also set up two big plastic tubs, along with lots of bottles of Nit-Out shampoo and gallon jugs of distilled water.

Brayden came bounding over. He had a set of trunks on, too. His upper body was also cut and muscled, like Jake's. But Jake had that pale skin and blond hair. Brayden's skin tone was olive, so even though it was autumn and none of us had seen the sun in about a week, Brayden looked tan and beach worthy.

Sahalia showed up just in time to see Brayden give Josie a big kiss. I guess Josie had gotten over her qualms about PDA. Maybe she just couldn't resist his bod.

DAY 8

Sahalia was not wearing a bathing suit, I noticed. I didn't expect her to. I didn't expect her to do anything anyone told her to do, actually.

Instead she was wearing a white T-shirt and short shorts, with long woolen leg warmers up over her knees.

In the moment I just supposed she had wanted to put together a cool delousing ensemble.

Josie told us that we would straddle a bin. Then she'd pour water over our head, wash our hair, rinse. Repeat and we'd be done.

So we were all gathered there. And there was a somewhat festive atmosphere going on, because it was a kind of a silly thing to be doing, having a group shampoo party in our bathing suits.

Josie was working on Ulysses and he was yelling and clowning around about how cold the water was.

"I'ms freesing!" he said, in his broken English. "Freesing col'!"

We were all laughing. And Josie had her hands full because he kept pulling away, but with a head full of frothy lather. It was getting everywhere.

Meanwhile, Sahalia, who I will remind you is thirteen, straddles the other bin, facing down the aisle away from us.

I'm standing with Niko and Jake and Brayden, all of us with towels over our shoulders, waiting our turn.

And Sahalia grabs a bottle of water and bends over the bin.

Now her behind is facing us, and they are *short* shorts she is wearing. So we can see . . . too much. We can see skin under the leg of her shorts. The creamy skin of her inner, inner thigh.

It was like a *Sports Illustrated* bikini-issue spread.

I looked away, as was only right.

But Jake and Brayden, not so much.

"Jesus, Sahalia," Josie quipped. "You're wasting water."

It was true. Sahalia had dumped more than half the gallon over her head while we had all stared, transfixed by her outrageous stance.

But it got worse (or better, depending on your POV).

She stood up and turned to face us.

And her T-shirt was all wet.

Now we could see her breasts outright, through the material of her shirt.

We could see the nipples. Everything about them, we could see.

It was hot. It was crazy.

I don't think she knew what she was doing. She was just a kid.

"Ha-ha," Max sang. "I can see your boobies, Sahalia."

Josie rushed over with a towel.

"Sahalia, your shirt is totally see-through," Josie clucked. Josie darted a glance at us and saw what we all were now trying to hide—that we had noticed what Sahalia wanted us to notice.

As Josie busied herself wrapping Sahalia in a towel I saw Sahalia look at Jake and at Brayden. A little smile played on her lips.

It was possible that Sahalia hadn't realized she was pretty much sticking her butt in our faces. And maybe she hadn't known just how sheer that shirt would get.

But it seemed to me she wanted us to see her body.

She wanted to be wanted.

When my turn came, I was glad to have the cold water poured over my hair. I very much needed to clear my head.

When it came time to wash Brayden's hair. I saw Josie be extra-loving, extra-sweet.

I watched her tenderly massage his thick, brown hair; saw

DAY 8

her dab away of any soap that threatened to run into his eyes; heard her murmur, "That okay?" and "How's that feel?"

Brayden had his eyes closed.

All her little kindnesses went unnoticed by him.

He was busy thinking his way up Sahalia's shorts.

CHAPTER TWENTY

WE GET HIGH

WHEN MY ALARM CLOCK RANG AT SEVEN, SOMEHOW I FELT
twice as bad as I had the day before. A glimpse in the pink
princess mirror Caroline had hung in the hall told me I had
two spectacular black eyes.

I brought the mirror really, really close to my face, so I could
see if my pupils were overly dilated. Maybe I had a concussion.

Max came bopping over. It was his turn to help in the kitchen.

"Dude," he said. "You look like a monster!"

I considered roaring or acting like a monster in some way,
but my head hurt too much.

On our way to the kitchen, I popped four Advils.

I fell asleep during breakfast. What can I say?

It sort of ran without me, with Max dishing out bowls of
cornflakes and boxed milk.

I had my head on the counter when Alex nudged me awake.

I saw that breakfast was over and everyone had left.

DAY 9

"What really happened?" he said. "You didn't fall off a shelf."

"Who cares?" I said and tried to go back to sleep.

"I care!" he said. "Tell me what happened."

"Go play with Niko," I said.

"What do you mean?"

"You're always off with him. Fixing everything. Running everything."

"Dean, what happened to your face?"

"Jake hit me, okay?"

"Why? What did you do?" he asked.

I just stared at him and he stared back. He had this look of exasperation on his face. Irritation and disappointment.

"What did you do?" he repeated.

It hurt my feelings so much, that he would assume I had done something stupid. That I was the screw-up.

Never mind that I had actually done something stupid.

I wanted him to take my side first and ask questions later.

Tears came to my eyes.

"Get out of here," I said.

"Dean—"

"Leave me alone!" I hollered. I turned my back and went into the pantry.

After a while, he left.

It was maybe an hour later. I had finished cleaning up breakfast and was just lying on the counter for a wee little nap, when Jake came by.

"Hey, books," he said. "How you feeling?"

"I feel like hell," I said.

"Yeah, I thought you might."

He slipped a couple foil packs out of his pocket.

"Let's get high," he said.

"Yes," I answered.

One of the EZ-melt pain pills from the day before and one triangular orange mystery pill later, I was flying.

I felt relaxed but energized. Loose and happy.

We decided to eat cookies.

We decided to eat one of every type of cookie in the very abundant cookie aisle.

"Friggin' Chips Ahoy," I said. "Classic."

"Soft or hard?" Jake said.

"They're not called soft, they're called chewy," I corrected him.

"Chewy!" He laughed. "You kill me."

He grabbed some bags off the shelf.

"Here's where we're going to get into trouble. Mint Milanos. Orange Milanos. Plain Milanos. Double dark chocolate Milanos. Why do they need so many Milanos?"

"Yeah," I agreed. "There's like a Milano for every human being in the world."

"Shoot," Jake drawled. "There probably is now. There's only twenty or so of us left!"

And we howled.

"Oh my God, I feel GREAT!" I said.

"I know. It's crazy," Jake said.

"Is this what you were taking the day of the elections?"

"Totally."

"Wow. You so blew it."

"I know."

This struck us as hilarious.

"What are you guys doing?" asked Max, coming down the aisle.

I turned and ROARED at him.

Like a monster.

DAY 9

He screamed and ran away.

Me and Jake thought this was the funniest thing ever.

"Hey, you want to know something screwed up?"

"Sure," I said.

"You know how they said the effects of the compounds on my blood type were, like, reproductive failure?"

"Yeah."

"I can't get it up," Jake said. "That's what they meant. I can't get it up for anyone anymore."

"Jeez!" I said. "For you? That's like a tragedy."

We started to laugh and laugh and laugh.

"Oh my God, I gotta piss," Jake said. "Come on. Let's go to the Dump."

As we passed the Sports Department, we heard Sahalia laughing.

"What do we have here?" Jake said.

We found Sahalia and Brayden playing air hockey.

Sahalia was wearing what I can best describe as a costume. A sexy carpenter costume. Maybe a sexy farmer.

She had on a giant pair of men's overalls, cut off at the knee. Under them she was wearing very little. A lace bra and matching lace panties. You could see the bra through them because the sides of overalls are totally open. You could also see the lace cutting over her hip. You could almost see where it connected with the thong part in the back but, hey, I wasn't staring . . . too much . . . I don't think.

"Hey, fellas!" said Brayden. "Want in on the game?"

"Aren't you two supposed to be working?" Jake joked.

"I'm in charge of restocking the Automotive section," Sahalia said sarcastically as she lined up a shot. "But I thought I'd take a break for an hour or three . . ."

"Friggin' Niko with his schedule," Brayden said. "He thinks he can tell everyone what to do at every moment of the day."

"What can we do, Bray, he was the people's choice," Jake said.

I was starting to feel woozy.

"What's with Geraldine?" Brayden asked.

"I'm good," I said.

"He's high," Jake said.

Sahalia and Brayden laughed.

"Some face you got on you, Dean," Brayden commented.

"You look like you got hit by a truck," Sahalia said.

"Nope, he got hit by me," Jake said, smiling at her. He flexed his biceps. "Feel that? Them's the guns what wrought such wreckage!"

Sahalia felt Jake's arm. She oohed and aahed.

"Jake's got size, but I've got definition," Brayden said, pushing Jake back and stepping up to Sahalia.

He made a muscle and she felt it. She pressed her body up against his and slid her hands up and down his bicep.

"Nice," she murmured.

"Excuse me," came Josie's voice. "What is going on here?"

Brayden stepped back from Sahalia.

"Nothing," he said.

"And what are you wearing, Sahalia?"

"Clothes, Josie," she answered.

Josie's face flushed and she grabbed Sahalia's arm and spun her around.

"Enough!" Josie said. "We get it, okay? You're sexy and you want to have sex with these guys. We get it. But, honey, it's not going to happen because you are thirteen. Thir. Teen. Do you understand what I'm saying?"

"I'm fourteen in less than an month," Sahalia answered.

DAY 9

"Go and put some clothes on," Josie commanded her, pushing her out of the aisle.

"Hey, guys——" Brayden said.

"People dress like this, you know," Sahalia said. "It's a style."

"Yeah, *prostitutes* dress like that!" Josie retorted.

This sort of reminded me of the discussion a controlling father might have with his teenage daughter. Except the teenage daughter was thirteen and the father was being played by a high school sophomore.

"You're not the boss of me!" Sahalia shouted.

"Oh yeah?" Josie countered. "I'm in charge of the little kids and you are one of them."

"I know more about sex than you do, you stuck-up bitch!"

Instead of yelling, Josie got up real close in Sahalia's face.

"You are a child!" she said.

Niko came jogging over. He was dirty and sweating.

"What happened?" he asked. "I heard shouting."

"Sahalia is throwing herself at the older boys," Josie said. "And the way they're responding, I don't know what could happen."

"Josie, we weren't doing anything," Brayden protested.

Josie turned on me. Me!

"And he's high! Dean, you of all people! You are the one we count on to be dependable."

"Okay, let's settle down," Jake slurred.

"She is thirteen," Josie said, turning to Niko. I could see the tears in her eyes. They were about to spill. "A thirteen-year-old child."

"I don't like it when people talk about me like I'm not here," Sahalia said. "I'm as grown-up as any of you. Jake and Bray know it. You're just mad because they like me more than you."

Sahalia threw her arms around Brayden's neck.

He got red in the face, then he ducked out of her embrace.

"Sahalia," he said. "You're a kid. We hang out with you, but we'd never, like, do anything with you. I'm sorry."

Her face crumpled.

For a moment, she really did look like the kid that she was. She turned and ran down the aisle.

"You're a jerk, Brayden," Josie said. "I thought maybe you could change . . ."

Josie stormed off in the opposite direction.

Brayden held his hands up.

"Jesus! I do the right thing and everyone is pissed at me!"

Niko glanced at the three of us and then turned and walked after Josie.

Brayden turned to Jake and me.

"I need some of whatever you're on."

I left them after Brayden took the pills. I didn't want any more. I didn't really want anything more to do with them, to tell the truth.

And I had to lie down. ASAP.

I needed a favor and I didn't have anyone else I could ask.

He was working at a desk near the kids. He had three or four different electronic devices spilled out on the desk and was grafting parts of them together.

"Alex," I said. "Can you please do lunch for me?"

He looked up at me, cool and hurt.

"I guess."

"And maybe dinner?"

"I don't know," he said, looking up at me. "Niko needs my help. Actual, real help. To run this place."

I shrugged.

DAY 9

"I just need a favor, Alex," I sighed. "I'm sorry."

And I was.

I went to my berth and climbed in my hammock and slept and slept and slept.

Through lunch. Through dinner.

In the middle of the night, I thought I was dreaming that Astrid was in my room.

I was dreaming that Astrid was in my little berth, standing at my side, looking down at me.

Then I got a whiff of her and I jerked awake for real.

Astrid *was* in my berth. And she smelled rank.

She looked beautiful in the iridescent glow of my crappy alarm clock. But she really did reek.

Stupidly, my first thought was that I was glad Jake had helped me take out the last cotton wads from my nose before I crashed.

There's vanity for you.

She grabbed my hair and wrenched my head up so I was looking in her face.

"Don't you ever spy on me again!" she spat at me.

"I'm sorry," I said.

"A-hole."

She let go of my hair and turned to go. The space was so small that her body was basically wedged against mine.

"And no more pain pills. They'll ruin you. They'll make you into an idiot."

"Astrid, please," I said.

"What?"

"I am really, really sorry."

I sat up, awkwardly, swinging one leg over the side on my hammock. My leg brushed her thigh and she didn't pull away.

"I was going to get my journal and I saw you two and . . . It was wrong. It was so wrong. Especially because . . ."

"Because what?" she said.

My mouth was dry. My heart was pounding.

"Because I . . . I care about you." I said, then I backtracked some. "I want you to feel better. I want you to come back and be with us."

In the glow from my clock, I couldn't see her that well. But I thought I caught a glimpse of a streak of tears on her face.

"Save it," she said. "Spying on me. Getting high. Scaring Max. It's not okay."

I felt so low. Like a worm.

"I need you to stay one of the good guys," she said softly.

And then she left.

DAY 9

CHAPTER TWENTY-ONE

THE HATCH

AT SEVEN A.M., I DIDN'T WAKE UP CHLOE. SHE WAS SUPPOSED to be my helper for the day. I bumped her and instead I woke up Max.

"Max," I whispered into the nest where he lay curled up with Ulysses and Batiste. The little kids didn't have hammocks. They slept on crib mattresses set side to side.

The three boys looked both feral and adorable, like wolf puppies in a den. Their hair was messed up, and the sheets and blankets were all twisted up. They looked like the wild boys from *Peter Pan*.

"Max," I said, shaking him gently.

"Yeah?"

"Will you be my helper today?"

"Again?"

"Yeah," I said. "I owe you."

"Two days in a row, you mean?"

"Yeah."

"Heck, yeah, I will!" he said as he lurched, still half asleep, to his feet.

As we walked to the Kitchen, he pulled on a fleece jacket. It seemed to be getting colder day by day. Maybe that's what happened when the sun's rays are blocked out by a giant metallic cloud.

"So, what's for breakfast?" I asked him.

"Sundaes."

"Like ice cream sundaes?" I asked.

"Exactly."

"Max, I don't think that's a good idea. We need food, real food, to start the day."

"Yeah," he said. "But still. You do owe me, like you said."

"Well, Max . . ."

"You were awful mean to me yesterday and you did make me cry . . ."

I should have said no. But I shrugged. "Okay."

Why not? We could serve nuts to put on top, or something . . .

We loaded the shopping cart with sundae accoutrements.

"You know who has the best sundaes? The Village Inn," Max said.

"Really?" I murmured. My head was aching again. The bruises, from what I'd seen, were even more brutal than the day before. There was some blood in my left eye.

To tell the truth, I thought I looked kind of tough.

But my head—I needed coffee and Advil.

"Once we was eating at the Village Inn and my mom went off to the bathroom," Max said as he tossed a bottle of strawberry syrup into the cart. "My mom took forever and then my dad went off to see what was taking her so long and they did

DAY 10

not come back for the longest time. And I sat there and waited and waited and waited and the waitress asked me if we wanted dessert and I said sure. So then she brought me a banana split, like I had asked for, and I ate it. And I was going to share it with my mom and dad but they took so terrible long I decided to eat the whole thing up and then I didn't feel so hot and I went to the bathroom to look for my dad and he wasn't even there so I just went back to the booth and then the waitress woke me up and she made me tell her my phone number and she called my mom and it turned out they had just plumb forgot me there and they had gone on home without me."

"Jeez, Max," I said. "That's terrible."

"That ever happen to you?" he asked me.

"Not really," I said.

"Yeah," Max said. "It's 'cause your folks probly don't drink like my folks do."

"No, not so much," I agreed.

"But you know what the upside was," Max said. "They forgot to charge us for the banana split!"

I had to hand it to him. That kid could really tell a story.

So we laid out the sundae bar. It was pretty impressive. We had nine flavors of ice cream, from vanilla to Chocolate Moose Tracks. Hot fudge, caramel, butterscotch, pineapple, strawberry. Every type of topping: crushed Oreos, gummy bears, gummy worms, all the nuts, chocolate chips, butterscotch morsels, white chocolate chips.

"They're gonna flip!" Max said.

"I agree. Hey, Max—"

"They're not going to believe it!"

"I know," I said. "Max, about yesterday. I'm sorry that I yelled at you. That wasn't a nice thing to do."

"Pshaw, yesterday's over. I never think about yesterday. If I did, I'd be dead meat."

He took a maraschino cherry out of the open jar and popped it in his mouth.

It seemed to me a pretty good life philosophy, actually.

Especially with the state of the world ruined as it was.

"Can you tie the stem in a knot?" he asked me. "There was this stripper named Bingo I met at Emerald's. She could tie a cherry stem in a knot around the handle of a plastic sword! All with her tongue!"

I shook my head no.

"But she had these buck teeth so maybe that was her secret weapon."

The ice cream was getting soft. I looked at the clock.

"When are they coming? Can I go get them?" Max asked.

It was eight thirty.

Where were they?

Suddenly I realized that the store was completely quiet.

We could hear no distant voices.

No early-morning quarrels among the little ones.

No husky laughing from Jake or Brayden.

No movement.

I started to run.

"What is it? Where are they?" Max yelled as he followed me.

The Train was completely empty.

I spun around.

Max ran up to me.

"Where is everybody?" he cried.

"Shhhhh!" I said.

And I heard, faintly, sounds coming from the storage room.

"They're in the back," I told Max. "Come on."

* * *

DAY 10

Just as we reached the doors, Alex came out.

"Dean," he said. "I was coming for you. There's people at the door!"

I pushed my way through the little kids to the front of the group, near the intercom.

The screen was a dull gray, with two shapes standing a bit off.

Niko: "They could be dangerous!"

Josie: "They need our help!"

Jake: "We can *not* trust them!"

Brayden: "But they know Mrs. Wooly!"

It was the last one that caught my attention.

"What?" I yelled. "They know Mrs. Wooly?"

"We're going to vote," Niko declared.

"WAIT!" I shouted. "Somebody tell me what's going on!"

"We were taking the trash to the Dump when Henry heard a voice," Josie told me. "I came back here and a man was asking us to let him in. Craig Appleton is his name."

"And he has a friend," Niko interrupted. "There's two of them."

"The friend knew Mrs. Wooly," Brayden added. "He's the maintenance guy from the grammar school."

"Yeah," said Chloe. "He fixed the buses and snowblower and stuff."

"How did they get through the guy?" I asked Niko. He looked at me blankly. "The *guy* guarding the store."

Now the little kids started asking what guy guarding the store and Niko shrugged.

"I didn't ask."

"Well, shoot," Jake said. "Let's ask them now."

So Niko stepped up to the intercom.

"Excuse me, sir, we have a question for you."

One of the shapes stepped up to the intercom. His face was wrapped in layers of some kind of plaid material. Maybe a wool throw rug?

"Yes, Niko, what's the question?"

"Well . . . There was a man. Who was deranged from the compounds. As we understood it, he had sort of decided the store was his and he wasn't letting anyone get—"

"Yes," said Craig Appleton. "We had to shoot him."

Niko told Josie to take the little kids, including Sahalia and Alex, back to the Living Room. Josie refused.

"I'm not going to be left out of this decision," she argued.

"Me either," said Sahalia.

Niko took a deep breath.

"I tell you what, Sahalia," Niko said. "If you take the kids to the Living Room and play with them, I will stop considering you a little kid. You'll have full big-kid status and all the privileges of a big kid."

"Oh, now I'm a big kid? You guys treat me like dirt but when you need something—"

"Sahalia!" Niko shouted. "I. Need. Your. Help!"

"Fine," she spat. "But I want my vote counted."

"And what's your vote?" Niko asked.

"Let them in. Maybe they can tell us what the hell's going on out there. Come on, guys," she said, rounding up the little kids.

"Let them in! Let them in!" shouted Chloe through the ruckus of little kids' voices.

"Hey, Sahalia," I called as she herded the kids off. "We set up a sundae bar . . ."

"For breakfast?" she said, disapproving.

"Mr. Appleton, you'll need to wait for a moment," Niko said into the intercom. "We need to discuss this and take a vote."

189

DAY 10

The man's muffled face came close to the monitor.

"We understand that you need time to decide," he said. "There's a lot of very scary people out here. But you can trust Robbie and me. That's why Mrs. Wooly told Robbie about where you were. She and Robbie are good friends.

"But now I am injured and we're out of supplies. Food and water are very scarce out here. If you could just help us stock up, we can give you the only thing we really have to trade."

"What's that?" Niko asked.

"Information," he said.

It was as heated a debate as we'd ever had. Niko and Jake made a good case for *not* letting them in.

Niko was really concerned that they had shot the O monster. They could use their gun (or guns) against us. We could end up their prisoners. They might take over and try to rule the Greenway.

"My job is to keep you safe," Niko said, his arms crossed. "They have guns and they are adults. They can take care of themselves."

"If they try to take over it'll be a total downer," Jake drawled. His eyes were glassy and strange. "They should just go on their way. We don't want strangers in here, telling us what to do."

Brayden shook Jake's arm.

"Dude, are you insane?" Brayden said. "They can tell us what's going on out there! We need to know! And we got tons of stuff. We trade stuff for information."

"I agree with Brayden. We should be generous and share what we have. We need to know what's going on outside. It's worth the risk," Josie said.

Alex was opposed to adding any variables into what was a stable environment.

What tipped it was the rules Brayden proposed.

And my vote.

Niko turned to all of us.

"I just want it on the record that I am against this. I am only doing it because I've been outvoted. I think it's a bad idea."

"Yeah, yeah," Brayden said. "Do you want to tell them or should I?"

Niko turned, sighing and pressed his finger onto the Talk button.

"We'll let you in," said Niko into the intercom. "On the following conditions. One, you give us your guns for the duration of your stay. Two, you agree to leave tomorrow morning, no matter what. Three, you promise to take no more than we give you, and four, you swear you will abide by our rules."

"Agreed," said Mr. Appleton, without consulting Robbie. "Now how can we help you open up this door?" he asked.

"We can't open it," Niko answered. "We'll throw you a ladder down from the roof."

I was banished from the storeroom, as were Niko and Brayden.

"You, too, Josie," Niko said.

"But we don't even know what type I am!" she protested.

"Exactly," said Niko.

Alex and Jake would be the ones to let the men in.

Jake and Alex got bundled up in layers of clothing as a preventative measure. Niko handed Jake the home security ladder and then Jake and Alex went up the metal staircase and worked on opening the hatch.

After the woman had been attacked, Niko had wanted the hatch to be really easy to open (though still airtight) in case we had another emergency.

DAY 10

I guess he'd made the hatch really darn easy because by the time we got back with baby wipes, two gallons of spring water, and fresh clothes for the two men, we could hear adult voices through the storeroom doors.

They sounded friendly. . . .

Josie, Niko, Brayden, and I waited impatiently outside the storeroom doors.

Eventually Alex came out holding two handguns. He held each by the grip, barrel facing down, held out away from his body. He held them the way you might hold a couple of dead rats. He also had a fanny pack filled with ammo looped around one shoulder.

"Guess what?" he said after he unwound a scarf from his face. "They have a dog! A nice one."

"I'll take the guns," Niko said. He held out a two-gallon Ziploc bag and Alex placed the guns and ammo into it. Niko wrapped it up neatly and headed off toward the Accessories Department. To hide them, I guess.

I gave Alex the clothes and cleaning supplies to take back into the storeroom.

"What are they like?" I asked Alex.

He shrugged.

"They're acting nice," he said. Then he looked at me. "Wouldn't you?"

Sahalia brought the kids over.

"I couldn't keep them away any longer," she said. "They're all hopped up on the idiotic amounts of sugar you set out for them."

They were pretty wired. They were buzzing around and laughing and shouting and pushing each other and bopping up and down.

Then the timbre of Mr. Appleton's voice came through the doors and they stopped talking.

A grown-up's voice. Grown-ups were among us.

Caroline and Henry were holding hands, and I saw Max and Ulysses grab on to each other.

The door swung open but it was just Alex again.

"They're changing their clothes and tidying up," he told us. "And guess what, you guys? They have a surprise!"

"What is it?" "What is it?" "What's the surprise?" "Are they staying forever?" "Are they here to rescue us?" "Is it anyone we know?" came the questions.

Josie motioned for the kids to follow her and she took them just a little ways back from the door.

"The two men are here to trade with us," she said. "We are going to give them food and water and let them spend the night here. In exchange, they are going to tell us how things are going outside."

"But . . . but . . . ," stammered Henry. He started to bawl. "I want to go home! I want my mommy! I'm tired of waiting and waiting!"

Josie hugged him and picked him up.

"I know, Henry," she said. "You and Caroline have been so patient. But maybe these guys can tell us how much longer we will have to wait. Come on, guys," she said to the little kids. "You can each pick out a welcome gift for the outsiders."

Off they went, chatting and chirping like a little flock of birds.

There was manly laughter from behind the doors. Meanwhile, for those of us on the other side, it felt like time had stood still.

"Aaaaaargh," Niko said under his breath. "I hope this wasn't a huge mistake."

DAY 10

"It'll be okay," I said. "Mrs. Wooly wouldn't have told them about us if she didn't trust them."

Niko sighed and ran his hands through his dark, straight hair.

"I will never forgive myself if something happens to one of us," he said. "Never."

"Lighten up, Scouty," Brayden said. "It'll be fine."

Chloe came back with two Snickers bars. Max and Ulysses lugged one big bottle of Gatorade each. Caroline and Henry had picked out some greeting cards. Batiste had two new bibles.

"Well, the Welcome Wagon's ready," Josie said.

And finally the doors swung open.

Mr. Appleton was tall, maybe six feet tall, and dressed now in a pair of khakis, a plaid flannel shirt, and a gray pullover sweater. The kind with patches on the elbows. His eyes had red rims, and his nose also was red around the nostrils. Besides that he looked pale and shaky. He had salt-and-pepper hair that was cut short and stood up pretty much straight. It was dirty— there was only so much you could do with a gallon of water and baby wipes, but it probably looked a lot better than it had before.

He was limping and there was already some new blood seeping through the khakis.

We should have brought medical supplies, I thought to myself.

Robbie was a good foot shorter. He was Latino and had a deeply tanned face with crinkle marks around his eyes. Smile lines. His eyes and nose were also red but he was grinning at us. And he held in his arms an old dog.

It was wet, and though Robbie had an awkward grip on it, the dog seemed patient and resigned to the indignity of being held. The dog was of no particular breed. A grayish-brownish-colored mutt with a scrunched-up face, white around the muzzle. It had one of those smushed-in faces dogs sometimes have, with one bottom tooth that stuck out over its upper lip. Ugly, but definitely lovable.

The kids cheered and oohed and aahed at the dog.

The dog woofed and wagged its stumpy tail politely.

"Everyone," Jake said. "This is Mr. Appleton and this is Robbie."

Robbie held the dog up.

"And this here is Luna," he said cheerfully.

Robbie let the dog down. She came forward to smell our feet. Luna had a length of twine as a leash.

We'd soon fix that. Luna would have every pet luxury a Greenway could provide.

The little kids pressed forward all at once, offering their gifts.

Mr. Appleton duly shook hands and tousled hair and accepted the offerings, then he seemed to sway and Robbie held out his arm to support him.

"Let's get you to the Pharmacy," said Niko.

"Or perhaps you could bring some bandages here," Mr. Appleton said as he slumped to the floor.

DAY 10

CHAPTER TWENTY-TWO

BREAKFAST WITH OUTSIDERS

MY FIRST IMPRESSION WAS THAT MR. APPLETON WAS AN ex-army guy. We had a lot of them in the area. He had that very good posture of the army men, and also the haircut. His haircut was the way army men let their hair grow out. They didn't quite want the buzz—maybe they felt they didn't deserve to wear a buzz anymore, but they didn't want their hair flopping over either.

Mr. Appleton seemed to tolerate the little kids, but I didn't have the sense he liked them one bit.

Robbie, on the other hand, was a family guy, you could see that straightaway. He looked like he was in heaven, surrounded by all the little kids. But it was the way he handled Ulysses that won me over.

After Niko went for medical supplies, the kids gathered around Robbie and Luna on the ground. Robbie was learning the names of the kids and introducing them to Luna. I saw him watching Ulysses, waiting for it to be Ulysses's turn to introduce himself.

And Ulysses said, "*Soy* Ulysses," and Robbie just reached out and grabbed him and hugged him. Spanish words poured out of the two of them and soon Ulysses was crying and Robbie was crying, too, and just holding him in a one-armed hug while the other arm held on to Luna, who decided she should begin washing their two faces with her tongue.

Ulysses, apparently, had had a lot to say this whole time. And only hadn't said much because none of us could understand him.

Why I had chosen to study French in high school I will never understand.

Niko returned with the supplies. He knelt down in front of Mr. Appleton and cut a slit on the cuff of his new chinos. Niko began splitting them up the leg.

There were two wounds on Mr. Appleton's leg. Near the ankle there was a horrible gash. I had never seen anything like it.

"Josie, maybe we should take the kids away?" I suggested feebly.

The wound looked like the guts of a fish, if that makes any sense. A big slash with pieces of flesh hanging out of it—green-and-yellow oozing flesh. It wasn't bleeding, but you could see lines of red running under the skin, going up the leg, following the course of his veins. The lines were red and also a bruised kind of green in places.

The blood was coming from a different wound. This one above the knee. It looked like a bite, kind of. There was a chunk of flesh missing.

"What happened to you?" Chloe demanded.

"Razor wire," Mr. Appleton said.

DAY 10

Niko poured hydrogen peroxide on the ankle wound and it hissed. Out loud.

"Come on, guys," I said, feeling a little woozy. "Let's give Niko some space to work. Everyone come help me in the Kitchen."

There were protests and awws, but the stink coming out of that ankle gash was pretty ripe and eventually me, Josie, Sahalia, and Alex got the little kids rounded up and led them to the kitchen.

They were like a bunch of crickets, hopping and jumping all around, so excited by the arrival of GROWN-UPS and a DOG!

"Batiste," I said, calling him over to me. "We need to fix something special."

"Two breakfasts?" he asked.

"Well, the first one was sundaes, for God's sake."

"Don't-take-the-Lord's-name-in-vain," he said quickly. Then "Yes! We'll make a feast of thanksgiving, but for breakfast."

Batiste ran ahead to the Food aisles. Chloe went with him to help. I guess they were starting to get along, somewhat.

I told Alex and Sahalia to throw away all the sundae stuff.

I got the other little kids busy making banana nut muffins under Josie's supervision while Batiste and I cranked in the Kitchen.

In just under forty-five minutes, Batiste and I prepared roasted vegetable quiches, hash browns, a kind of a fruit salad Batiste told me was called ambrosia, and the last four packages of bacon.

Niko led the men into the Kitchen, just as the coffee finished brewing. Mr. Appleton was now equipped with crutches, which I hadn't known we even had.

"Ay Dios!" Robbie exclaimed. "Look at all of this food!"

"And we made muffins for you!" shouted Max.

"And mine is the biggest!" shouted Chloe.

The little kids were a-boppin' again, all yelling at the same time. And then Luna started barking.

"Shhh, you guys!" Josie said.

But they didn't listen.

"Quiet! QUIET!" Mr. Appleton shouted.

The kids shut up immediately.

The silence was tense.

"I'm sorry," Mr. Appleton said. "It's just . . . we're . . . I'm a little shell-shocked. It was very chaotic. Outside. And I'm not used to so much . . . noise."

"We understand," said Josie. "You've been through a lot."

"Please sit down and I'll get you two some food," I said.

"Are you the chef?" Robbie asked me.

"Ah, yes," said Mr. Appleton. I could see he was straining to be jovial. Trying to recover. "Who can we thank for this food?"

"I'm Dean. I do most of the cooking," I said. "But Batiste here is the one who put this together."

Robbie shook our hands heartily. Then Mr. Appleton shook them as well. His hand was papery but strong.

"Pleased to meet you," Mr. Appleton said to us.

"Yes, sir," Batiste said.

"I'm in charge of the food," I said. "So I guess I will be the one who loads you up with provisions. I'll be sure to give you lots of good stuff for when you leave."

Somehow I felt strongly compelled to remind them that they'd be leaving sooner than later.

Maybe it was because they were eyeing the food like animals.

Everyone ate, but those two men really *ate*.

Halfway through their meal, Robbie stopped eating and said an impromptu prayer in Spanish.

DAY 10

He winked at Ulysses and then explained to all of us, "I was so hungry, I forgot to give thanks to *El Señor* for sending us here to this little paradise of a Greenway, filled with *angelitos*."

"Amen!" Batiste said. "I'm always telling these sinners we should pray before each and every meal."

Robbie chucked Ulysses under the chin. The boy shined like a new minted penny.

"Well, now we said thanks, so I'm gonna eat more!"

There was laughter at this and I gave him thirds.

CHAPTER TWENTY-THREE

MR. APPLETON'S STORY

NIKO AND JOSIE DISCUSSED WHAT TO DO WITH THE LITTLE KIDS while we all met with the grown-ups.

"I don't want to miss out on the meeting," she said firmly.

"I understand that, but I don't think Sahalia will watch them either."

Sahalia was skulking against the wall, eyeing Brayden with venom.

Niko looked over to me.

"No way," I said.

"Well, somebody's got to keep them away!"

"I have an idea," I said.

I walked over to the kids.

"Okay, you guys, I have a problem and I need your help. Me and the big kids and the men need to have a meeting. But Luna really, really needs a bath. Do any of you know how to give a dog a bath?"

Caroline and Henry's hands shot up like arrows.

DAY 10

"Oh, oh, oh!" they chorused.

"I do, too!" yelled Chloe. "My nana has a Bernese mountain dog and I wash him all by myself!"

"Great!" I said. "We have three experts. You guys need to get all the supplies and bring them all here. Then wash the dog. Then dry her. Then comb her hair."

"Then we'll make her a bed and give her some food!" Max shouted.

"Then we'll sing her to sleep!" Caroline added.

Josie watched me, nodding her head.

"Nice one, Dean," she said. "I'm impressed."

"Let's start our meeting now," Niko said to the men.

So Mr. Appleton and Robbie held court in the Living Room. Robbie groaned as he lowered himself down onto one of the futon couches and patted his belly.

"I feel so happy now," he said, smiling at all of us. "I thank God he brought us to this place."

Mr. Appleton chose a straight-backed desk chair. He put his bad foot up on an end table. I tried to ignore the smell.

"What would you like to know?" he asked us.

"Maybe you could just start at the beginning and go from there," Niko said. "We've been here since the hailstorm, so any information you can give us about what has happened outside would be good."

"Fine."

He took a moment and began: "The hailstorm caused a significant disruption for everyone, as you can imagine. There was panic when the Network went down, as no one could reach 911. However, it was the news of the disaster on the East Coast that created what I would consider to be a chaotic environment. Many people gathered at the VFW to watch the news coverage, such as it was, on an old television set. It was a time of mourning and there was a sense of camaraderie that was admirable.

"I am proud to say there was no rioting or looting at any of the stores in town. At the stores whose riot gates had not deployed, people stood quietly in lines and purchased only necessities. From what I understand, people in Colorado Springs were not as well behaved.

"I set out for the hardware store first thing the next morning. My Land Cruiser was garaged, so it was undamaged by the hail, which is more than I can say for most of the cars in town.

"I was surprised to find the store was closed. There were some employees gathered in front of the store who weren't sure if the store would be opening or not. There was a spirit of confusion and discouragement among the employees and the few customers who had arrived.

"Then the earthquake hit. People fell and were hit with some debris. A part of the roof of the store collapsed and the windows shattered. There were some minor injuries among those of us gathered around the store.

"There was discussion among those of us uninjured about how to best care for those who had been injured. I am fully trained in first aid, so for about an hour, I issued directions and tried to oversee the care of the injured. I went into the store and found a basic first aid kit. I decided we should move the injured away from the store in case further aftershocks brought more of the building down.

"It was at that moment that I detected the change in the color of the air. I saw a black plume rising in the sky toward Colorado Springs.

"In a matter of minutes, the people around me started acting in ways that were beyond my comprehension."

DAY 10

Mr. Appleton stopped to wipe sweat from his forehead. He was staring straight ahead, as if watching a movie of the events he was describing to us.

"I was helping a young employee of the store carry a female employee who had a broken leg. She was quite heavy. African-American descent. I would estimate two-hundred to two-hundred-fifty pounds.

"As we carried her across the parking lot, the air turned around us. Everything became quite green. The woman's skin erupted in blisters. They started small, but as we continued to carry her they grew and burst. She began to scream and writhe. We were forced to set her down, not only because she was moving but because her blood was spurting from the many lesions and she became too slick. Just as I realized that she was dead the young man I had been assisting gave a furious cry and attacked me."

Mr. Appleton was now rocking slightly front and back as he spoke. This small movement was a metronome and the story kept coming out of him at a steady, even pace.

"I fought the young man off for a moment, but he might have injured me seriously if he had not been attacked in turn by another person. It was an elderly man who had earlier told me he was there for chicken wire. I watched as the old man and the young man fought each other to the death. The young man was the winner."

Suddenly Mr. Appleton seemed to come back to the present moment.

"Are you sure you want the younger ones hearing this?" he asked Niko, pointing toward Sahalia and Alex.

Sahalia huffed.

"It's okay," Niko said. "They're big kids. They have all the rights and privileges of us high school kids."

Mr. Appleton continued.

"The light got more and more dim and soon it was as if night had fallen. The sounds around me were horrific. I heard screams of rage intermixed with the screams of the murdered and the gurgling sounds of what I assumed to be people choking on their own blood.

"I pulled my sweater over my face and began to walk to my car. I got in my car and took care not to turn on the lights. I turned on the radio and heard the emergency broadcast that explained what was happening around me. I attempted to drive back to my home. The highways had become glutted with cars and none were moving. Around me, in the cars, I could see some people blistering up and dying. In other cars I saw people begin to attack each other. And in a few cases I locked eyes with other people who seemed to be just as sane and frightened as I felt.

"I was sure that if I tried to walk home on foot I would be attacked, so I drove my car over the median and made my way over the land. This was made difficult because of the hail, but my Land Cruiser has four-wheel drive.

"However, as I neared my home, I could see that the development was on fire. All of Woodmoor was ablaze. The fire had spread quickly from house to house. Among the burning homes, I could see many people running and screaming. I decided not to try to get to my house, but instead to go try to take shelter in one of my schools."

"What do you mean, one of your schools?" Niko asked.

We all looked at Mr. Appleton.

"Well," Mr. Appleton said, "I'm the chancellor of schools for El Paso County."

Sahalia groaned out loud, which was so startlingly funny that I burst out laughing.

DAY 10

Everyone laughed, even Mr. Appleton.

"Sorry," he said. "But it's true."

Mr. Appleton went on, in his measured, efficient way, to tell us that he'd met up with Robbie at Lewis Palmer. Robbie had told him that Mrs. Wooly had come to see about getting a bus to get a bunch of kids home who were currently stranded in the Greenway (that was us).

"Yeah, I was at the school during the hailstorm," Robbie told us. "It was me and some teachers. They left, after the storm, but I stayed. That's when Mrs. Wooly showed up. She told us you were safe here."

"Is she okay?" Niko asked. "Where is she?"

"I'm not sure."

"What do you mean?" Josie asked. Robbie looked flustered.

"We were trying to calm people down because some parents were coming, looking for their kids."

"What parents?" Alex interrupted. "Did Mrs. Wooly tell them we're here? Do you know the names of the parents?"

"Well, no. Not really. Because, well . . ."

"There were a group of us there," Mr. Appleton took over. "We gathered together, sharing the resources and information. We were trying to create a secure, uncontaminated area that everyone could bring their families to. But we were attacked."

"By who?" Jake asked.

"By people with O-type blood," Niko said softly.

Mr. Appleton nodded.

"They were all killed."

This landed like a punch to the stomach.

"Mrs. Wooly?" asked Niko.

"I'm not sure," Mr. Appleton answered. "It was very chaotic."

"I think she got free," Robbie said.

"But if she'd gotten free she would have come for us," Alex said.

"So what's it like out there now?" Niko interrupted.

All of us fell silent to listen.

Mr. Appleton took a drink off his water bottle. He looked greenish and not at all well.

"It's dangerous," Mr. Appleton said. "Most people are staying inside. Those who have no water are out, trying to find it. The O-affected are out and raving mad. They lie in wait and attack foragers."

"There's some cadets, from the Academy, that have made, like, a gang," Robbie added. "They have been attacking people's houses, if they think people are inside with food and water."

"All in all," Mr. Appleton said, "You are the luckiest children in Monument, Colorado. Very lucky to be holed up here with enough food and water to last you for . . . months?"

"Years," Alex said. "We've been looking at the inventory. I think we could stay here for up to twenty to twenty-four months, given the supplies we have. Fresh oxygen and power are bigger issues than food and water, for us."

Mr. Appleton rubbed his hand over his forehead. He was sweating.

"Niko," he said. "Can you show me to the latrines? I think I ate too quickly."

Niko stood and offered Mr. Appleton his arm.

He led him toward the Dump.

"You guys, get some beds set up," Niko directed.

"Yes, sir, Niko, sir," Brayden snapped.

Robbie smiled at Brayden.

"He's pretty serious, huh?" Robbie asked quietly.

"He's our very own dictator," Brayden answered.

DAY 10

"That's not fair," Josie protested.

"Come on," I said to Alex. "Let's set up the beds."

Alex and I made a space in a back part of the Automotive aisle with air mattresses, sheets, blankets, and a little battery-powered floor lamp and flashlights to help them get around in the darkened store.

Niko and Brayden came over with the men a couple of minutes after we'd finished.

Mr. Appleton looked a little better. He had some antibiotic foil packs in his hand.

"Thank you," Mr. Appleton said. "I'll sleep for a few hours now, I think. And you have my word, tomorrow morning, we leave."

"Yes," Niko said. "That's our deal."

Robbie helped Mr. Appleton to lower down onto the wobbly air mattress.

"I have to hand it to you kids," Mr. Appleton said, looking up at us. "The way you have arranged things here is smart. Ingenious, actually."

Hmmm. How did this make us feel? It was dark and the only light came from the one table lamp, so I couldn't see the other kids' reactions but I thought I saw Niko cross his arms.

He really didn't like these men.

I felt Alex, who was standing next to me, straighten up somewhat. I could tell he was pleased by the compliment.

And Alex deserved praise. He *had* worked really hard to help our little colony thrive.

Brayden, I'm sure, was rolling his eyes.

I felt a profound uneasiness.

The compliments seemed like the type of compliments that

come when you're doing something and then a grown-up comes and takes it over from you.

Robbie turned to follow us away.

"Aren't you going to rest?" Mr. Appleton asked.

"Me? Naw. I want to get a look at that bus," Robbie answered.

DAY 10

CHAPTER TWENTY-FOUR

BUSES HAVE TYPES, TOO

AS WE NEARED THE KITCHEN, AND THE BUS, THE KIDS SWARMED out to greet us with a happy, fluffy Luna.

She was white under all that grime!

Robbie laughed. He had such a broad, good-natured laugh.

"I had no idea you were white, *mi angelito*!" Robbie said, bending down to gather her in his arms.

All the little kids talked at once, regaling him with the adventures of giving Luna a bath.

I looked at the kitchen. A kiddie-pool full of filthy water stood in the center of the dining area of the Pizza Shack. Water was everywhere, along with towels, empty shampoo bottles. It was a mess. Whatever—it had been an activity that bought us enough time to hear the outsiders' story.

Josie came and stood next to me.

"I'll help clean it up," she offered.

"Good," I said.

* * *

Robbie went over to the bus, so all the kids, big and little, followed him. He walked around it with an appraising eye, Luna still in his arms. Then he let her down and got on his back and slid under the front of it.

"*Oye*, can somebody bring me a flashlight?"

Many pairs of little feet went pattering off to fulfill his request.

Apparently there are several types of school buses—the one that had delivered us all safely into the Greenway was a type D.

Now, the high school bus had been a type C, that's the kind that has an engine up front. The front of it has a hood and an engine. You can open the hood and fix the engine the way you would any car.

But a type D bus has a flat face.

The engine is under the body of the bus. And that's why Mrs. Wooly's bus weathered the storm so well. And that's why it could still run—the hail hadn't damaged the engine one bit.

The tires were another story.

There were six tires total on the bus. Two up front and four in the back—two on each rear axle.

One of the front tires was flat.

"This one is no problem," Robbie said, showing Niko. "We patch it with a kit. They have them in Automotive. Then we reinflate."

Then he walked around and shone the flashlight under the bus, at one of the back sets of tires.

"But the inside one, here, see it's melted? That's not good."

The inside tire was collapsed and had a gaping, melted hole.

"Can the bus run on just the outside tire?" Alex asked.

"Maybe for a short distance," Robbie answered.

"Well, thanks for taking a look at it," Niko said.

DAY 10

"I'll try to patch it," Robbie said. "I'll try this crazy thing I saw on TV—they filled a tire with tennis balls and then used fiberlace."

"Cool!" Brayden said.

"We should fix the bus up," Robbie said. "Change the oil, tune up the engine. You could have it running in case of an emergency."

"That's a really good idea," Alex said.

"It would probably take more than one day, though," Niko said. "Thanks anyway."

"The kids could help me."

"Niko, we should totally do it," Brayden urged. "In case of emergency."

"Of course you can work on it," Niko snapped. "I just doubt you'll be able to fix it in one day. And these guys leave tomorrow. That's all."

"Aw," complained Chloe. "I don't want him to leave. Not ever."

"Me either!" said Max. The other kids agreed.

Niko walked away.

I looked at Robbie, smiling and rustling the hair of the little kids who were gathered around him.

It didn't seem to me like it would be the worst thing in the world if Robbie stayed more than one day, either.

He grabbed Chloe and Max and lifted them off the floor. They squealed, delighted.

Robbie appointed Chloe the note taker. She kept a log of the repairs needed as Robbie inspected the bus: Pound out dents in roof; replace broken windshield; replace windows; repair seats; tune engine; fix tires.

Henry suggested they paint racing stripes on the bus and Robbie told Chloe to put it on the list.

Robbie had a good sense of kids and how to manage them

in a crowd. He sent Brayden and Alex off to get some supplies from Automotive and then he told the little kids that the first thing to do was to clear a working space around the bus. The kids set to work pushing the carts away and cleaning up any pieces of glass or debris that had been missed before.

"I'm good with engines. I have experience. Wanna know why, Mr. Robbie?" Max said in his cheerful way. "Because my dad sometimes works at a chop shop."

"What's a chop shop?" Chloe demanded.

"It's a secret club where you go to take cars apart. It's really fun."

"What's so fun about that?"

"Because it's a secret and you can't tell nobody! Especially not the police, because they're never allowed in the club. They're always so jealous. The cops would give anything to get in a chop shop."

Robbie caught my eye and he grinned. I had to grin back.

"And sometimes the cars are really fancy, too," Max continued. "BMW, Lexus, Subarus . . ."

"Wow," Batiste said.

"Our mom drives a Subaru!" Caroline said, her sweet little voice excited and proud.

"It's a Forester!" Henry added.

"Cool," Max said.

They were pretty cute, our kids. I could see why Robbie liked to hug them. They were definitely huggable. At times.

I decided I'd better get working on lunch.

As I turned and headed into the Kitchen I saw that Sahalia was sitting on top of the low dividing wall between the Pizza Shack and the cart corral where the bus was sitting.

She was biting her cuticles with determination. She looked really left out and downhearted. I felt bad for her, but not that

DAY 10

bad, since she'd been such a pain in the ass to us all in the last couple of days.

I saw Robbie notice Sahalia and walk over.

"We need everyone to help if we're going to get this bus in shape," he said softly.

"It looks like you have enough helpers to me," she said.

"Yeah, but they're little," Robbie said. "I need people who can actually help." He smiled at her and patted her on the knee. "Grown-ups."

Was Sahalia a grown-up? Not really.

But he knew exactly what to say.

Sahalia smiled. She gathered her hair up and twisted it in a knot.

"Okay," she said. "Show me what to do."

"That's my girl," he said, giving her knee a squeeze.

CHAPTER TWENTY-FIVE

HANDS

I LET MAX HELP FIX THE BUS INSTEAD OF MAKING HIM COME do KP with me.

They were having a great time.

While Robbie, Brayden, and Sahalia worked on the tires and then on the engine, the little kids washed the bus with baby wipes, which was absurd but very cute.

Robbie gave Alex the task of figuring out how to replace the windshield and broken windows. Alex set off into the store to forage for Plexiglas. This was exactly his kind of challenge.

I made tuna sandwiches for lunch, with some peas and carrots on the side. I figured Robbie and Mr. Appleton could use the protein from the tuna and fresh (frozen) vegetables are something grown-ups seem to enjoy.

Mr. Appleton was still sleeping, so he didn't come to lunch, which, truth be told, probably made lunch all the more fun. That guy was a grump.

And Niko had come, taken a plate of food and left, so we

also didn't have him there to be worrying in our faces and bringing us down.

Robbie had all the little kids play a guessing game called I'm Thinking of an Animal.

"I'm thinking of an animal," said Chloe. "It's black and white and wears a tuxedo!"

"A penguin!" Max shouted. "Now, I'm thinking of an animal. It's brown and lives in the woods."

"A bear?" asked Caroline.

"A squirrel?" guessed Batiste.

"It roars and eats people!" Max added.

"A bear!" Caroline insisted.

"No, a lion!" Max announced.

"They don't live in the woods!" Batiste said.

"Yes, they do!"

"They're not brown," Chloe objected. "They're yellow."

"I'm think of animal," Ulysses offered, interrupting the spat. He was more confident now, with Robbie around. "I'm think of animal—it's a dog!" he said.

We all laughed.

Everyone was in their finest form.

Josie came and sat with me and Alex.

"What do you guys think about the outsiders?" she asked us quickly.

"I really like Robbie," Alex said eagerly. "He knows so much about engines. I'm going to show him my video walkie-talkies later."

Josie turned to me.

"Dean?"

"I don't know," I said. "I like Robbie. I mean, everyone likes Robbie. But Mr. Appleton is pretty heavy."

Josie nodded, chewing her sandwich.

"You know what troubles me? That Niko doesn't like them."

I was glad, for Niko's sake, that Josie had even noticed his feelings at all. She seemed pretty oblivious to him, most of the time.

"I worry what the effect on the kids would be, if we all want them to stay and Niko still wants them to go . . ."

I had been wondering the same thing.

"God," Josie said with a yawn. "Is it really just lunch time? This day already feels a million years long."

"It's because so much has happened," Alex said through a mouthful of tuna. "Our whole universe has changed in just a few hours."

Alex was right. As usual.

Everyone worked on the bus in the afternoon except Jake (high), Niko (pissy), Mr. Appleton (sleeping), and Astrid (AWOL).

Robbie, Brayden, and Sahalia got the engine purring nicely.

Robbie and Sahalia got along really well. It turned out that if you treated her like an adult, she acted like one.

Josie helped Alex with the windows. For the front windshield they used Plexiglas that Alex had taken out of the Media Department display cases. The side windows they decided to just cover with wooden shelves from the Home Improvement section. Robbie helped them screw them into place.

The little kids were given the delightful task of putting epoxy glue into every dent, chip, nook, or cranny that looked like it might let air into the bus.

Josie and Alex used the same epoxy to seal around the windows.

"Looking good," I heard Robbie say, inspecting their work at the end of the day. "Looking very good."

He boarded the bus and walked down the aisle.

DAY 10

I couldn't resist, I put down my spatula and went over to see how they'd done.

"Look, Dean," Alex said, showing me the interior.

The inside of the bus was dark, now. Most of the side windows had been replaced by wood.

It smelled kind of dank in there.

All in all, I did not like being on a bus again.

"We have a little more work to do," Robbie said.

He pointed up.

We could see slivers and shards of light coming in through the dented roof.

"I guess you guys can do it tomorrow," Robbie said. "After we're gone . . ."

"No," Alex said. "Niko will let you guys stay longer. I know he will. Now that he sees how helpful you guys are. Don't you think, Dean?"

I shrugged.

"A deal is a deal." Robbie sighed.

The atmosphere at dinner was completely different than it had been at lunch.

Mr. Appleton came over, looking a lot better for his day's sleep.

"Look what we did, Mr. Appleton," Max said, bounding over to him. "We fixed the bus!"

"My goodness," Mr. Appleton said. "What good work."

Robbie walked over to him.

"You're looking better," Robbie said.

Chloe came over and snuggled up to Robbie. Robbie tousled her hair.

I saw a flicker of surprise on Mr. Appleton's face at Chloe's gesture of closeness.

"Thank you, Robbie," Mr. Appleton said. "I must be feeling better, because I feel like I could eat a horse!"

Anticipating this, I had prepared like eight bags of chicken alfredo frozen pasta.

Mr. Appleton clapped Niko on the shoulder. "Niko, I think we hit on the right antibiotics. I am feeling a lot better."

"Good," Niko said. "Then you two will be ready to leave in the morning."

"Of course we will. Perhaps you'll lend me an alarm clock so we can wake up at a reasonable hour. Then we're on our way."

All the friendly chitter chatter of dinner stopped suddenly.

"What?" Chloe said. "Who died? Why'd everyone stop talking?"

"Niko's going to make Robbie and Mr. Appleton leave tomorrow," Sahalia said.

"Nooo!" shouted half the kids, and the others screamed, "You have to let them stay!"

"We have a deal!" Niko shouted, but the ruckus was too loud.

Ulysses was crying in Spanish and Robbie drew him onto his lap. Those fat tears welled up in Ulysses's eyes and he put his head down on Robbie's shoulder.

"We have a deal with these men and they can only stay for one day," Niko repeated.

"Now, kids," Mr. Appleton tried. "Be reasonable now . . ."

"I hate you!" Chloe screamed at Niko. "I wish we had elected Jake president! He wouldn't care if they stayed."

Niko turned to me and Josie.

"How about some backup here?" he asked us.

But it was basically futile to try to talk to the kids when they were so worked up.

DAY 10

"This doesn't make any sense," shouted Alex. "They should stay at least until we're finished fixing the bus and Mr. Appleton is feeling better."

Part of me was happy that Alex was now mad at Niko, his hero.

But truly Alex was right. What would a couple more days do? The men were safe. They could be trusted. Why couldn't they stay a little longer?

"We made a deal," Niko insisted.

"If you make them go, I'm going with them," Brayden shouted.

"Whoa now," Mr. Appleton said, holding his hands up.

"Me, too!" Sahalia announced. "I'd rather take my chances out there than stay here with you losers!"

This caused more screaming and crying from the little kids, who, I think, were less insulted by being called losers than afraid their new "family" was breaking apart.

"Everyone, please quiet down," Mr. Appleton said. "Quiet down!"

The kids tried to rein in their distress, sniffling and hiccuping back their tears.

"Right. Good," Niko said sarcastically. "Listen to him, but not to me."

Mr. Appleton turned to Niko.

"Niko," he said. "I give you my word that we will leave. But the truth is . . . my leg is worse than I thought. Robbie could finish fixing the bus. I could rest . . . If perhaps we could stay one or two more days . . ."

The chorus of whining "pleases" went up from the kids and Niko stormed off.

Josie got up.

"I want you all to settle down," she said to the little kids. "I am going to talk to Niko and see if we can't work something out. Dean?" she said, turning to me.

"Yeah." I rose and followed her.

"I'm coming, too," Alex said.

"No, Alex," I said. "You're too upset. You won't be impartial."

He nodded, looking down at the table. He prided himself on remaining impartial.

"You think he's just insecure about losing his power?" Josie asked me as we looked for Niko.

"I guess. I don't know. He's so disciplined. Maybe he just really wants them to stick to the deal, even though it makes sense for them to stay."

Niko wasn't in the storeroom or in the Living Room.

We passed the towel aisle.

Jake was lying on a hammock, strung between the aisles.

"Hey, Jake, you seen Niko?" I asked.

"Naw," he drawled.

There were shadow circles under Jake's eyes. His sunny blond hair looked gray and dirty. He looked like his own evil twin.

"What's all the ruckus?" he asked us.

"Everyone wants the outsiders to stay, but Niko says they have to go."

"Oh."

That was it?

He didn't have an opinion?

He reached out his foot to the shelf and pushed himself into a gentle sway.

"Don't you think they should stay?" Josie asked him.

"Who cares?" he said. "We're all gonna die anyway."

He looked up at us.

DAY 10

His blue eyes were dark like a stormy nighttime sky.

"Maybe Niko's in the Train," I said, steering Josie away.

We hurried away.

Josie stepped into the Train.

"I'll knock on his door," she said.

A moment later I heard, "Dean, can you come here?"

I opened the door to Niko's berth. Josie was standing there, looking around, totally transfixed.

Niko's berth had a hammock, like mine.

It was the only thing in the berth, besides drawings.

Drawings covered all three walls.

Each drawing or sketch was meticulously stuck into the soft wall with thumbtacks. The drawings were on all different-size pieces of paper. Some eleven by fourteen. Some no bigger than a Post-it. There was a little edge of the fuzzy, orange Greenway dressing-room wall showing between them. The berth looked ordered and neat, and at the same time, it was wonderful and wild. It boggled my mind.

For one thing, who had any secrets left?

We were all with one another all the time.

This guy, the leader of our group, had kept his drawing a secret. How did he do it? I guess I'd seen him sketching on his clipboard at times. I think I just assumed he was making lists or something.

I looked more closely at the drawings. On one whole wall, there were hands, lots of hands. They were rendered in charcoal or felt-tip pen. Some in plain old ballpoint pen.

On the other walls the drawings were varied. There was a drawing of Henry and Caroline, looking at a book. One of me, cooking something. From the grimace on my face, I guess I'd burned it. I looked taller than I remembered myself. There was a drawing of the bus, broken-down and leaning on its two flat tires near the front entrance. There was a beautiful color pastel of Josie. She looked radiant and glowing, her brown skin captured in a spectrum of chocolate and mocha tones.

"Did you see this?" I asked her, pointing.

She nodded yes.

"It's beautiful," I said.

There was a sketch of the ink cloud pouring up into the sky. A drawing of our memorial circle—the one we'd had after Josie woke up. A really crazy-good drawing of Luna, which he had to have made in the last twelve hours . . .

Josie had her back to me, looking at the wall with the hands.

I saw that they were all different hands. Hands from different people. They were labeled at the bottom-right corner in Niko's neat block printing: Dad. Grandpa. Tim. Mrs. Miccio. I saw Chloe's chubby little mitt. And one of Jake's big meat paws.

Josie was looking at one drawing in the center of the wall. Tears were streaming down her face.

I knew whose hands they were before I read the label. The hands were open, as if welcoming, or calling someone into them. The palms seemed soft, drawn with gentle lines and a sort of a rosy effect from the charcoal. The fingers were long and thin and tapered off at the tips. A wedding band and engagement ring were on the ring finger, but you only saw the back of the rings because of how the hands were opened.

They were the hands of Niko's mother.

Sometimes, when you'd least expect it, the grief would chop your legs out from under you.

DAY 10

And that's how it was with me when I saw that drawing there.

"What are you guys doing in here?" Niko said from the doorway.

"Oh, Niko," Josie said, turning to him. "Your drawings are so beautiful."

"And private," he said. He motioned for us to leave.

"I'm sorry," I said. "We were looking for you."

"Please get out of my room!" he said, raising his voice.

We went into the Living Room and he followed.

"Thanks for making me the enemy with the kids, by the way," he said derisively. "I'm trying to keep everyone safe and now everyone hates me. I really appreciate it."

His jaw was tight. I could see this was pretty much Niko at his worst—uptight, being a stickler for the rules, going for sarcasm to try to defend himself.

"We just want to understand your logic here," I said.

"We made a deal. One. Day. That's my logic."

"But, Niko, Robbie is really helpful and the kids love him,"

"I know," Niko said. "But don't you think he might just be trying to win everyone over so we'll let them stay?"

"But Mr. Appleton needs more time to recover," I protested.

"I know! Look," Niko turned to us. "Robbie's just . . ."

"Just what?" Josie asked.

"I don't like him."

"What do you mean?" I asked. "Why?"

"The way . . . I don't know. The way he's all over everyone. It doesn't feel right."

"Come on, Niko," I protested.

"I saw him put his arm around Sahalia. They were going to get motor oil. He had his arm around her. It just wasn't right."

"Niko, she's thirteen," Josie said. "You can't think . . ."

"I don't know what I think!" he exclaimed. "Except that everyone is putting pressure on me to do something that feels wrong."

He looked from my face to Josie's face. Back and forth.

"Don't you feel it?"

"I'm sorry," I said. "I mean, Mr. Appleton is kind of a jerk, but everyone loves Robbie. He's friendly. He's nice. He's helping us to fix the bus. Ulysses *loves* him."

"Can we compromise, Niko?" Josie said and for the first time, I saw warmth toward him from her. "What if we just let them stay for two more days? Long enough for Robbie to finish fixing the bus and for Mr. Appleton to rest."

Niko turned away from her.

"You can't back me up on this?" he asked us.

"Just two days, Niko. I think the little kids really need some grown-up time. And it would also give Brayden and Sahalia some time to get used to the idea that they can't go with them. I can get everyone used to the idea, if I just have some more time . . ."

Niko sighed. He shrugged.

"Okay, Josie. If that's what you want to do. Fine."

Josie told everyone that Robbie and Mr. Appleton could stay two more days.

Robbie and Ulysses hugged.

Mr. Appleton nodded and I think he even smiled.

That was about as positive as I'd seen him.

DAY 10

* * *

Robbie took over Josie's job of storyteller that night.

On the floor of the Living Room, the kids gathered around him like he was a campfire.

He told them fables from Mexico about turtles and rabbits and frogs and crows.

You never saw a happier bunch of kids or a happier man.

I was so glad Niko had changed his mind.

CHAPTER TWENTY-SIX

"EVACULATION"

AFTER BREAKFAST THE NEXT MORNING (CHLOE WAS MY HELPER and she said, "Just do whatever, Dean. I want to hang out with Robbie!"), Josie and Alex gave Robbie a tour of the store. All the little kids went along, shining their flashlights all over the place.

I was getting lunch on the table when Jake wandered into the Kitchen and slung himself down at a booth.

He looked worse than he had the day before, if such a thing was possible.

"You okay?" I asked him.

"Dean. Dude. Is there any coffee?"

"Sure, Jake," I said. "You take cream and sugar, right?"

He nodded and his low-hung head began to bob. He was crying, I realized.

I put my hand on his shoulder as I set the coffee down.

"It's gonna be okay," I said.

DAY 11

"It's not. It's never gonna be okay again."

I just stayed standing where I was. I felt like if I sat down, he'd stop talking.

"I keep taking these pills. But everytime, they're working less. It's like I squeezed all the good feeling out of my brain and now I'm out. I drained it all out and I'm done."

"Jake, you gotta lay off the pills."

"I know. I know," he mumbled. "I'll stop today."

He turned to go, just as Sahalia came over.

She was wearing leggings, a tank top, and some kind of blazer.

"Have you guys seen Robbie?" she asked.

"He's with Josie and Alex and the little kids," I said. "They're touring the store."

"Sweet," she said. "See ya."

Robbie was definitely the big man on campus.

As I was plating the food, Mr. Appleton walked in. He was definitely looking better.

"Mmmmm," he said, eyeing the steaming-hot orange chicken I was dumping into a bowl. "Chinese?"

"Yup," I answered. "I'm serving fried rice, too."

"Have you seen Niko?" Mr. Appleton asked me. "I want to start packing up."

That was interesting to me. I had sort of assumed that Mr. Appleton wanted to stay, as Robbie clearly did.

"LUNCH!" I yelled.

Mr. Appleton jumped.

"Sorry," I said. Then I hollered again. "LUNCH! Come and get it!"

I heard the sound of the hungry hordes moving toward the Kitchen.

"You're feeling like you can travel?" I asked Mr. Appleton as I set out the plates, forks, and napkins.

"I want to honor our agreement," he said. "And, yes, I guess I am anxious to get on the way."

"Why?"

"Well, we need to have another meeting," Mr. Appleton said. "So I can tell you about Denver."

The kids swarmed in.

"Mmmm! Chinese!" Max said.

"I love Chinese!" chirped Caroline.

"Wait," I said to Mr. A. "What about Denver?"

Niko came in. He had his arms crossed over his chest.

He stood behind Batiste on line.

"Oh, Niko," Mr. Appleton said. "I want to talk to you about our departure plan."

"Really?" Niko said. "Okay. Good."

"And I realized we haven't told you about Denver yet."

"What about Denver?" I said, shooing Ulysses and Max off to a table.

"What's this now?" Robbie said, ambling up.

"They're evacuating people," Mr. Appleton said to Niko and me. "If you can get yourself to the Denver International Airport, you can be evacuated."

"What do you mean '*evaculated*'?" Chloe demanded, cutting into the line.

By now most of the kids had their plates and were seated.

Mr. Appleton turned to face them. It looked like a class set in a Pizza Shack. Weird.

"Well, children," Mr. Appleton said. "When there is a crisis in an area, the government comes and evacuates the people living in that area. Evacuation is the transfer of large groups of people to a safer place."

DAY 11

"What do you mean?" Batiste interrupted.

"Many people in this area are making their way to the Denver airport," Mr. Appleton explained. "It is rumored that the government is flying people out by helicopter and taking them to Alaska."

Caroline raised her hand.

"Do you mean like our mommy?" she asked. "Like our mommy might be going to Denver to go away in a helicopter?"

"Possibly," Mr. Appleton said.

All at once everyone was talking, screaming, shouting: Denver, Denver, Denver. We had to go to Denver. We could drive the bus to Denver. We had to leave today for Denver.

Niko was shaking his head, already imagining the chaos this news was going to create.

"Whoa, whoa, whoa!" Mr. Appleton said, holding his hands up. The kids gradually fell silent though Henry had the hiccups. "It's not at all feasible for you kids to make it to Denver. Absolutely not. It's too dangerous out there for you."

"But we want to find our mommy!" Caroline said.

Her freckled face was so sad. It was hard not to just sweep her into a hug.

"I understand that, Caroline," Mr. Appleton said. "And that is why Robbie and I are going to Denver. We will be airlifted to Alaska, and then we will find your parents and tell them where you are so they can come for you."

The little kids started smiling. They started clapping and grinning, wiping their tears away.

Niko was grinning.

This was the happiest I'd ever seen Niko and I understood why: The men were leaving; he hadn't had to make them leave, so he didn't look like the bad guy anymore; and on top of it all, now there was a prayer we might be rescued.

Hope. It was a real glimmer of hope Mr. Appleton had just given us.

Everyone talked with excitement. Niko, Alex, and Mr. Appleton started talking about what supplies the men would need.

Only one person looked unhappy: Robbie.

I could tell that he really had wanted to stay with us.

He stalked away.

Sahalia watched him go, then started after him.

I thought she was probably going to beg him to take her along.

I didn't think about it too long, because Mr. Appleton said, "Now, if you kids will please go to your school area, you may each write a letter to your parents for Robbie and me to deliver."

I was throwing away the remains of our meal when Alex came back. He held a small storage bin with some electronics in it.

"Can I show you something?" he asked me.

"Of course."

I was happy he was even bothering to show me anything. We weren't getting along like we should be.

Alex took two video walkie-talkies out of the bin. One of them had an extra-long antenna attached and some extra wiring, all held together by some blue electrical tape.

"It's a video walkie-talkie but I amped up the transmitter with this antenna," he explained. "I've been testing it and, so far, it works pretty well in the confines of the store."

"That's cool," I said. "Are you thinking we could use it as, like, an intercom?"

"No," he said. "I thought maybe Mr. Appleton would take it with him. That way we could see what's going on outside."

Again, again, again, like always, I was bowled over by my brother's brilliance.

DAY 11

"That's incredible, Alex," I said. "That's such a great idea. They're going to love it."

He went off to show it to Niko and Mr. Appleton.

I sat down to write my letter to our parents.

I tried to tell them what had happened to us. I wrote that Alex and I were taking care of each other and that I'd make sure to keep him safe, no matter what.

I had to do a better job of that.

But it's hard to take care of someone who doesn't want or really even need your help.

Mr. Appleton and Robbie came to the Kitchen with Niko and Alex a little while later.

I had seen the four of them in the bicycle aisle. They had picked out two sturdy high-end mountain bikes. Now that their success was linked to our dreams of finding our parents, we wanted them to have everything they wanted. They could take the whole store, if they wanted. Just get us our parents back.

"Dean," Niko said. "Have you given some thought to the food we can send with these guys?"

I had.

I had a plastic storage bin filled with stuff:

2 boxes of granola bars
1 box protein bars
2 bags trail mix
4 cans RavioliOs
4 cans of beans
1 bag of dried beans
1 bag of rice
1 box instant oatmeal

2 jars of instant coffee
1 box powdered milk

I had also set out four gallon bottles of water and six liter bottles of Gatorade. I don't know, that seemed like the most they'd be able to carry.

"You guys can take as much dog food as you want," I offered.

Robbie shrugged.

"Luna does pretty well for herself," he said. He seemed down. He was looking at the floor.

He didn't want to leave. That was clear.

Mr. Appleton started rummaging through the plastic box.

I went over to Alex.

"Are they going to take the walkie-talkies?" I asked him.

"Yeah! They thought it was a great idea. Mr. Appleton said I am very ingenious."

His serious face looked proud.

I put my arm around his shoulder and kind of gave him a hug. He shrugged it off and went to stand next to Niko.

They were best buds again, I guess.

I tried not to care.

Mr. Appleton lifted the tub, and seemed okay with the weight. Going through it, though, he discarded the RavioliOs.

"Do you have any beef jerky?" he asked me.

"Sure," I said. And I turned to go get it for them.

"I'll go with him," Robbie said.

Robbie and I went back toward the snack food aisle.

"I feel like I can trust you," Robbie said to me, putting his hand on my shoulder. "I'm in a bind and I don't know what to do."

"What's wrong?" I said.

DAY 11

"Craig wants to leave right away. But I don't think he's well enough to go."

"I know that Niko had said you guys could stay at least another day," I said.

"Yeah! And now Craig wants to go today. He wants to go right now and I'm just not sure he's up to it."

We had reached the jerky and he skimmed his hand over some packs.

"I think he's afraid he's gonna die. He wants to try to get to Denver before he dies."

Robbie turned to me.

"I think the longer we stay, the better. I mean, I want to get your letters to your folks. I do. But I don't know what kind of chance we have with him the way he is."

I had to agree.

"I feel really bad, Robbie," I said. "But I don't know what to do. Truthfully, I think before we all knew about Denver, most of us would have wanted you to just stay. Like forever."

Maybe it was too much to say that. Maybe I had crossed a line, but I felt bad. To have to go back out there after everything he'd been through, when it was safe in the store and we all wanted him to stay. It was rough.

"But I also have to say"—and this was the truth in every way—"if you can go to Alaska and find our parents, you would be our hero forever and ever."

Robbie sighed.

"That's true," he said. "I would like to help you kids."

When we got back, Niko was helping Mr. Appleton pack up two large-frame backpacks and two bicycle saddlebags. I saw on the ground two small camping stoves—the kind that are just a can of fuel and a metal thing that goes on top. Also two thermal sleeping bags—the very thin space-blanket kind. And a bunch of matches and some Ziploc bags. Ponchos, flares, camping stuff from the Sports Department. Alex's video gear was in a heap next to the clothing. Most key: a Ziploc bag containing a list of our names and our letters.

Niko and Mr. Appleton were methodically packing the stuff up.

"Mr. Appleton, I was just wondering." I had to try, on Robbie's behalf. "I mean, it's fine with us for you to spend some more time here. We all want you to make it to Denver with our messages, why don't you just wait until you feel a little better?"

"I have already discussed this with Niko," he said stiffly.

"We don't know when the evacuation began," Niko said. "So if they wait too long, they might miss it."

"Besides, we've hit on the right antibiotics and I'm already starting to feel better," Mr. Appleton added.

Okay. Those were sound arguments, but why wouldn't he meet my eyes?

"We'll have dinner with you and then we'll go," he said.

Robbie was staring at Mr. Appleton with irritation and maybe anger on his face. When Robbie saw me looking at him, he gave me a weak smile.

DAY 11

CHAPTER TWENTY-SEVEN

THE BIG SEND-OFF

BATISTE AND I REALLY WENT TO TOWN FOR THE FAREWELL dinner.

After the men left, I was going to ask Niko if Batiste could just become my permanent helper. He really had a way with food and I think everyone was getting tired of the ridiculous meals my other helpers picked (for one lunch Ulysses had picked only foods with cherries in them—Cherry Pop-Tarts, cherry pie, black cherry ice cream, etc.)

Batiste and I oven-roasted the last of the fresh-frozen chicken. He made a corn soufflé using Egg Beaters and frozen corn, with some other stuff. For dessert we made three cakes: yellow with chocolate frosting, devil's food with marshmallow icing, and a pink cake with vanilla frosting and sprinkles, for novelty effect.

It was a really good meal. Everyone said so, except for Jake, who took a plate and slunk away to eat by himself, and Astrid, who was still MIA.

Mr. Appleton and Niko had joined forces, clearly. They sat together, discussing the trip. Alex sat with them, listening in, and happy, I imagine, at being allowed in on this important conversation.

After dinner Mr. Appleton gave a speech.

He stood up and dabbed his forehead with a napkin.

"I want to thank you all for taking us in and taking such good care of us," he said. "You are some of the brightest and most determined children I have had the pleasure of knowing. I am proud that you are in my school district."

He swabbed his head again. Why was he sweating so much? It wasn't warm in the kitchen. It was chilly, like the rest of the store.

"Robbie and I will make it our mission to find your parents and tell them you are here."

The kids cheered.

"Can you please ask my mom to tell Mr. Mittens that I mi[ss] him?" little Caroline asked Mr. Appleton.

"Sure," he said. Then he closed his eyes. He put a hand ou[t] so he could lean on the tabletop.

Niko stood up. At his signal, Alex handed out plastic flutes filled with sparkling apple juice.

"And, Mr. Appleton and Robbie, we are very glad you came. It has been our honor to prepare you for the journey ahead and we thank you very much for taking our letters to our parents. To Mr. Appleton and Robbie!"

We toasted with our faux champagne.

"Okay," Mr. Appleton said. "I think it's time we headed out."

The kids groaned.

"I don't get it." Chloe pouted. "At least wait until the morning. Nobody travels at night."

DAY 11

"It doesn't really matter," Mr. Appleton said. "It's night all the time out there."

"And less people are out at night. So there's less of a chance we'll run into dangerous people," Robbie added.

Chloe shivered.

Ulysses was sitting on Robbie's lap. Robbie kissed him on the top of the head. Ulysses snuggled into him and wrapped his arms around Robbie's neck.

This was going to suck for Ulysses, their leaving.

"Come on, Robbie," Mr. Appleton said. "It's time."

Mr. Appleton stood up.

"Thank you again," Niko said.

"It's our duty and our pleasure," Mr. Appleton said. His color was not good.

He seemed to squint at Niko, reaching out to shake his hand. But he couldn't find it.

Mr. Appleton put a hand out to steady himself against the tabletop, but the hand missed.

Slowly, sideways, Mr. Appleton crumpled to the ground.

Niko, Robbie, Brayden, and I carried him back to their sleeping area.

"I knew he wasn't feeling up to it," Robbie said. "He has this sense of duty toward you kids. Wanted to get those letters to your parents."

They set Mr. Appleton down. His head lolled back. He was out.

"Do you think he's okay?" I asked.

"Someone go get smelling salts," Niko ordered.

"I'll go," Brayden volunteered. He took off for the Pharmacy.

"We need to get him to the hospital," Niko said. He turned

to Mr. Appleton. "Do you think you could get him there, if we made some kind of sled for you? It's not too far . . ."

"No, no, no," Robbie protested. "The hospital's closed. It was one of the first things to go. There were like hundreds of people trying to get in. It was mobbed."

Niko thought about that. I saw him look to Robbie. He didn't trust him.

"Believe me, I swear to God above, this is the best place for Craig. This is the only place he has a chance."

"Great," said Niko. His hands were in fists.

Brayden came back after a while with smelling salts. A little bottle from the Pharmacy. I'd never seen them before.

Niko expertly uncapped the bottle and held it a hand's length away from Mr. Appleton's nose. He wafted the fumes toward him.

Mr. Appleton recoiled. He was super-groggy.

"My gun," he said, and he grabbed for Niko's shirt, then he groaned, a long, bull-like sound, and he fell back to sleep.

"He must have overexerted himself," Niko said on the way back to the Kitchen.

"He's sick," I said.

"Dude, his leg is rotting off," Brayden said, always one with words.

"I don't know," I said. "He almost seemed stoned to me. Maybe he overdid it on pain pills."

"That's possible," Niko said. "I gave him a lot of them to take along."

Niko exhaled.

"Now we're stuck with them," he murmured darkly.

"Don't worry, Niko," I said. "Robbie's not so bad."

DAY 11

We assigned watches for taking care of Mr. Appleton. Niko would watch from bedtime until midnight. Robbie insisted on taking the second shift. And I volunteered for three to six a.m.

When Niko told the little kids that the grown-ups would be staying for a few more days, they were delighted.

Ulysses started break dancing, which was just funny enough to break the grimness of the moment.

Even Niko had to smile as Ulysses jigged and jagged and did ye olde robot. The chubby kid really had some moves.

CHAPTER TWENTY-EIGHT

THE BIG SEND-OFF:

PART TWO

EVERYTHING WAS QUIET AND DARK IN THE STORE WHEN WE woke to the sound of Luna barking and Astrid yelling her head off:

"JAKENIKODEANBRAYDENGETOVERHERE!"

We ripped through the store, scrambling over each other in our half-asleep state, but awake as soon as our feet hit the linoleum.

We ran toward her voice and the dim light of a lantern.

I rounded the head of the aisle and I saw an air mattress, half covered by a twisted sheet. And Robbie, lying on it in his underwear. And Astrid.

Astrid stood above Robbie, holding a handgun, aiming at his chest.

Luna was standing like a fireplug and barking her head off.

Then I saw Sahalia.

She was crying and basically naked. Just wearing a thong. She sat on the floor, clutching her nightgown to her chest.

DAY 11

Sahalia and Robbie had been . . .

Sahalia and Robbie had been . . .

Sahalia and Robbie had been . . . what?

"What the hell?" Jake said.

"Take the gun," Astrid said.

Jake took the gun from her, pointing it at Robbie's midsection.

"This is intense. This is too intense," Jake said, and I saw his hand was trembling.

"What happened?" Niko asked.

"Nothing!" Robbie protested.

Sahalia was weeping, clinging to Astrid as if she was a life raft. Astrid was making calming sounds and trying to both cover her up and gather her from the floor at the same time.

"It's okay," Astrid said. "You're fine. You're fine. Just get up."

Sahalia clutched her nightgown to her chest and Astrid moved her toward the Train.

"Guys," Robbie said. "It's not what you think. I was just lying here sleeping, and I woke up and she was on top of me. She said she wanted me to take her with me and she could be my girlfriend. I said no!" He held his hands up.

"You're a liar!" Niko said.

"I'm telling you the truth," Robbie continued. "I know how bad this looks, but really, I said no. Really. *Te lo juro!*"

Luna was still barking and growling.

"Come here, Luna." Robbie called the dog over to him.

He scratched her ears and petted her, calming her down.

Trying to calm us all down.

"It's all a misunderstanding," he said to the dog. "These kids would never hurt anyone. It's a big misunderstanding."

I looked at the guys. Did they buy it? Did I buy it?

"She's crazy, that girl," Robbie said. "She kept talking about how none of you think she's a grown-up but how she is, and she wanted to prove it to you, and honestly, I was trying to get her to put back her nightgown on when that other crazy girl came with the gun."

"All right!" Niko shouted. "That's enough! Just don't talk. Let me think."

Robbie murmured soothing sounds to Luna.

"You guys stay here and keep the gun on him," Niko told us, gesturing to me, Brayden, and Jake, who still held the gun. "Keep the gun on him no matter what he says. I'm gonna go talk to Sahalia. I'll find out what happened here and then we'll know what to do."

Niko sprinted down the aisle.

"Oh God," Jake said. The hand that held the gun was shaking violently. "I think I'm gonna be sick."

He bent over.

"Give me the gun," Brayden said, moving toward Jake.

But then Robbie was reaching up. Lurching up.

I was too slow. A beat behind.

Robbie grabbed the gun from Jake, just as Brayden reached for it.

"No!" Brayden shouted. He snatched at the gun and in the scuffle the gun fired with a deafening BANG.

Brayden slipped down to the floor, looking confused.

"Brayden!" I shouted.

Jake lurched toward Robbie and tried to get the gun away.

Niko came vaulting back down the aisle and launched himself at Robbie and had him around the neck, and the three of them went toppling backward onto the floor.

Robbie punched Jake and elbowed Niko to the head and grabbed the gun out of Jake's hands.

I rushed to Brayden. He looked at me with shock in his eyes.

DAY 11

When I looked up, Robbie had the gun right at Niko's head.

"Get back!" Robbie shouted. "I'll shoot! I'll shoot him! I will!"

Jake scooted away, hands up.

Robbie cursed in Spanish, rising to his feet. He wiped blood from the corner of his mouth.

"*Maldita sea!* I told you it wasn't me! She wanted to be my girlfriend. Why couldn't you just believe me? You," he said, turning on Niko, "you had it in for me from the start!"

Robbie lashed out and struck Niko across the face with the barrel of the pistol. Niko fell.

"You don't get to decide who goes and who stays!" Robbie screamed at Niko's fallen form. "Who lives and dies!"

He raised up his gun.

And *BWAM*!

A gunshot murdered my ears.

Robbie was flung backward, led by his head.

He hit the shelving unit behind him and slumped to the ground.

He was shot.

There was *Josie*, holding the other handgun, coming out of the shadows down the aisle.

On the ground just behind her lay the two-gallon Ziploc bag that Niko had stored the guns in.

Had the other gun just been laying there on the floor the whole time?

Josie dropped the gun, shaking her arm out.

She sank to her knees, covered her face, and howled.

CHAPTER TWENTY-NINE

BLOOD, BLEACH, AND LIES

THE LITTLE KIDS CAME SCREAMING OVER TO SEE WHAT HAD happened, and I grabbed Max and Ulysses and pushed them all back toward the Train.

"Go back to the Train!" I shouted. "This is an emergency! Go! Go! Go!"

They could *not* be allowed to see what had happened.

I yelled at them every step back to the Train.

I pushed them inside and pulled one of the futon sofas in front of the door.

"You stay in there until it's safe!" I shouted. "We'll come and get you when it's safe."

They cried and sobbed inside, banging on the door.

Astrid and Sahalia were curled up together on the other futon couch in the Living Room.

Astrid was singing to Sahalia.

Robbie was dead. Brayden had been shot, and now Astrid

DAY 11

was singing to Sahalia. I had to keep the facts straight or I might go crazy. Those were the facts.

I raced back to my friends.

"This is bad, this is bad," Jake kept repeating. It must have all felt like a very bad trip to him.

Josie was crying on the floor, the gun lying next to her on the linoleum.

Niko had Brayden lying on the floor and was pressing both his hands down on Brayden's shoulder. Blood was all over Niko's arms and shirt. Brayden was soaking with it.

"I'm trying to stop the bleeding but I don't know what to do," Niko said, looking up at me with pure panic in his eyes.

I ran to the Pharmacy.

Alex was there, scrambling to gather as many bandages in his arms as he could.

It was dark. It was hard to find anything because the store was so dark.

"Bring those to Niko and then go turn the lights on, okay?" I said.

"But the power!" he protested.

"We need light!" I answered. "We need to see what we're doing."

"Okay." He gulped and ran off to obey.

I needed something to stop the bleeding. I knew stuff existed because once our neighbor fell off a ladder and opened up a huge gash on the back of her head.

The EMTs had sprinkled a powder on it. Some kind of powder to stop bleeding.

I jumped over the pharmacy counter. The place was a mess.

What the hell has Jake been up to back here? I thought.

The lights came blinking and twittering back on.

I squinted, at first.

Then I started scanning the shelves.

I grabbed the pain pills Jake had given me. Those would help Brayden.

I couldn't find that bleeding stuff. I didn't know what it was called or anything.

I grabbed some of the antibiotics Niko had given to Mr. Appleton and I ran back.

The crime scene looked much, much worse with the lights on.

"We gotta get this body out of here!" Jake was nearly crying.

"We will, Jake. We will," Niko said tersely. "Shut up about it."

Robbie had been pushed backward by the force of the bullet and lay slumped against the shelves.

Blood and clumps of tissue (brain) were spattered over the decorative steering-wheel covers behind him.

And under his legs an oil slick of blood was spreading slowly.

Niko had made a square pad of bandages out of the supplies Alex had brought and was pressing down on Brayden's shoulder with all his might.

"I couldn't find that blood stuff," I huffed, out of breath.

"It's slowed," Niko said. "I think the bleeding's slowed. But he's lost so much blood."

I took Brayden's uninjured arm and tried to find a pulse.

"He's cold," I said to Niko.

"I know."

DAY 11

"Where's Josie?" I asked.

"Astrid came and got her."

"We have to do something about the body, guys!" Jake wailed. "It's freaking me out."

Niko looked at me.

"Can you get rid of it?" he asked.

"You don't need my help?" I said.

"Alex will be right back," Niko said.

I turned to Jake.

"Okay, I'll get rid of the body," I said. "But you have to help."

Jake was crying now, tears streaming down his face.

"It's my fault, it's my fault," he moaned.

"Stop, Jake. I need your help."

"I can't do this," he said.

"Yes, you can. Just . . . just don't look at him," I told Jake.

I grabbed Robbie's hand.

It was cold and heavy. Like clay. A clay body.

I took the one hand and Jake took the other.

"Oh God," Jake groaned.

We flopped Robbie onto the air mattress. His body landed with a sick, wet sound.

I picked up the comforter, which had been lying on the floor, and covered the body with it.

"Come on," I told Jake. "Pull."

We pulled the air mattress back to the storeroom, leaving a grisly trail behind—blood running in parallel lines—as if the air mattress was a flat paintbrush trailing firehouse red.

Jake had blood all over the center of his body and his arms. We looked like we'd just butchered a cow.

"I'm scared," Jake said.

"I know, Jake," I said.

"I don't want Brayden to die," he said, breaking into sobs. "Christ! I have to get myself together."

He wiped the tears away with his forearm, which was spattered with blood.

Jake and Alex were assigned to cleaning up the blood, while I helped Niko to bandage Brayden.

We cut Brayden's shirt off. Niko swabbed him down with that orange stuff and then asked me to hold the bandage down hard while he wrapped the whole shoulder with gauze.

It was wet and disgusting to do this. The bullet had taken a chunk off the shoulder. The flesh was raw meat, horrible and messy. I could see white bone under the torn meat.

I tried not to black out.

"Keep the pressure on!" Niko commanded.

I closed my eyes and pressed down hard.

Niko didn't think we should move him too much, so I went and got a new inflatable mattress.

Me, Niko, Jake, and Alex lifted him, as carefully as we could, onto the air mattress.

Niko sent Alex for space blankets and Gatorade.

Niko continued to attend to Brayden while I helped Alex and Jake finish cleaning up.

By the time we finished, there were eight trash bags filled with blood-soaked paper towels, dirty wet wipes, empty bottles of bleach, etc.

After what felt like hours and hours of hard, gruesome work, the kind of work nobody ever, ever wanted to have to do, Niko finally said:

"I think he's stabilized enough."

DAY 11

"Stabilized enough for what?" I said. Maybe he was in good enough shape that we could wash up and change clothes. We looked gruesome beyond belief.

"Stabilized enough for us to go talk to Sahalia."

Sahalia was still lying with Astrid on one of the futon couches. They were just lying together, spooning, their bodies curled together in one doubled *S*.

Neither of the girls was asleep. Their eyes were wide-awake, staring forward.

Josie was curled up on the butterfly chair, staring ahead. Someone (probably Astrid) had thrown a blanket over her.

There were no sounds from inside the Train, but the futon I had put in front of the door had been removed, so I gathered that everything was okay inside.

"Sahalia," Niko said gently, kneeling down beside the futon. "We need to know what happened."

Sahalia simply closed her eyes.

"Come on, Sasha," Jake tried. "We have to know."

"No one blames you at all for what happened," I said.

"Robbie was lying to us and we need to know the truth," Niko said.

"He said he would take me with him," Sahalia said quietly. "He said we were just alike and we could make it together. I thought it would be, like, as a team. But then . . . he . . ."

Tears were sliding down her face. She made no move to wipe them away.

"He said that I should be, like, his girlfriend. And I guess I thought I could, you know, do what all he wanted me to do. But then I didn't want to and . . ."

"I was keeping an eye on him," Astrid said. "I didn't trust him. She said no. And he wouldn't stop—"

Josie grabbed my sleeve, pushing her way through to the center of the group.

"So I was right. Right? He was bad. He was bad?"

She was breathing fast, tears pooled in her eyes.

"He was a bad guy and I had no choice but to do what I did. Right?"

"Yes." "Of course." "Absolutely." We answered, but she didn't seem to hear us.

Niko took her by the arms and looked right into her eyes.

"Josie," he said. "Robbie was bad. You saved my life by shooting him. You did the right thing."

Josie swooned, her knees buckling out from under her. Niko steered her down onto the futon, next to Astrid and Sahalia.

Astrid put her other arm around Josie and now she had Sahalia on one side and Josie on the other.

"I heard the shot and I came running," Josie said.

I understood she needed to tell us all her story.

"There, in the middle of the aisle, was the bag on the floor and the second gun just laying there. I took it. I wasn't going to shoot anyone. I just thought . . . a gun shouldn't just be laying on the floor."

She wiped at her eyes.

"I didn't even want to pick it up. But I did. And then I saw Robbie hurting Niko. I didn't even think," she whispered. "I just shot him. It felt so natural. As if shooting people is something I do all the time."

"You did the right thing," I said.

"Because he was going to hurt Niko, right? He was going to shoot Niko."

"He had already hit me with the gun," Niko said. "And I think he was going to shoot me."

"Yes," she said. "I did the right thing. I did."

DAY 11

Josie pulled her head back and looked at us all of a sudden. Niko, Jake, Alex, me. My shirt and my arms.

"Are you guys covered in *blood*?" she asked. "You have to get cleaned up," she said, staggering to her feet. "What will the kids think?"

CHAPTER THIRTY

A KISS

AS BONE WEARY AS WE ALL WERE, ONLY SAHALIA, JAKE, AND Alex could sleep.

Sahalia was curled up on the futon couch.

Alex on the butterfly chair.

Jake had lain down in front of the futon on the floor. "Just to rest my eyes for a sec." And soon he was snoring away.

"I'm ready to work," Josie said. "I'll take the first watch over Brayden and Mr. Appleton while you guys get some sleep."

Astrid stood up. She walked over to the door to the Train and looked in, scratching her head.

"Do you want me to show you where your bunk is?" I asked her.

"I guess you're pretty tired," she said, looking at me.

"Why?"

"I think I might have lice."

"Yeah," I said. "You probably do." I explained to her that we'd all had lice and that Josie washed our hair.

DAY 11

"I can wash yours for you," I said.

"You're not too tired?" Astrid asked me.

I had been totally wiped out just a moment before, but talking to Astrid. Just the idea of . . . well, the idea of washing her hair, made me feel really, very awake.

"No," I said. "I can always spare a moment to delouse a friend." She smiled.

We walked over to the Dump. Astrid darted away near Office Supplies.

"What are you doing?" I asked.

She came back holding a pair of scissors.

"I have four brothers," she said. "I've had lice three times. And there's no way to get them out of long hair like this. You're gonna have to give me a haircut."

"You know I'll suck at it, right?"

"I would be shocked if you didn't," she said.

And there—she smiled at me.

The same smile I'd been seeing in my dreams since I was a freshman.

The hair-washing stuff was still set up in the Dump, complete with extra towels and everything.

"Cut away," she said as she sat on one of the stools.

"God help me," I said.

I took a towel and wrapped it around her.

I started chopping. The golden tresses that had absolutely transfixed me were now drab and mousy. They were almost like dreadlocks. One big clump was all fused together and I just hacked at it with the scissors until I had cut the whole thing away.

Astrid shivered.

"Does it feel weird?" I asked her.

"Light," she said. "My head feels free."

I cut and chopped until it was mostly gone. It looked god-awful. Down to the scalp in some places, wispy in others. Matted down in places and kookily long in others.

"I think I need to wash it so I can make it look . . . uniform . . . somehow . . . or better . . . maybe . . . ," I said.

She laughed.

The most elegant way to wash someone's head over a basin, Josie had figured out by the end of the delousing episode, was to have two stools set together. The washee sits facing away from the basin and the washer sits closer to the basin, sideways. Then the washee leans back so that they are lying down, their torso resting on your knees. You put the basin under their head and you have a bottle of water and the shampoo at an arm's reach.

I explained this to Astrid, so she sat down facing away from me and then leaned back onto my lap.

And there she was. So beautiful, laid out on my knees. She had her eyes closed, and for a moment, I just looked at her. Dirty face. Lips drawn together, chapped and rosy. Eyes red rimmed. The rise of her cheekbones. Eyebrows and lashes golden honey–colored. Some brown, dried freckle-dots that could be blood on her jawline.

Astrid Heyman. I tried to memorize how beautiful she was.

"Okay," she said. "I'm ready."

"I'm sorry," I told her, "it's going to be cold."

I poured the water over her head.

"It's freezing!"

I put the pitch-smelling shampoo into my hands and started

DAY 11

rubbing. I moved my fingers in small circles over the surface of her grimy scalp.

"Mmmmmm," she said and it was all I could do not to bring her to me and kiss her.

A trickle of water had run over her forehead to her eye. I took the edge of the towel and dabbed it away softly.

In the ruse of brushing away water, I ran my thumb over her eyebrow. It was a marvel of God, how perfect it felt under my thumb.

Brayden shot and Mr. Appleton dying and all I could think of was that perfect eyebrow.

I rinsed the shampoo out.

She shivered and I saw goose bumps go up on her forearms.

After it was done I put my hands under her shoulders and helped her sit up.

She towel-dried her hair and put her hands up to feel her head.

"Oh my God," she said. "I'm bald!"

She turned and looked at me, her blue eyes shining.

Her hair was fluffy and standing up in all directions.

"You look like a baby chick!" I said.

She let me trim it some. I cut away the long, draggly tendrils.

In the end, she looked not so much like a baby chick, but maybe an orphan boy from a Charles Dickens book.

"It's cold," she said, shivering.

And I realized I had a hat! It got cold sometimes in the early morning in the Kitchen so I'd taken to keeping one in my back pocket.

It was an orange knit ski cap with a band of blue around near the edge.

"Thanks," she said and she put it on.

"There's like a dozen different styles in the Men's Department, if you want a different one," I said.

I didn't want her to feel some kind of pressure to wear it. And if she replaced it, it would have made me feel better to know that I had given her the idea.

"I like yours," she said.

I didn't know what to say to that.

"I'm going to go check on everybody," I told her.

"I'm gonna go change," she said. "I smell, don't I?"

"Yes, you do." I told her. "Also, you have a terrible haircut."

She gave me a smile. A shining golden smile, flashing in the center of our dark, lost world.

We had moved Brayden near Mr. Appleton to make it easier to take care of them.

Josie and Niko were looking at Brayden.

"Can't sleep?" asked Josie.

"Not so much," I answered. "How is he?"

Brayden looked ashen and weak.

"If the wound doesn't become infected, I think he'll be okay," Niko said.

"And if it does?" Josie asked.

I guess I expected Niko to say something about antibiotics.

"Maybe I could take him in the bus."

"To where?" Josie asked.

"The hospital," Niko answered.

"You know what Robbie said. It's shut down. There is no one there."

"But think about it," Niko said. "Robbie wanted to stay here. He was probably lying. The hospital might be open."

"We can't risk it," I said.

"I know," he snapped.

DAY 11

"Brayden's going to be okay," Josie said. She pressed a damp washcloth to his forehead. "You gotta pull through, Brayden. We need you to pull through."

Brayden's breathing was shallow but steady. Maybe he'd be okay . . .

"Now you two go to sleep. And I mean it," Josie said.

I was following Niko back to the Train, only he didn't go to the Train. He went to the bus.

"Hey, what are you doing?" I asked.

He came out with some supplies—caulk guns, some spackle, some rags.

He set them down and then headed off toward House-wares.

"What are you doing?" I called to his back.

He went to the Storage section and took a stack of big plastic bins.

"Can you get the lids?" he asked.

"Sure," I answered. "But, Niko, don't you think we should sleep? At least for a few hours?"

"You should. I'm going to stock the bus."

"You don't really think you're going to get to the hospital."

"Don't you remember my motto? Always be prepared."

He laughed. A dry chuff of a laugh.

"Get it?" he said. "It's a Boy Scout joke."

It wasn't much of a joke, but I got it all right.

We were going to stock the bus.

I got us some carts, which we definitely needed.

We filled them with water. Cases and cases of water. That was the first thing we loaded.

Then we put in the plastic storage bins, which we had filled with food.

Trail mix, beef jerky, protein bars, nuts, cookies . . . All the things you'd think to bring on, say, a hike. Then Niko also added canned soup, oatmeal, tins of tuna and chicken meat, and I realized he was preparing for us to survive for a long, long time, from the food he was bringing.

"In case we get to DIA and have to wait," he explained.

And that's how I came to understand what we were packing the bus for.

It wasn't to take Brayden to the hospital.

It was to make it to Denver.

"What about the tire?" I said. "Isn't there one sketchy tire?"

Niko shrugged.

"Robbie fixed it the best he could. And it's coupled with a tire that's okay . . ."

After a few more minutes of quiet packing, I said, "I bet Brayden's fine."

"Yeah," Niko answered. "He has to be."

We got all the food and drinks we might need for two weeks or so onto the bus.

Niko told me to go get medical supplies.

He was going to finish caulking the roof of the bus.

When I came back with my four big tubs of antibiotics, pain medicine, bandages, Bactine, Benadryl, hydrogen peroxide, and the like, Astrid was there, helping Niko.

"Hey," she said, with a nod of her head.

"Hey."

She had on a pair of jeans, new sneakers, and a pink fleece.

I noticed she was still wearing my hat.

DAY 11

Niko had apparently sent her to get blankets and sleeping bags and now she had a big pile of them.

"Put two sleeping bags and two blankets under each seat, okay?" Niko asked her.

"Sure thing," she said, and started bringing them on board.

"What's next?" I asked.

He sent me to Home Improvement, for flashlights, battery-powered lanterns, and some assorted tools he thought we should have.

I came back and Astrid and Niko were sitting, resting against the side of the bus, discussing what else we needed.

"We have gas masks for each person. Food, water, first aid stuff. Do we have Benadryl?"

"All of it in the store," I said.

He continued his list.

"Rope, matches, tarps, backpacks, oil, knives . . . We have two guns and some bullets . . ."

He rubbed his eyes.

"What about some money? Or some jewelry? Stuff to barter, maybe."

"I'll get it," Astrid volunteered.

"Niko!" Josie came stumbling into our clearing.

Niko jumped up. "What? Oh God, what?"

"It's Mr. Appleton. Not Brayden. Not Brayden. Brayden's okay," Josie said, tears streaming down her face.

She stumbled toward Niko and fell into his arms.

"Mr. Appleton's dead," she said.

Niko held her to him, encircling her dark shoulders and pulling her into his body.

She looked up at him and he looked at her and then they were kissing.

Astrid and I didn't look at each other, but we each knew to walk away.

We left them alone, together.

DAY 11

CHAPTER THIRTY-ONE

RECONNAISSANCE

MR. APPLETON'S STILL BODY LAY ON ITS AIR MATTRESS HALFWAY down the Automotive aisle. Josie must have tried to drag him away from Brayden, when she realized Mr. Appleton was dead. He looked waxen and fake in death. Like a model of his own self.

Jake was sitting there next to Brayden. Jake's eyes were glazed over and he stared blankly ahead, rocking back and forth.

Luna was lying next to Jake. She raised her head at me and gave her stump of a tail four weary thumps.

"Hey, Jake, how are you doing?" I asked him.

"Bad," he answered, waving the question away.

I put my hand on Brayden's forehead. It was clammy.

His eyelids fluttered and he seemed to recognize me for a moment.

Astrid knelt down next to Brayden and tipped his head up a bit. She poured a little water into his mouth.

He sputtered, choking on it.

"If only we could get him to the hospital," Astrid said.

"If only we knew if it was even open," I said. "We just don't have enough information."

Suddenly I had an idea.

"Alex's video walkie-talkies!" I said, standing up.

"What?" Jake said.

"I'll be right back," I told them. And I ran for Niko.

"Niko!" I shouted as I hurdled through the store.

I came into the clearing where Niko was with Josie. They jumped apart. As if it mattered that I saw them together!

"Alex's video walkie-talkies!" I said, breathless. "Listen, Brayden's got to get to the hospital. We don't know if it's open. I can put on the walkie-talkie and go to the hospital. That way you guys can see what's going on out there. You can see if it's safe."

"What?" Niko said.

I explained it to him again as we hurried to the Train.

I wanted to wake Alex up and ask him if it was possible.

"I'll wear the transmitter and you guys will be able to see what's out there," I said as we came to the Living Room. "I can even go to the highway and see if it's clear."

"But it's not safe to go out!" Josie protested.

"What do we know?!" I nearly shouted. "Can we trust anything those guys told us? Robbie didn't want us going out. He wanted to stay here. He could have said anything to keep us here. Maybe the hospital is open!"

I was raving a little. It was possible that exhaustion had pushed me over some kind of edge, but the idea seemed so smart.

"Reconnaissance!" I said.

Alex was awake now. And Sahalia was stirring.

"I'll do reconnaissance! That's what it's called."

I turned and addressed Alex.

DAY 11

"Would it work for me to take the walkie-talkies out and go to the hospital and see if it's safe?"

"No," came Jake's voice. "It wouldn't."

I turned to stare at Jake.

"But it would work for *me* to go," he said.

Niko shook his head, but Jake kept on talking.

"I know, I've been a screw-up. I got . . . messed up. But I'm fast. I'm in good shape and I'm type B. No blisters, no hallucinations, no rage."

"I don't think you can handle it," Niko said. "I'm sorry. It's too dangerous."

"You gotta let me do something for Brayden. He's my friend. He's my best friend, and if he dies because I let Robbie get the gun . . ."

He looked at us.

"Please, let me go."

Astrid had come over during this speech.

"I don't understand this plan," she interrupted. "Jake is going to go out?"

"Yeah, and you'll be able to see what I'm seeing," Jake answered.

"What if you're attacked?" she asked.

"He could take a gun," Niko said.

She hung her head, backing away. Jake rose and went to her.

They went a little ways away, but we could still hear them.

And we could see them, too, now that the store was fully lit.

It seemed indecent, somehow, to have the whole store lit that way.

"I have to do it for Brayden," Jake said to Astrid. "It's my fault that he got shot. If I hadn't been using, it wouldn't have happened."

"You're going to die, just to try to save him," she said.

"Please," he said softly. "I want to do something. I want to do something right. For once."

They embraced and I looked away.

She loved him and he loved her. And that was how it was. I could wash her hair from here to Grand Junction—she loved Jake.

I glanced up and saw my brother looking at me with pity in his eyes.

Just what I needed.

It was at this moment that Ulysses appeared at the door, rubbing his eyes.

"I want Robbie," he said.

The kids were awake.

It was the morning.

DAY 11

JAKE TV

NIKO, ALEX, AND JAKE WENT AWAY TO PREPARE JAKE FOR HIS trip.

Astrid volunteered to go take care of Brayden.

Which left Josie and me to lie to the kids.

"What happened?" Max said, as he came to the door.

The little kids came out cross and sullen and unforgiving. They blinked and looked dazed in the full light of the store.

And Josie and I pulled ourselves up and lied and lied and lied.

"Kids, some bad stuff happened last night," Josie told them. "Mr. Appleton took a turn for the worse after you all went to sleep, so Robbie said he wanted to go out and get help, right, Dean?"

"That's right. And then Brayden went to get the men's guns from where we had hidden them and he fell . . ."

"Yes, that was the shot you heard." Josie stepped in. "Brayden shot himself in the shoulder. Fortunately, he's okay. He's going to be just fine."

The kids looked so puzzled, you could almost see question marks spinning in their eyes.

"But there were two shots," Max protested.

I looked at Josie.

"No," she said. "That was just the ricochet."

"The what?" Chloe asked.

"A ricochet," Josie repeated. "Like an echo."

"I don't think so," Max said, crossing his arms.

"Where's Robbie?" Ulysses asked.

"Well, that's the thing," I said, bending down. "Robbie left. He wanted to go and find our parents as soon as possible."

"And get help for Mr. Appleton," I added. I just didn't have it in me to tell them he'd died.

I looked at Josie and my look conveyed: Let them accept the bad news about Robbie first, then we'll tell them about Mr. Appleton later.

It must have conveyed that, because she said, "Yes, Mr. Appleton is sleeping now. A very deep sleep. We must not disturb him."

Caroline and Henry started crying. Ulysses was already dissolving in tears.

"But there is good news," I said, scrambling. "Robbie left Luna behind. He said he wanted Ulysses to have Luna, because he's such a good boy."

Ulysses buried his face in Josie's shirt.

"Let's call her now," Josie said. "Luna! Luna!"

The kids started calling Luna in their sweet little voices.

Josie looked up at me.

"Breakfast," she said. "Something with a lot of protein."

By the time I had fed the kids their breakfast of egg-and-cheese Hot Pockets, Niko and Alex had Jake all geared up. I brought

DAY 12

a tray with food on it to them, where they were getting ready, in the Media Department.

Jake wore layer upon layer of sweatpants and sweatshirts—M through XXL. He looked like a padded dummy. They hadn't wrapped his head yet so he sort of had a pinhead effect going on—this very round, puffy body with Jake's regular-size head poking out and grinning at us all.

"What are you doing?" Max asked.

The kids all laughed at Jake. He looked so silly.

Niko shot me a look that said, You didn't tell them?

I sighed and shrugged my shoulders. We'd had plenty to tell them, already.

Jake had a backpack, which I saw was stocked with jerky, trail mix, and water, as well as two extra flashlights.

I knew he also had one of the guns.

God, I hoped it was enough to keep him safe.

Alex was finishing the hookup of the video walkie-talkie.

The walkie-talkie was strapped to Jake's torso by layer upon layer of duct tape. This gave the chest section of Jake's ensemble a weird, girdled look. The camera side of the walkie-talkie pointed out. An earpiece was wired up Jake's neck, taped down to his skin, as if he was a narc going on a drug bust, or maybe an FBI guy.

"How do I look, booker?" Jake asked me.

He looked like a fat super-gadget-oriented exercise fanatic.

"You look tough, man," I answered.

"Liar." He laughed.

It was good to see him with some purpose again. He still looked pale and bedraggled, but at least he was smiling.

All the kids gathered around, but still gave us space to work. Josie patiently explained what was about to happen.

The kids were amped.

Chloe squeezed Luna hard. That dog was going to have to get used to a lot of love.

She was a good dog, just licked Chloe's face until Chloe released her.

Alex switched on the walkie-talkie and then crossed to a bigtab. It was one that had been in a box, so it hadn't been damaged at all by the quake. Now, it was plugged in to the power system and had a cable slotted into its AV IN port, which ran to the other walkie-talkie.

Alex turned it on, and suddenly an image came up—it was Caroline and Henry, who happened to be standing right in front of Jake, huddled together and sucking their thumbs.

"Hey!" they said in unison, seeing themselves on the bigtab.

We all cheered.

Jake turned his body, and as he did, the image on the monitor panned across us.

The light was dim. It was hard to make us out totally, but there we were. Dirty, I noticed. We all looked a lot dirtier and scrawnier on camera than we did to my eye.

Maybe I'd just gotten used to our level of grime.

"This is awesome," Jake said.

He bounced up and down and the image bounced up and down on the screen. He got all up in Max's face and the image on the screen zoomed in on a very happy Max, sticking out his tongue and making a silly face.

"Okay," Alex said. "Say something."

"What up, what up?" Jake said. "I am broadcasting to you live from the Greenway on the Old Denver Highway in Monument, Colorado!"

The volume was way too low, but we could hear his faint, tinny voice coming out of the walkie-talkie.

"See if you can hear me," Alex said.

DAY 12

Alex sat on the ground next to the walkie-talkie.

"Can you hear me, Jake?" he said into it.

"Yes. Jesus, it's loud in my ear," Jake complained with a grin. "Man, this is awesome. I feel like an astronaut!"

Niko stepped forward.

"Are you sure you want to do this?" Niko said. "We know it's dangerous out there, Jake."

"Dude," Jake said. "I got it all under control, Niko Knacko."

"Niko Knacko," Max echoed with a smile.

Jake was back. Fun-loving Jake.

This was what he had needed, I thought to myself. Jake needed a chance to be a hero again.

Astrid appeared.

"Brayden's temperature is rising," she said. "I don't like how he looks. He's thrashing around."

"Then there's no time to waste," said Jake. "Let's get this thing going."

Astrid looked away.

"I'm going to go sit with Brayden," she said.

"I'll keep you company," Sahalia said.

Sahalia seemed subdued and quiet now. The two girls went off together.

Astrid couldn't meet Jake's eyes.

"See you soon, Astrid," he said.

"Yeah," she said.

"Let's get your head wrapped," Niko said to Jake.

Alex and Niko had figured out a system of an air mask, with several of those fleece ski masks with the eyes and nose cut out, over the top of the whole thing.

Niko brought the heavy rubber air mask down over Jake's face.

Jake put his hand up and futzed with the earpiece and the microphone, getting them in a comfortable place under the mask.

"Jake, can you hear me?" Alex asked as Niko began putting the ski masks over Jake's head. It was hard to get them over the air mask.

"It's okay," Jake said, trying to wave Niko off.

"No," Niko said. "Just give me a second."

So Jake stood still while Niko fitted the fleece balaclavas into place.

"Can you say something?" Alex repeated.

"Testing, testing, one-two-three," Jake said. His voice came muffled—both through the mask and through the small speakers of the walkie-talkie.

Alex looked at all of us.

"It's a go," he said. "We're a go."

"Okay, let's go," Niko said.

Everyone started to walk toward the storeroom to see Jake off.

"Wait!" I yelled. "You guys can't all go back there."

"Why not?" Niko asked.

"There's *stuff* back there," I said, willing him to remember that Jake and I had stowed Robbie's bloody, destroyed body back there.

"Oh yeah," Jake said, the sound muffled through the mask.

"And the compounds."

"You're right," Niko said. "Alex can help Jake up onto the roof."

This meant Alex needed to outfit himself with a gas mask and a couple of layers of clothing, too.

"Guys," Chloe said to the kids. "Let's get chairs and popcorn and treats for the show!"

DAY 12

The other kids ran, giggling and excited, to go bring over comfy furniture from the Living Room.

Ulysses was the only one of them who still seemed sad about Robbie and Mr. Appleton. The rest of them were psyched to be watching TV.

"Good luck, Jake," I said, while we waited for Alex to gear up.

Jake shook my hand, then Niko's.

"Hurry back," Niko added.

The kids were still off foraging for snacks, when, on the screen, Jake walked past Robbie's body on the air mattress. I stood in front of the monitor to block it, just in case one of them came back.

On the bigtab, I saw as Jake and Alex walked up the metal staircase leading to the hatch.

Alex pulled a big metal pin out of a socket and the hatch swung down.

Jake must have gone first. Then on the monitor, I saw Alex's masked face. Alex handed up to Jake a bundle of chains and rungs. The safety ladder, I realized. Then Jake extended his hand and helped Alex onto the roof.

Just the thought of Alex being up on the roof scared me.

Jake clipped the safety ladder to the side of the building and then the rungs fell down away from the camera, into darkness.

Jake turned back to Alex and shook his hand.

"Hey, little man, don't worry." Jake's voice came through the walkie-talkie. "I'll be fine."

Alex said something we couldn't hear.

"You got it," Jake answered.

The kids came running back with pillows and beanbag chairs. Chloe came from the opposite direction with a big bag of popcorn, a bag of miniature candy bars and a six-pack of Mountain Dew. Yikes.

The image moved as he went rung by rung, down the ladder, but it was very dark.

"I can't see anything!" Chloe complained.

"Me either," echoed Max.

"Make it lighter!" demanded Chloe.

She moved to touch the walkie-talkie.

"Nobody touches that but Alex!" Niko shouted.

Chloe jumped.

"Where is he, then?"

"He's pulling the ladder back onto the roof and then he has to wipe down. Now shut up and watch!"

I'd never heard him so stern. But I was glad. I just wanted to watch Jake TV.

It was hard, actually, to make anything out. Every step Jake took made everything shaky, and it was so dark.

"Can you stand still for a moment so we can see what you're seeing?" Niko asked softly into the walkie-talkie.

"All right, what you're seeing here is the sky and the horizon."

Jake stopped and we saw, well, not much, really. A dark sky and a dark ground and a glowing strip of light between them.

To me, it looked like black-and-white footage of the sky before dawn. But I knew it was at least eight a.m. Maybe ten.

"We're not seeing much," Niko said. "Are *you* able to see?"

"It's dark," Jake said. "But I can see. I don't want to turn on a flashlight because I feel like it would attract attention. But I'll tell you, it's darker than I expected out here."

So now we knew something. It was darker out there than we were expecting.

The image jounced with his footsteps. We could see faint

DAY 12

spots of color and different areas of grayness, but we couldn't make out anything.

"I'm in the parking lot. The cars are still here from the storm. They're all beat to heck. Check this out."

He brought his torso close to a car. In the light reflected from the walkie-talkie, we got a close-up of the surface of the car. It looked rough and pitted. Wafers of paint sat atop the rusty, flaky surface.

"I think the compounds are eating away at the metal. . . ."

We could tell he started walking again by the loping bounce of the image.

"Just picking up the pace a bit," Jake said. "My eyes have sort of adjusted out here. Don't want to waste any time."

According to the route we had all worked out, Jake was now heading through the parking lot and across Old Denver Highway. He had maybe a quarter of a mile to go to reach I-25.

Just past it, on the other side of Struthers Road, was the Lewis-Palmer Regional Hospital.

"Okay, now. I can see the highway," Jake said. "There's lights, actually."

"Oh my God!" Josie said, excited.

Alex came running back.

His face was red, fresh-scrubbed, and he wore new clothes.

"Did I miss anything?" he asked us. He went right to the walkie-talkie and took his place in front of it.

"He's walking through the parking lot," Niko said. "There's lights near the highway."

On the screen we could see circles of light, the size of a Tic Tac, bouncing in the distance.

"There's the lights!" shouted Henry.

Jake's footfalls sped up for a moment, and then they slowed.

Suddenly, the image went black.

"Someone's coming," he whispered.

"What's happening?" Chloe said. "Why can't we see?"

"I think he's crouching down," I said.

We waited.

"Ask him if he's okay," Alex said to Niko.

"No," Niko said. "If he's in danger, they could hear the sound from his earpiece."

Finally Jake spoke.

"They're gone," he said.

"Who was it?" Niko asked. "Could you tell?"

"It was two people. Walking together. They have suitcases. The rolling kind."

Two postapocalyptic nomads with rolling suitcases. Surreal.

"They were all bundled up so I couldn't see if they were women or men or anything."

"Jesus," Josie moaned. She looked stricken. "They could be anybody."

It was true. They could be people we knew. But Jake couldn't stop them and ask them. They might rob him or kill him or God knows what.

But they could have been people we knew (and loved).

Like our parents.

I looked behind me and caught sight of Astrid. I guess she'd left Brayden in Sahalia's care.

Astrid was sitting cross-legged on the floor at the back of the group. Luna had her head in Astrid's lap and Astrid was rubbing the old dog's head absentmindedly.

On the screen, the lights got steadily bigger. Every few moments they would dip or blink off, as Jake's motions took his torso away from them, but then they would come back.

DAY 12

"The ground's real boggy," Jake said. "The plants are all dead and everything is, like, rotting."

He slowed.

We could hear his breathing, amplified by the face mask he was wearing.

We all shifted in our seats. Caroline and Henry were gripped on to each other like they were a life raft.

"Here's what I'm seeing," Jake whispered to us. "The highway is mostly clear. There are cars every once in a while, but at least one lane is clear. There are some kind of military-looking lights at the side of the road in intervals of, I don't know, fifty yards apart, maybe.

"There are lots of cars pulled off on the sides. Looks like they've broken down, but I can't tell how long they've been there. Could be from the hail, or more recent. The road's in bad shape. The quake broke it up in places. The quake broke everything up."

Jake's breaths were rhythmic and steady. It seemed too intimate a thing, to listen to his breathing like that.

And then it grew faster.

"Just . . . picking up . . . the pace a bit . . . ," he said, slightly breathless. "Hard to breathe in this thing."

There were a few streetlights on, which was somehow surprising to me.

"Okay," Jake said. "Just a nice stroll on a nice quiet street." His voice was nervous.

"The streetlights are on?" Niko asked into the walkie-talkie.

"Yeah, and I've got the gun out. Just in case anyone's watching me."

Jake walked in the darkness, for what seemed like forever.

The kids ate their popcorn and I wanted to shush them, but I couldn't even spare the breath.

Jake approached the hospital.

"It's not looking good," he said quietly. "It's dark. No lights anywhere."

We saw a ghost of a building, windows crashed out.

"The hospital's dead," Jake said. "There's nobody here."

"Shoot." Niko dropped his head into his hands. "What are we going to do?"

On the screen, the walls of the hospital seemed to be fluttering, moving.

"What are we seeing?" Alex asked into the walkie-talkie, taking it over from Niko.

"There's flyers up. Letters, notes, pictures," Jake said.

He drew close so we could see.

A flyer of a photo of a middle-aged man: "Missing, Mark Bintner. Last seen on Mount Herman Road."

"Have you seen my daughter?" A photo of a pretty blond toddler.

A hastily scribbled note: "Grandma, I'm still alive! Going to Denver."

"Everyone's gone," Jake said as he continued to scan over the flyers.

There were multiple flyers saying the same thing: ALL SURVIVORS GO TO DENVER TO BE AIRLIFTED TO ALASKA. DEPARTURES EVERY 5 DAYS ON THE FIVES.

"Every five days on the fives," I said.

"What day is it?" Josie murmured.

"It's the twenty-eighth," Niko answered grimly.

There was a photo of a girl in a prom dress.

A photocopy showing someone's grandmother.

A picture of a woman taped to a paper: "Anne Marie, Find me at DIA!—Lou"

And there, our Christmas card.

DAY 12

"Stop!" I screamed. "Tell him to go back. That's our Christmas card! That's our Christmas card!"

Niko told Jake to go back and he found the card.

My mother, my father, Alex, and me.

Standing in front of our house.

Smiling, waving.

I grabbed my hair with both hands.

"What does it say?"

Jake took the card off the wall. He held it in his hands and opened it.

"Seasons Greetings from the Grieders!" it said in pretty red writing. And below that:

DEAN AND ALEX, in my father's neat print.

WE DIDN'T DIE. STAY SAFE OR GET TO DENVER.

WE LOVE YOU ALWAYS.

Alex and I launched ourselves at each other and embraced.

Everyone seemed to be crying along with us and I felt myself hugged, embraced by bodies from every side.

Josie, Chloe, Batiste, and Ulysses were hugging us. Henry and Caroline, Niko, even Astrid. We were at the center of the group and everyone was hanging on to each other.

I don't know if we were crying that they might be alive or they might be dead or if it was just that contact had been made.

"Oh God," said Jake's voice. His voice was thick with tears. "I'm sorry. I'm sorry, guys."

He moved away from the hospital.

"I'm not . . . I'm not coming back. I can't do it anymore."

"What?!" Astrid said, breaking away from the group.

"What did Jake say?"

There was the sound of tape ripping and the bungling sound of clothing being rearranged.

"What is he doing?" Astrid asked.

The angle of our feed changed suddenly and I realized Jake was taking the video walkie-talkie off his chest.

"Tell Astrid I'm sorry," was the last thing we heard him say.

We all stood in front of the monitor and watched.

Jake set down the video walkie-talkie on the street.

We could just see his boots. The pavement. The darkness beyond.

Jake walked away from us. Away from the camera.

And all we could do was watch him walk away, disappearing into the black day-night.

"No!" Astrid wailed.

The kids were clinging to each other and to us, sobbing.

Niko strode away, his hands in fists at his sides.

Astrid slid down on the floor. Caroline and Henry heaped themselves onto her lap, hugging her and crying. Astrid buried her face in Caroline's hair and wept.

Maybe two minutes later we heard a mechanical growl. An engine *VROOM*-ing to life. Luna started to bark. The sound came from the opposite end of the store.

It was the bus.

Niko had started the engine.

DAY 12

CHAPTER THIRTY-THREE

THE BUS

THE SOUND OF THE BUS RUMBLED THROUGH THE STORE.

As if in a daze, we wandered over to it. Like the engine's roar was casting a spell on us.

The engine shut off, just as we drew near.

It was sitting there by the front doors, where it had always waited. Niko came to the door of the bus.

"You all have ten minutes to get a bag packed. It should be mostly clothes. You can bring one special toy," Niko said to us.

"Wait!" Astrid said. "What are we doing?"

"Brayden needs a doctor. So we're going to take him to one."

"To where?" asked Max.

"We're going to Denver."

The screaming, the hoorays, the giddy laughing were all deafening.

I felt sick to my stomach.

"Are you sure?" I asked. "Can't we talk about it?"

Niko walked over to me as the little kids skittered away to pack. Alex came to stand at his side.

"Brayden's worse. The wound is infected. He looks green!" Niko said.

"But the roads!" I said. "They could be damaged or blocked—"

"He's going to die if we stay here."

"But, Niko—"

"You have ten minutes to put together a bag. You know the bus is stocked. We'll be fine."

"Dean," Alex said. "It could be our only way to see Mom and Dad again!"

"You want to see your parents?" Niko asked.

"Of course I do," I shouted. "But I don't want to turn into a blood-drinking, bone-chewing monster on a bus with a bunch of eight-year-olds!"

"We're going to sedate you," Niko said. "Alex and I discussed it."

He nodded to Alex.

"What?" I asked.

"We're going to sedate the three of you with O-type blood, and also tie you up, as a precaution," Alex said.

"Thanks for having my back," I said.

It was logical, but it still felt like a betrayal, especially with the two of them trying to convince me together.

"Plus, maybe the compounds have dissipated a bit by now," Alex said. "Your reaction could be less severe."

"I don't have time to argue about this anymore," Niko said. "It's my decision and if it's wrong, I'll live with it. But I can't let him die and not do anything about it."

"Niko, you're supposed to be the smart one," I said. "Cautious and smart and thinking everything through."

DAY 12

"This bus is a tank," he said to me. "It will get us there, I know it."

"We have to go," Alex said. "It's our only chance to see them."

"And if we're going, we have to go now. The next evacuation is in two days."

I turned and walked away.

"Where are you going?" Alex called.

"To pack my bag, of course," I spat out. "What choice do I have?"

"Hurry," Niko called after me. "I need your help to load Brayden onto the bus."

I went and grabbed a backpack from Sporting Goods and then I went to Men's Clothing.

Inside, I was ranting.

It was stupid. It was a big mistake. They didn't understand what the compounds would make me do.

And what about the roads? What about the bandits?

"It's a bad idea," came a soft voice behind me.

It was Astrid. She looked small and scared under the bright fluorescent lights of the store.

"I know," I said.

"We shouldn't go," she said.

"I know. Niko is so scared Brayden will die that he's risking everyone."

Astrid stepped close to me and embraced me.

She pressed her face to my chest and held me tight.

It felt so good. Like we were magnets, meant to be fitted together. I put my arms around her and held her to me.

"Stay," she said. "Stay with me, Dean."

"What?"

"I'm not going," she said, pulling away to look up at me. "And I want you to stay with me."

My heart was in my throat. My vision was swimming.

She was going to stay and she wanted me to stay with her?

"You want me to stay with you?" I said. "Me?"

She pulled out of my arms and drew back a step, putting her hands in the pockets of her vest.

"I mean . . ." She blushed. She was blushing.

"I'm not going," she said, not meeting my eyes. "I can't. And neither should you. The compounds will make us into monsters. They don't know what it's like. We do. You and me and Chloe, we need to stay."

So . . . what? Huh? That's what I felt like saying: huh?

She was asking me to stay because I had the same blood type? She was advising me to stay because of the compounds?

What had the hug meant?

It felt like it meant everything.

I guess she was hugging me because . . . I was a nice guy. I was her friend.

I stuffed a couple sweatshirts into my backpack.

"Well?" she said.

"I don't know what to say, Astrid. I have to go with my brother. We have to stick together."

"Then get him to stay, too. He's logical. Alex will know it's the right thing to stay."

"No, he wants to go. He thinks this is our only chance to find our parents. He'd never stay."

"We can't go! We'll kill somebody!"

I turned to her.

Tears were streaming down her face. She wiped at them with the back of her hand.

"Please, Dean." Every time she said my name it was like a warm knife, slicing my heart right through.

"Astrid," I said. "We'll wear gas masks the whole way. They're

DAY 12

going to sedate us and tie us up. We won't be able to help them, but we won't kill them either."

I shoved some jeans in my bag.

"Who knows? Maybe Niko is right. Maybe we'll make it just fine."

"No," she said, near hysterics. "I can't go. I can't go. I can't go!"

"You'll be fine—"

"I'm gonna have a baby."

"What?" I said.

She crossed her arms over her chest.

"I'm pregnant."

"Are you sure?"

She nodded. "Been sure for a while now. I'm four months. Maybe more."

"Four *months*?"

She lifted up her sweater and undershirt.

I saw the creamy skin of her beautiful diver's body. And yes, there was a bump there. A swelling. Right under the navel, a rise. How had I not noticed it before?

She dropped her shirt and put her hands up to cover her face. She was crying softly.

"Oh, Astrid," I said. And I stepped to her. Took her in my arms and held her.

"But don't you think it means we *have* to go?" I said quietly. "We should go so we can find a doctor. Don't you think?"

"I thought about that," she said. "But what will happen to the, you know, the fetus, if he's exposed to the compounds? What if he's like us, Dean?"

And then she lowered her voice. "Or what if he blisters?"

I will not share the grisly images that came into my mind.

"What the heck, you guys?" Chloe said, charging into the aisle. "We're almost ready to go."

It was mayhem, everybody scrambling and putting things on the bus and then Josie taking some of the things off ("No, Caroline, you can't bring wind chimes for your mom!" "But Dean said we could!" "Okay, fine!"), and Niko trying to get everything into some kind of order.

"Finally!" he said when he saw us.

Niko had just finished making Chloe take a sleeping pill. He had ground it up in a teaspoon of jelly.

"I gave her the full dose," he said. "Hopefully she'll sleep the whole way. I'm gonna dose you now, but first I want you to help me get Brayden on board."

Josie and Sahalia were helping the kids get into their layers of clothing.

"Okay," Niko said as we walked toward the Automotive aisle where Brayden was.

He took out a piece of paper from his pocket.

It was a checklist.

"We have food, water, first aid, extra clothes, valuables to trade—"

We heard Luna barking.

"Shoot," he said. "We need dog food."

"Max," I called back. "Food for Luna!"

He nodded and ran for the Pet Department.

Niko kept reading: "Air masks, layers of clothing, rope, matches, tarps, backpacks, oil, knives, one gun, bullets."

He looked up at me.

"What else?"

DAY 12

It was an impressive list.

"I can't think of anything," I said.

Sahalia was with Brayden. She had taken over his care and now seemed somewhat territorial about him.

She was wearing her own layers of clothing and was struggling to get Brayden into his.

"We'll help," I told her.

Niko was right, Brayden looked green.

As carefully as we could, we put zip-front hoodies onto him. Niko dealt with the sweatpants.

"Brayden," Niko said softly. "We're going to move you onto the bus."

Brayden didn't acknowledge he'd heard Niko. He was limp and clammy.

"Let's slide the mattress over, then we'll lift him in."

So the three of us slid the air mattress to the bus.

All the while I was thinking about what the hell I was going to do.

Josie lay down blankets for Brayden on the second seat of the bus.

Niko and Josie and Sahalia and Alex and I lifted Brayden awkwardly and got him onto the bus. He was able to walk, a little, when we got him up, but then he collapsed into his seat.

"We're going to get you help, Brayden," Sahalia said. "You're going to feel better soon."

As Niko and I left the bus she asked Niko, "We have pain meds, right? And antibiotics."

"A whole bin full," Niko assured her.

Sahalia had grown up a lot in the last couple days.

* * *

I wish I was the strong and silent type who never cries and never shows emotion.

But I saw my brother standing there, working with Astrid to take down the plywood wall over the gate, and tears welled up, making everything blurry and shiny.

My dear, serious, smart brother.

How could I do this to him?

"Don't start taking down that plywood until we are all in our clothes and have our face masks on!" Niko said to them.

"Jeez, what about the gate?" I said, turning to Niko.

"I figured out how to retract it," Alex said.

I nodded and looked away from him, turning my head so he wouldn't see the anguish building up in me.

All the others were already in their many layers of clothes. They all had their masks in their hands. Sahalia came off the bus to get her mask.

They were ready.

"Where's Chloe?" Niko said.

"She got very, very sleepy, so I put her in the bus to have a rest," Josie said.

I guess a sleeping pill works pretty fast on an eight-year-old.

"Alex, can I talk to you?" I said.

"Here are your layers, Dean," Josie said, handing me a stack of sweatpants. "And I have your 'vitamins,' too."

"I want vitamins!" Caroline said.

"Me too!" said Henry.

Josie shushed them.

"Alex, I need to talk to you," I said.

"You can talk on the bus," Niko said, pulling on his clothes. "Put your layers on."

I looked to Astrid. Josie was dressing her, pulling sweatshirts

DAY 12

over Astrid's head and helping her to stick her arms through the sleeves.

"Come on, Astrid," Josie said. "Help me out here."

Astrid was crying. She caught my eye, pleading with me over the heads of our busy friends. Our best friends. Our family.

"No," I said. "I'm not going."

Heads turned.

"Astrid and I are staying."

Josie looked at Astrid's face.

"What is he talking about?" she asked.

Astrid nodded, miserable.

"That's not funny, Dean," Alex said. He took the sweatshirt Josie was still holding and pushed it into my hands.

"Put it on!"

"We're staying," I said.

"No, you're not!" he shouted.

"We have to stay."

"You have to *come*!" Alex yelled. Tears were springing to his eyes. His lips were drawn in a straight line.

"It's not safe for us to be on the bus," I said.

"Niko, tell them they have to come! Make them come!"

Niko continued to dress himself.

"Niko!" Alex yelled. "Tell them!"

"No," Niko said. "They're right. It's safer for them and safer for us if they stay."

Alex screamed and hit Niko. Then turned and attacked me.

I grabbed him and hugged him tight to me.

"Alex, listen to me," I begged him. "You are going to find our parents."

"No."

"And you will know exactly where I am. And you'll all come get me."

"Please, Dean. Please!"

"It's safer for us and safer for you if we stay," I repeated what Niko had said.

"You're staying . . ." He struggled for a breath. "You're staying . . ."

He pushed away from me and wiped the snot off his face.

"You're staying for a girl!" he spat at me. "You're choosing her over me! Over our mom and dad!"

He walked away from me.

"You love her so much you're never going to see your family again! I hate you!"

And he turned and boarded the bus.

"Alex," I said, tears streaming down my face.

Niko put his hand on my arm. He had all his layers on by that point.

"If you guys are staying we need to rethink how we deal with the gate," he said. "Also, I think you should keep Chloe."

I looked at Astrid and she nodded.

"She's not going to like it," Josie said. "Being left behind."

She would be furious, when she woke up.

But, really, she would be safe with us and the others would be safe from her.

I carried her warm, heavy body off the bus and laid her on Brayden's dirty air mattress.

"Is there anyone else who doesn't want to go?" Niko asked the little kids.

They all were silent.

They looked terrified, clutching their gas masks.

But none of them came forward.

We only took down the center panels. The side panels could stay up because the bus only needed to go through the center doors.

DAY 12

And after refusing to put on the layers so dramatically, Astrid and I did end up putting them on, along with the face masks, because the compounds were going to come into our space.

We'd have to put the wall back up as soon as we could.

"Come on, guys, hurry. Say good-byes and get on board now," Niko said. "We're wasting time."

Max and Batiste and Henry and Caroline all surged over to us and we hugged them. I felt a tug on my hand and Ulysses tugged on my fat, padded arm.

He pressed Luna's leash into my hand.

"Keep Luna," he said. "And you memember me."

He hugged me hard and then got on the bus.

Saying good-bye to them hurt like I was getting stabbed in the heart.

Little Caroline and Henry were weeping. They clung to me until Josie pried them off and sent them up the stairs.

"Dean," Caroline called. "You have to come. You're our favorite!"

"I'm sorry, Caroline. I have to stay here and keep Astrid and Chloe safe."

"Tell Chloe we said 'bye', okay?" she said.

Tears rolled down her freckled cheeks. This was agony.

Alex was sitting near Brayden at the front of the bus. He wouldn't look at me. Niko had gone and tried to talk him out, but Alex wouldn't come. Not even to put up the gate. He'd given instructions to Niko to give to Astrid.

"So when you hear the air horn," Niko told her now. "That means press the retract sign, but only for the center gate. Then when you hear it a second time, that means put it back up."

Astrid nodded.

"I'm sorry, Niko," she said. "I'm sorry we can't go with you."

"I know," he said.

"You were a great leader," she told him.

I hated hearing this conversation. Everything had this terribly final feel to it.

"Good luck," he said.

"You, too."

And Astrid went to wait for the air horn.

The bus was running now.

Josie and Sahalia were standing by with their air masks on.

All we had to do was take down the last panels and then blow the horn for Astrid to retract the center gate.

"Wait!" I said.

I had an idea. I turned from Niko and I ran.

"Dean! We have to go!!!" Niko shouted.

I hurdled through the store.

Searching for what I needed.

I was breathless when I got back.

I saw Josie and Sahalia were on the bus. I had forfeited my chance to say good-bye to them. It didn't matter.

I took the stairs to the bus in two steps.

There he was. Front row.

"Alex," I said. "Take this."

I held out a blank journal, just like mine, and a box of pens.

"You take this and you write down everything that happens. You write it all and you write it to *me*. Tell it to me."

He was sobbing and he reached his many-layered arms to me and we hugged.

"That way I'll know what happens to you," I said.

"I will," he said. "I promise."

* * *

DAY 12

Niko and I unscrewed the last of the screws.

Luna was tied to a four-top in the kitchen. Chloe lay on the air mattress.

All the children were seat-belted into their seats.

I stood at one corner of the final section and Niko at the other.

We pulled and the four remaining plywood sheets came crashing down. I dragged two out of the way. Niko dragged the other two.

Josie stood on the steps of the bus. She has been waiting for the wood to come down. That was her cue.

BWRAAAM! She hit the air horn and tossed it aside.

But under the wood, we had covered the gate in thick woolen blankets and layers of plastic. I had forgotten that.

I reached up, wondering if we should pull down the blankets.

But then the gate started up with a loud mechanical drone. Too late.

The gate went up, chucking and whining with the added padding of the blankets and plastic, but still retracting.

And there was the dark parking lot. The broken asphalt. The ruined cars. The dots of light, far in the distance, that were the emergency lights on the highway.

There was the world.

We had blocked it out for so long.

The engine of the bus roared as Niko put it into reverse and backed out into the lot.

It worked! It rolled! The bus could drive.

Niko honked the horn.

I knew inside they were shouting good-bye, probably crying, but I couldn't hear them . . .

They were leaving now. Without us.

I hit the air horn: *BWRAAAM!*

The bus drove forward into the lot.

But then it stopped. The doors opened.

What was happening?!

Two bundled-up children got off the bus and started running clumsily back to me.

My heart was in my gut. My stomach was in my throat. My nerves were jangling and I rushed forward, outside, my arms out to them, whoever they were.

Then, behind me, the gate started to lower.

I ran to them and slid on the slimy, sticky pavement. I darted past the cracked sections, trying not to fall.

I picked the two children up and ran for the store. The gate was coming down, shutting out the light of the Greenway. It was slicing down, cutting off the view of the Kitchen, the cash registers, the empty carts waiting in their corral.

I threw the children onto the ground, pushing first one and then the other under the gate.

I squeezed under it. My coat—my stupid layers—made it harder. The gate was crushing my chest. The two kids pulling at me, trying to get me in.

I pushed up and to the side, and somehow, I got in.

It had my sneaker but I pulled my foot out of it. The sneaker got left outside, but my foot made it in.

We were inside. Back to our blessed home. Our bright commercial sanctuary from the dark, grisly, true world. Our Greenway.

The two children took off their balaclavas and removed their masks. They were Caroline and Henry.

DAY 12

"We want to stay with you," Caroline said.

"You'll keep us safe," Henry added.

"Can we stay?" Caroline asked. She looked up at me, her face streaked with grime and tears.

"Of course," I said. "Of course you can stay."

Astrid came out from the storeroom.

"Oh!" she cried when she saw them.

They ran to her.

She sank to her knees and covered their faces with kisses. Just took their little, grimy, stained faces in her hands and kissed them all over.

Then she hugged them.

And Astrid had them in her arms, she looked up at me, welcoming me with her eyes and I joined them.

Alex was gone.

And Niko and Josie and Brayden and the rest.

Jake was gone, too.

But we had Caroline and Henry and Chloe.

And we had each other.

We were five.

ACKNOWLEDGMENTS

Heartfelt thanks go to my agent, Susanna Einstein, who supported *Monument 14* from the moment I told her the first glimmer of the idea, to this very draft you've just read. Jean Feiwel, my editor and publisher, thank you for your vision and dedication to making *M14* the best book it could be. I feel tremendously fortunate to work with you. Holly West, thanks for loving the book so much and taking such great care of it.

Big thanks to Gregory Casimir and Vinny at Target for all their insider know-how. And thanks to the Boy Scouts from Upstate New York that I met at that Chuckwagon Dinner in Colorado Springs. Your openness, intelligence, and honesty made me decide to make Niko a Boy Scout. I hope he does you proud.

I would also like to acknowledge Jane and Bob Stine, who gave me the opportunity to write my first book way back when. Bill Gifford, Terry Culleton, Richard Walter, and Howard

Suber are all educators who made a big difference to me and I want them to know it.

Marina Dominguez, I wouldn't have found my way back to a creative life if I hadn't had you to help with the kids.

Thank you to my early readers: Amy Baily, Cate Baily, Andrew Bair, Kristin Bair, Wendy Shanker, and Kevin Maher; and my always readers: Kit and Gerry Laybourne (my very own parents).

Thanks to Patricia Hasegawa and the Parent Your Dream group. To the Warriors. To the Heartless Floozies. To my e-mail vibe group. (It turns out, I run on groups.) How lucky I am to have you all!

And Greg, thank you for being my advocate and my hero.

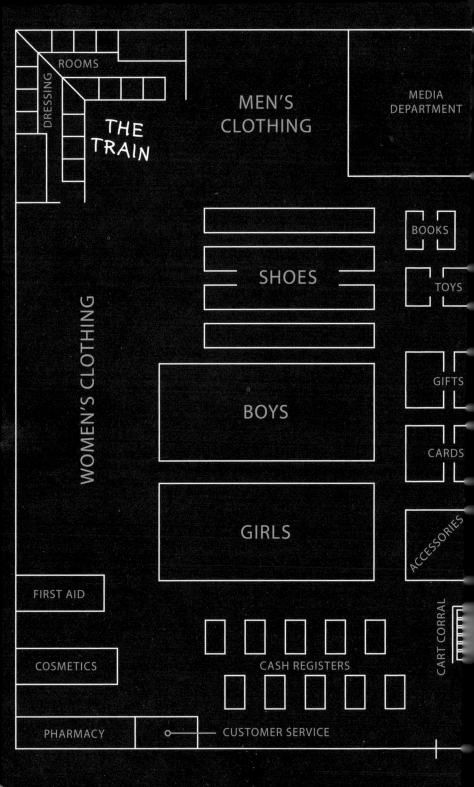